TOXIC WHISPERS

A COLLATERAL DAMAGE NOVEL

CANDICE WRIGHT

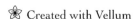 Created with Vellum

For Mallory and Miss T
My wifey and my side chick.
Because misery loves company and I wouldn't have survived
this without you.

PROLOGUE

SIX

*M*y fingertips are numb. It's so cold in here, I can see my breath puff out in front of my face.

I wrap my hands around the icy bars of my cage and try to see who else might be awake. It's so quiet that if I didn't know there were ten of us down here, I would think I was alone.

The others will be sleeping like they are supposed to be. They are better at following orders than I am. That's why I spend more time in the hole than they do.

Mama always said I was different. Wild spirited and precocious. I don't know what that means, and mama is gone now so I can't ask her. Not that she would have told me anyway. She got mad when I asked questions. Questions led to trouble, or at least that's what she said.

I shift from one foot to the other. My toes are so cold I can't feel them anymore.

The metal lock on the door clanks as it opens and I rush to the back corner of my cage and bury my head in my hands.

I sit as still as I can and I don't make a peep. I think small like mama taught me, back before they took her away.

The doors to some of the cages open. Not mine though. I don't know if I should be happy that nobody wants to hurt me today or sad that I won't see the sun.

"Nine, Four, Three—line up." One of the guards' metal sticks hits the bars of one of the cages.

I tuck myself even smaller. I don't like those sticks. They hurt so bad when they touch me, making me shake so much I usually wet myself.

Somebody cries. Three, I think. She hasn't been here very long. She replaced the old Three when she left, but this one cries a lot.

I tried to tell her that tears make them mad, but she doesn't listen to me.

The sound of footsteps moves past my cage. Some of them are loud as they walk by with heavy boots. Some make hardly any sound as their bare feet whisper against the cold stone floor. Then there is the other sound. The shuffling, scratching sound of people being dragged along because their feet won't carry them anymore. That's the sound that makes me feel sad inside because those people don't usually come back.

When the door slams closed, I take a deep breath and let my tears slip free. I don't make a noise though—I know how to be quiet. Plus, I don't want the others to think I'm a baby, even if I am the youngest here since two left last week.

We've never had so many leave at once before. I don't

2

understand what's happening, but I heard the guards talking through the vents about the location being compromised.

I don't know what compromised means, but it sounds bad.

Maybe they will have to move us all again. Maybe in my new cage, I can have a window. That way I'll be able to see the sun whenever I want.

I let my eyes close, tip my head back, and imagine I can feel the warmth of the sun's rays on my skin.

I pretend I'm not cold or scared or alone or hungry.

I pretend I'm free, somewhere outside where it's big enough for me to spin in circles with my arms out wide.

I want to spin until I'm dizzy and all the colors of the world blur together.

But slaves don't spin, they kneel.

They don't see colors. They see darkness and they don't get to taste freedom.

They suck dick and sometimes that's enough to buy them one more day.

CHAPTER ONE

SIX

"*S*ix."

I look up at the sound of my name, careful not to make eye contact. I stare at M's shoulder as she addresses me.

"It's time. R will be taking you to the drop-off point tonight where you will be collected by your new owner. I expect you to be on your best behavior. I have a reputation to uphold after all."

She steps closer before gripping my jaw tightly and tipping my head back. Still, I don't make eye contact. I've fallen for that too many times before.

"This time if you misbehave, it will not be me who corrects your behavior. It will be your new owner and I doubt he will be as lenient as me. Do you understand?"

"Yes, mistress," I reply quietly.

She lets go of me, shoving me harder than necessary, trying to make me fall out of my pose. But I'm used to her tricks now so I braced myself in anticipation.

As soon as she steps back, I lower my gaze and make sure my hands are in the correct position—palms up on my thighs. I've been kneeling next to X for so long, my legs are going to sleep. But I don't let so much as a muscle twitch. I keep my legs spread apart, my back straight, and my chest out.

X strokes my hair lazily and no one says anything for a further fifteen minutes.

Out of all the trainers here, X is the one I like the most. Or hate the least. I'm not sure which anymore, or if it even matters.

An odd pall hangs in the room—a sadness that seems to have sucked all the air, making this vast space feel small and confining. If I didn't know better, I would think that X will miss me. But I do know better. X doesn't have feelings—none of the trainers do—and by the time the slaves are sent out to their owners, neither do they.

In my world, emotions will get you killed. You learn early on how to shut them off, or you become a master at pretending you don't feel anything like me.

"Time to get you ready, pet. Your new master is a lucky duck."

I don't reply. He hasn't asked me a direct question. He doesn't want my input. Besides, what can I say? I know where I'm heading will make this place seem like those picnics Ten used to tell me about.

Memories of Ten make my eyes slip closed for a minute before I catch myself.

He would talk to me all night through the bars of our cells. When he was sold, my heart cracked into two jagged pieces. It had been different with my mother. I was so young when she was taken that I can't remember much about her, other than the rules she tried to teach me. She was neither loving nor gentle, but that wasn't because she didn't care. She just knew that girls like me don't get to be dreamers. She tried to keep me safe in the only way she could, but that meant keeping a distance between us I never realized was there until Ten came along.

I was branded a slave while still in my mother's womb. My destiny was cast before I was little more than a bundle of cells.

I never knew anything beyond my cage. But Ten, he was different.

He and his family had been fleeing their war-torn country when everyone except him was killed.

He was brought here to be trained and sold to the leader of the very people who killed his family. They never kept that a secret from him, but instead of it breaking him, it made him strong. It sparked a fire inside him that was both terrifying and awe-inspiring as he plotted his revenge, swearing he would avenge his family and return home a hero.

The day he left, a piece of me went with him.

Six months later, he returned to have his behavior corrected. He didn't talk anymore and his eyes were haunted with ghosts, but he still offered me his quiet smiles when nobody was looking.

I had him back. He wasn't the same, but he was still mine. Until one day he wasn't.

I woke up to what felt like arms wrapped around me. I'd

never been hugged before, but I knew instinctively that's what it was.

For the first time in forever, I felt safe. Then I opened my eyes and saw him hanging from the cage bars. His eyes were open but the boy I called mine was gone. I don't know how, but I know down to my soul it was Ten hugging me goodbye as he left me here alone once more.

"You have permission to leave, Six." X snaps me away from my bleakest memory.

I climb to my feet, ignoring the shooting pain through my shins and calves from being in one position for too long.

I walk toward the door slowly, hiding my wince as X stands and follows beside me with a possessive hand on my hip. He raps his knuckles against the door and steps back before it opens, revealing two guards that will escort me back to my room.

X releases his hold on me, his fingertips glancing deliberately over the curve of my bare ass.

"Good luck, Six," he whispers sadly.

"Thank you, master," I reply, even though I know better than to speak out of turn.

He doesn't reprimand me though. He smiles and turns away.

I hope my voice haunts him for the rest of his days.

It's a fanciful wish made by the dreamer inside me that my mother couldn't stamp out.

X will be inside another slave before the hour is over. He always is after a session with me and from what I hear, he is particularly brutal on those days.

Poor X. It must be frustrating not being able to fuck me the way he so desperately wants.

That's what makes me different from the others here. The virgin sex slave. It's what my owner had insisted on. A virgin in every way except one, and bad oral sex would be intolerable.

I follow the guards with a blank expression, even though my brain is a swirling mass of emotion.

I spent my whole life being trained to be the perfect slave, waiting for my number to be called. Now that the time has arrived, I want nothing more than to hide in my cell.

I'm so distracted by my runaway thoughts, I almost crash into the back of the guard when he opens my door for me.

With a snarl, he grabs my arm and shoves me inside.

"You have ten minutes," he tells me, slamming the door shut behind him.

I stay in my spot for a minute and look around the cell that has been my home for the last five years. I'd been to three different facilities and this one was the nicest. I have a real toilet and a warm blanket on my bed.

I look at that blanket and for a minute I picture myself doing what Ten did all those years ago, but I can't. I'm not ready to give up yet. I still haven't seen a rainbow. How can I leave this earth before witnessing that?

I move to my bed and see a simple white dress on the end of it. I look at it, assuming I should put it on, but the thought of wearing clothes is odd.

I pick it up and smell it. It doesn't smell of anything, though I'm not sure what I was expecting.

Slipping it over my head, I let it drift down my body.

It has thin straps that leave my shoulders bare, but it covers my breasts and goes all the way down to my knees. It's not exactly tight but I feel somehow restricted wearing it. The material is rough against my skin. If this is what clothes feel like, I think I'd rather not wear them at all.

With a sigh, I look around the room once more.

I have nothing to pack, nothing at all to take with me. All I have is this scratchy dress and my name.

I stand at the door and wait for the guard, wondering if by the end of the week I'll even have those.

CHAPTER TWO

WILL

The wind was the first thing that registered. I open my eyes and groan, slamming them shut again as a swirl of nausea rises in my stomach.

"I am never drinking again," I mutter. My mouth tastes like a damn ashtray and the half-empty bottle of whiskey on the floor near my hand lets me know I won't be in any fit state to drive today.

I roll over with another groan and remind myself that at my age I can't drink whiskey like it's water and expect to function the next day.

The birds circle above me chipping away loudly, much to my annoyance. My pounding head wants nothing more than for me to lift my gun and shoot the fuckers from the sky, but that seems like an awful lot of effort.

Wait. Birds?

I open my eyes again and this time wait for everything to come into focus.

That's when I realize I didn't even make it to bed. I passed out cold on my deck like a frat boy at a kegger. Guess I should be glad I didn't wake up in a pool of my own vomit.

With a sigh, I drag myself into a sitting position and look out over the lake, hoping to find some kind of peace, but that's doubtful. Not when I remember why I needed to get drunk in the first place.

What the hell was I thinking, bidding for a slave? Yes, it was a ploy to gain us access to the network. We were looking for a way to target the man who was after Jenna. When that all blew up in our faces, I forgot to pull out. Kidnapping and bullets to the chest tend to distract a man, even if those things happened to my friends and not me, but it's no excuse.

I'm stuck now and I'm not sure the best way to play this.

My first instinct had been to refuse. Hell fucking no did I want to get caught up in human trafficking. The problem is, my conscience couldn't let me walk away that easily. What would happen to the person I had bought? Would they be resold, to someone far worse than me, or would they be terminated? I have more blood on my hands than I care to admit but I've always had lines I wouldn't cross. The thought of someone innocent being killed because I simply forgot to cancel my order made me feel sick to my stomach.

I didn't care about the money either. I had more money than I'd ever be able to spend in this lifetime or the next. Every time I close my eyes, I can't shake the feeling that if I do nothing it will haunt me forever.

This leads me to today. In less than three hours I'll be

collecting my latest purchase. It just so happened this purchase is made of blood and bone.

"Fuck." I swipe my hand over my face and climb to my feet, finding no comfort in the view. The only way the lake will bring me peace today is if I drown myself in it.

I take in the scene that had me buying this house before I'd even seen the rest of the place. The huge midnight blue lake is surrounded by trees as far as the eye can see.

The whole place is completely isolated, the nearest neighbor about ten miles out, which is just as well now that I'd converted the basement to a dungeon—and not the sexy fun kind.

In this line of work, a dungeon is pretty much standard practice, just not many have one as part of their home. Unless they are a serial killer.

Even Viddy, who is usually slightly more unhinged than me, doesn't have one at her creepy haunted house. She has a kill house, of course, in the middle of nowhere. Most hunters do. They just don't usually hunt humans.

I turn from the view and head through the glass doors, snagging the whiskey bottle along the way. In the kitchen, I pour the amber liquid down the sink so I'm not tempted to finish it and make myself a pot of coffee.

I head up to my bedroom to take a shower while it brews, stripping out of my dirty clothes and tossing them into the corner of my room.

The shower makes me feel human again and when I step out and look at myself in the mirror, I'm relieved to see my eyes don't look as bloodshot.

Even though I can't be bothered, I reach for my razor and lather up my face in shaving foam.

I have an impression to uphold in this world, which means I can't turn up looking anything but cool, calm, and deadly. If my enemies see a weakness, they will somehow find a way to use it to their advantage.

I finish shaving and wipe the rest of the foam from my face, checking to make sure I haven't missed any.

My dark hair is threaded with more silver than I'd like, reminding me I'm not a spring chicken anymore. I make it work for me. It's a touch longer than usual. I've been too busy to get it cut but after styling it the way I want, I realize it adds a kind of edginess to my look, so I'm not complaining.

I walk into my room naked and head straight for my closet, selecting an expensive black suit with a white shirt and a black tie.

I also snag a pair of sunglasses while I'm there, knowing, thanks to the whiskey, I'll need them later.

I get dressed, then slip on silver cufflinks that were a gift from my mother, before heading down for my much-needed coffee.

The pot is full when I get there so I pour myself a large mugful and add a splash of milk before taking a sip.

My cell chimes as I look out the window, making a mental note of all the things I need to take care of later. A glance at the screen tells me James is waiting outside.

I let him know I'm on my way, which means I'll be there in ten minutes. There is no way I'll make it through the day without a second cup. At least not without shooting someone.

I finish the first and refill my mug before grabbing my guns and knife and securing them to me. By the time I've finished the second cup, I'm more alert and ready to get this shit over with. With my cell in my hand, I leave knowing when

I come back, my once peaceful home is going to feel very different.

"James." I greet him as I climb into the back of the car and lean back, slipping the sunglasses over my eyes.

"Rough night?" he jokes as he climbs back into the driver's seat.

"You have no idea. Chopper ready? I don't want to have to hang around any longer than necessary."

"Gene messaged me just before I texted you to tell me they were just refueling. They'll be done before we arrive."

"Good."

When he doesn't say anything else, I close my eyes and try to think about what little information I have on the person I bought, which isn't much.

I know she's female, young, and has red hair. I had to pick my preference, but that's all I know. Most places have photos, making the selection process easier, but not this one. What makes this place unique is the ability to return the slave and select a new one if the customer is unhappy. A try-it-before-you-buy-it deal that makes my stomach roll.

I can't begin to figure out how that works logistically, let alone anything else. I can only assume the return rate is low.

Still, the lack of any real information about the woman doesn't sit well with me. I'm a details man who likes to weigh all the variables, but right now I'm so far out of the loop it's not funny. Hell, I don't even know how old she is, although I did specify that I had no interest in anyone under eighteen. That at least has to be my one saving grace in all this. If I'd accidentally bought a kid—I shake my head, feeling sick once more at the thought. Trying to help a traumatized woman is going to be tough enough, but a kid?

15

Jesus fuck, what am I doing?

I turn to look out the window, unable to think clearly any longer.

I've already weighed all the options, from every angle, and there is no other move I can make.

It doesn't matter how I justify it, I'm still picking up a woman who has been subjected to god only knows what. Instead of setting her free, I'm taking her home and making her my prisoner.

CHAPTER THREE

SIX

I don't know how long we've been traveling. Whatever drug they gave me to make me sleep has long worn off. The woman next to me still seems out of it. I can't see her through the material of the dark hoods over our heads, but I can feel her beside me.

I roll as the van turns, my body too tired to resist. I bump into the side panel and bite my lip when my chin hits the metal.

When the van seems to slow, I tense and prepare myself. For what, I don't know. Whatever happens, I'll need my wits about me. My mind drifts to my companion. I wonder if I should pretend I'm still out of it like she is. It might make the driver let his guard down.

A ringing fills the van and after a brief moment, I recognize R's voice. "No, they are both still out cold. No issues at all.

Yeah, Mr. Ajax is arriving first. He will collect Two before Six is picked up." He pauses for a moment.

"No, I understand and I can assure you neither woman has a mark on them." He sighs as the other person speaks.

"It's out of your hands, X. Six was born for this. You know what's at stake here. She won't last. He'll toss her aside once he's bored. And he will get bored. He always does. When she's broken in, she'll be returned. Six won't be a virgin then, so you'll be free to do what you want to her. For now, there is nothing you or I can do until this plays out."

He's quiet once more as I swallow down the rush of vomit in the back of my throat. Why buy me and wait so long to collect me if, by the sound of it, I'll be tossed back soon? None of this makes sense. Unless…I picture all the damage a man could do to my body until I'm of no use anymore. Maybe sex isn't this man's primary need but violence. Oh god. I just about manage to bite back a whimper as R speaks again.

"Nah, no idea who Two's buyer is. Some old rich fucktard who bought her at one of our auctions. You know as well as I do how much people need to hide their identity. He has money and means. That's all that matters."

I tune out his words for a minute, not understanding everything he's talking about. I know enough that I do not want my buyer to get his hands on me. I thought I'd prepared for everything, but the thought of possibly dying with someone's hands around my throat before I've even had a chance to live makes me want to scream at the injustice of it all.

I feel fear start to spiral wildly out of control inside me, but I lock it down before panic consumes me. Rolling closer to who I now know is Two, I press my hand against her thigh and pinch her slightly.

Maybe if I can get her to wake up we could overpower R and make a run for it. I don't care where I end up as long as it's not with a man who wants nothing more than to break me.

When Two doesn't stir, I slide my hands up her body to tap her face. My hands stall on her chest.

A chest that isn't moving.

I bite my lip to keep from crying out. I keep my hands on her, hoping I'm wrong and I'll feel something. There's nothing.

Ever so carefully, I slide my hand up to my face and lift the sack so I can see her.

I wince against the light but focus on Two's chest. When it still doesn't move, I reach over with shaky hands and slide her hood up over her face.

When dead eyes stare back at me, I almost scream. Somehow, I bite it back.

Her eyes look so much like Ten's did all those years ago, looking at me but not seeing me at all.

I tug the hood back down, unable to bear the sight any longer. I'd never spoken a single word to her. She had been kept in a room on the far side of the compound from mine. The guards frequented it a lot. Day and night, they entered her room. In the silence, I could make out the soft grunts and squeak of the springs. In the beginning, I'd hear Two's sobs. As time passed, the crying grew fainter until I realized one day I hadn't heard her cry for a while. She'd learned the hard way, like the rest of us, that tears didn't bring you anything but trouble.

I heard two of the guards talking once as I pretended to sleep that Two was so popular because she looks like me, or what I suppose an older sister would look like. She has the same color hair as me, maybe a shade darker, the same sprinkling of freckles across the bridge of her nose, and similar eye color—although hers are bluer than my gray ones. Some days I pretended she was my sister, and we would somehow team up and break free.

The little girl inside me that refused to give up dreaming loved the idea of having that bond with someone even though I knew it would never amount to anything. Sometimes all a person has is hope.

But now hope is lying dead beside me and all I feel is despair.

I stare at the hood covering her face, feeling so sad for the woman who came to mean something to me without knowing it. I hate to think what they will do with her body once they realize she's gone.

At least now she is finally free.

I look from the crudely scrawled number two on her hood that's covering her dead eyes and look over the rest of her. Not a mark mars her body. It's as if she simply gave up.

I notice she's in the same dress I am. I guess they must be standard issue for slave deliveries, I think bitterly. With her bare feet and blemish-free skin, her identity is erased as if she never existed. She's just another lost girl in a dirty white dress and a numbered hood over her head. Trash to be thrown away, just like me.

I suck in a sharp breath and tug off my hood for a moment. I twist it and see it has a blue number six on the front.

I stare at it for a beat before my eyes drift to the hood marked with a two and make a split decision based on nothing more than instinct.

I tug Two's hood free and carefully slide mine over her face before climbing over her and switching places.

I look up at the front of the van but there is a partition dividing the back from the front. I might not be able to see R, but I can hear him still talking and not paying attention to us. I blow out a deep breath, trying to calm my racing heart as I pull Two's mask over my head and lie back down.

Only then do I allow myself to cry.

CHAPTER FOUR

WILL

*T*he chopper lands and I wait for the blades to stop rotating before climbing out.

I button up my suit jacket. The air is damp and I wonder if a storm might be heading in. If so, I want to be back home before it drops. Checking into a hotel with a slave would likely be frowned upon.

I climb into the back seat of the waiting car and tell James to step on it.

I'm not sure if it's the changing weather, but a sense of urgency strikes me. I learned long ago to listen to my instincts.

"When we get there, I want you to stay in the car and keep the motor running. I don't want to spend a second longer there than necessary. You made sure this car is untraceable?"

"Yes, sir. The plates are fake, but it won't matter anyway

because as soon as you're back on the chopper, the car will get collected and destroyed."

"Good. You have the decoy car in place too?"

"Same make of car, same plates. Everything is good, sir. If we get a tail, the other car will draw them away while we wait them out."

I nod. "I know you've got this, James. I'm not questioning your skill set. I just don't want any of this to follow us back home. My friends have had enough to deal with lately without bringing more shit to their door. And as much as I'd like to keep things from spilling over, it always does."

He chuckles at that. He knows that's the damn truth. He's been with me since I was a kid.

"Do you ever get sick of this life, James?" I ask him on a whim as we pull out of the airfield and head to the coordinates sent to me.

"Some days, sure. It's not a life suited to everyone, but then the good outweighs the bad."

"Oh yeah, like what?"

"Claire and I couldn't have children of our own and when she passed, I just couldn't bear the thought of lying down with another woman and considering starting a family with them. But you…God, Claire loved you like you were hers. You were the son we never had and if living in this world means being close to you, then so be it. Because I don't regret the choices I've made for a single second."

I swallow around the lump in my throat. I'm forty-one fucking years old but shit, that's humbling to hear.

"My parents—"

"Were both a waste of space. I only stayed as long as I did for you. Trust me, if Claire hadn't gotten sick, she'd have fought to remain your nanny until you were eighteen, and then pulled you out of that mausoleum your parents called home and adopted you. I'd have been happy to call you mine, even if by that point you'd have had more hair on your balls than me."

I grin at that rather disturbing image.

"How the fuck do you know how many hairs I have on my balls? You been looking, old man?"

He rolls his eyes at me in the rearview mirror.

"It's in the attitude. Men who shave their backs, cracks, and sacks are pussies. You are not a pussy."

I throw my head back and laugh, forgetting about my headache as I'm caught up in the hilarity of the moment.

"You sure do have a way with words."

"I just call it like I see it."

I shake my head and continue to chuckle as the road narrows and steepens.

We don't talk after that, but the mood is lighter until we reach the peak of the hill we just climbed. I send a message to my team and hit send.

"Five miles to go. I've let the others know we're at the checkpoint. Fisher said he will talk to the local PD and see if they can watch this place. I don't know if they pick these drop-off spots at random or if there is a pattern they might be able to spot," I tell him, sliding my cell back into my pocket after reading Fisher's text.

"I hope so. Buying and selling people is fucked-up. I'm sure it went on back in my day, but I didn't hear much about it. Now it's everywhere."

"Trafficking is one of the world's richest enterprises. It has no space for morals or conscience. You have to be a special kind of asshole to be able to justify that shit and still sleep at night."

"Ain't that the truth? But it does bring me to my next question. What are you gonna do about this girl?"

"Honestly? I have no fucking clue. Kai said to make her the housekeeper. Let her earn a living while showing her I'm not going to use her body like whoever else might have hurt her. It's a way to earn her trust."

"You can try but I don't think this will be as simple as you are hoping. Trust is a fragile thing. It's harder to give to someone than it is to break it. Once it's broken, even if both parties take the time to glue the pieces back together again there will always be cracks. It might still be functional, maybe even beautiful, but it will never be the way it was before."

I scrub my hand over my face. "I'm not sure what else I can do, James. I'm really out of options if I plan on staying out of jail and keeping this woman away from the next buyer who might not be as nice of a guy as me."

"Call me crazy, but maybe you could just try to be her friend. At the risk of sounding like a pussy myself, she could probably use one."

I mull over his words and realize his idea holds merit. I'm not saying I won't go down the housekeeper route, it gives her something to focus on and a legitimate reason for me to give her money, money she will need once I deem it safe enough for her to leave.

"This is it, Will," James tells me quietly. Pulling into a wide clearing in the middle of the woods gives credence to this place being used as a regular drop-off point because it's not the kind of place you just stumble upon.

A nondescript white van is parked at the far edge of the

clearing. I slip my shades back on and catch myself in the rearview mirror once more.

"Don't play the hero. If anything goes down, you grab the girl and you get the fuck out of Dodge."

"Will," James protests, but my look shuts him up. He knows I can handle myself, but I don't want the woman getting caught in any potential crossfire.

"Fine, but if I have to stitch you up later, I won't be gentle about it."

I smirk before wiping my face clean of emotion and stepping out of the car.

I don't approach the van. I lean against my side window and wait. No matter the truth behind my actions, all they need to know is I paid a fuck-ton of money for this girl. I expect them to wrap her in a golden ribbon and carry her to me.

After a few minutes, a man climbs out of the driver's seat. It's hard to make out his height from here but he's fair-skinned, wearing shades like mine, and sporting an unruly full dark beard. I can't make out his hair as he is wearing a navy blue skull cap. His clothes are basic. Nothing too expensive, nothing too cheap. Just a plain navy blue jacket over dark jeans. The whole look is unremarkable, which I can only assume is exactly what he is going for.

He doesn't look in my direction. He moves to the back of the van and reaches inside. The door obscures my view of him, which I don't like one bit. I keep my eyes glued to the door, looking for anything suspicious, knowing Viddy will be pissed as hell if I get shot. I tense when the man steps back and the door closes.

He has a woman thrown over his shoulder, her body limp in his arms. The sight has my heart thumping in my chest.

Fuck, the first thing I need to do is get this woman to a damn doctor, or at least get a doctor to come to us.

I don't know if she's been physically knocked out or if she's been drugged, but neither option makes me happy.

The man walks toward me with a lazy gait and a smile on his face, completely at ease with the situation. Right off the bat I know he's done this a million times before. He's confident in his actions. There is no worry, no fear. But pride makes a man cocky. At any time, I could have pulled my gun and shot him, taking the girl with me anyway.

"Mr. Ajax, I presume. I have your gift."

Thankfully, this asshole only knows me by one of my aliases.

I nod curtly. "I must admit, this area was not what I was expecting. Seems a little too out in the open for my liking," I complain.

"Not to worry. This place is protected. If any unexpected guests arrive, they will quickly find the error of their ways."

Right. So we are being watched. Good to know. Snipers at a guess and the reason for his ease. Glad my instincts stopped me from drawing on him like I wanted to.

I incline my head, making it seem like I'm impressed. Really, I'd love to wrap my hands around his throat and squeeze his neck until his eyeballs pop out of their sockets.

"Anything I need to know?" I question, looking at the woman in his arms as he swings her down and offers her to me.

I hold my arms out without hesitation and accept her, only I hold her bridal style.

A bizarre feeling of rightness washes over me just as I feel her tense, but when I blink, she's relaxed again and I wonder if I imagined it.

"Your slave, your rules. We do offer a money-back guarantee." He laughs like he's a fucking comedian. I'd like to see him laugh with no tongue.

"If you're not happy with your purchase, you can return her within thirty days and we will correct her behavior. Or you can try out a different girl. I will say it is very rare that our clients are unhappy."

"Good. I'm sure I won't have any issues. I'm more than capable of reminding her of who her master is."

His grin spreads over his face and it's as cold as the bitter wind. This is a man who likes his job. If I have to bleed myself dry doing it, I'll make sure he ends up with his dick cut off and shoved up his ass. As much as I'd like to gut him where he stands, I don't doubt for a second his words about us being watched.

If I reached for my gun, I'd be dead before I could aim it his way. That's okay. I'm a patient man.

I school my features to hide my anger.

"Nice doing business with you." He smirks, taking a step back, but he doesn't go back to his van.

Not wanting to raise his suspicions, I walk to the back of the car and pop the trunk.

I carefully place the girl inside and close the lid without looking at her.

"If you'll excuse me, I find I'm excited to go home." I offer him a lecherous grin, which makes him chuckle as I open my door and climb inside.

I close it without further conversation.

"Let's get out of here," I growl at James. "And for the love of god, try to avoid potholes."

CHAPTER FIVE

SIX

I lie in the dark and let my tears fall. Better to get it out of my system now than later when I need to be strong. I thought coming with this guy might have been the safer option but after the conversation he just had with R, I'm not so sure. I can't really be surprised. It was a long shot anyway.

Maybe it won't be as bad as I'm building it up to be. Whoever this man is, he hasn't hurt me yet. He didn't do anything to prove himself the bigger man to R and I've seen that happen with the guards before. One of the others, I forget who, called it alpha male bullshit. I'm not sure what that means but I guess it's when they try to outdo each other.

I don't understand how you can be proud of being more of a monster than the man beside you.

My head pounds, the rumbling of the car not helping at all, and the coarse material of the hood scratches my skin. The constant reminder of the hood makes me feel like I can't breathe. I try to think of Ten and his stories, but it's not helping right now. I need to get out. I need air. I can feel my chest move faster and faster and yet I feel like I'm getting less air than before. I don't know what's happening to me. Am I dying? Did R do something? Is that why Two died?

At the thought of Two, I give in to the darkness and let it take me under. I'm feeling too many things at once and I don't know how to shut everything off. As scared as I am right now, the darkness is the only thing that promises me peace.

The peace is short-lived. It feels like I've only just passed out when I jolt awake. The road is bumpy and I bounce a while, which makes me feel sick to my stomach. Not that I have anything inside me to throw up.

I feel the car slow and nervous anticipation spreads over me. It's not fear per se. I'm not sure I've processed everything enough to feel anything beyond this need to survive. All I have is my will to live and a knowing that whatever comes now will change my life forever.

Logically I'm aware I should be terrified. Lots of people over the years had told me there is something wrong with me for not feeling a certain way about things—fear mostly. But it's not that I don't feel emotions, it's that I hide them in a tiny box in the back of my mind so they don't beat against my skin like a butterfly trying to escape from its chrysalis.

None of the slaves I had been with over the years, and

there had been many, had been held in captivity longer than me. That's not to say that there weren't thousands of people treated worse, because there were. If I hadn't been sold at such a young age with the explicit instructions that I had to be kept pure, my fate would have been much the same.

The thing that made me so different from the others was my view of the world. My tiny sliver of life had been dark and uninformative. I knew how to kneel, how to present, how to walk, how to address a master. I also knew how to make a man come with my mouth and how to swallow him without gagging.

What I didn't know was what chocolate tasted like on my tongue or what the ocean felt like on my feet. I didn't know how it felt to dance in the rain or to make angel wings in the snow. The only time I left my windowless room, apart from when I was receiving my training, was to be relocated to another windowless room in a new compound somewhere.

I was born in darkness, raised in darkness, and like a flower reaching for the sun, I crave the light I know I've been missing. Where others lost hope, I held on to mine, cultivating it until it was the only thing keeping me going.

So even though I know I should be scared, craving the light outweighs everything else.

The hum of the engine turns off and I hear the door open — no, two doors opening — and a set of footsteps heading my way.

Not sure of the best option, I figure it might be safer to continue to pretend I'm asleep. That's what I do when the trunk opens moments later.

I try not to tense when I feel a hand touch my leg, but it's difficult fighting against your instincts when they are telling you to run and hide.

I wait for him to drag me out and throw me over his shoulder. Instead, a hand slides under my legs and one behind my back before lifting me as if I weigh next to nothing.

I find myself pressed against a hard chest as he carries me somewhere. I like the way he smells. It's nothing I recognize, but it smells clean and that's something I haven't felt in a long time.

It's hard to feel clean when you're living in the dirt. I'm not talking about the earthy kind of dirt you grow flowers in.

"I know you're awake," he murmurs to me.

Only years of training stop me from reacting.

"I understand you have no reason to trust me and that's okay. I'm not expecting you to. But know this, I will not hurt you." His quiet words wash over me, making that hope buried inside me bloom like a seed shooting from the ground. I lock it up tight, knowing this is likely a trick and I refuse to fall at the first hurdle.

I heard what R said. This man has thirty days to return me if he's unhappy. I might not know what life outside of my cage holds for me, but I know I can't go back. I won't be protected like I was before. My memory flashes back to the revolving guards in and out of the Two's cell and I shiver before I can hold it in.

The man holds me tighter. I feel us shifting around and then I'm sitting in his lap.

"The hood needs to stay on until I get you home, as a safety precaution," he tells me as he drops his arms. I can feel him moving and the rustle of fabric makes me bite my lip hard enough to draw blood.

Oh god, I'm not ready.

When I feel something touch my bare shoulder, I jump.

Something warm and heavy that smells of this man is wrapped around me, warding off the chill.

"Alright, let's go!" he says louder than before. When we don't move, I realize it's not me he's talking to.

Moments later, a loud whoop–whooping noise has my body going rigid as I squeeze my hands into fists.

My stomach flips and dips and then it feels like we're moving, but not like when we were in the car.

The man turns me until I'm tucked up under his chin and a warm hand rests on my thigh.

"It will take a little while before we get home. Just rest. Everything's going to be okay now. You'll see."

He sounds so sure, but liars always do.

I find my eyes drifting closed as his warmth and smell surround me, seeping into my bones and making me slowly but surely relax.

Just as I'm about to fall asleep, he asks me a question. Because I'm more asleep than awake and it's taking more strength than usual to keep that door in my brain tightly closed, I answer with the truth and not with the designation of the dead woman I left in the back of a van. Once it's out, it's too late to take it back.

"I'm Six."

CHAPTER SIX

WILL

She slept the entire flight, only stirring when I transferred her from the chopper to the waiting car.

I don't know why I've kept her on my lap the whole time, but try as I might, I cannot put her down.

I want nothing more than to yank the stupid black hood from her face, but I don't want her to see where we're going. I live so far out that she'd never find her way off my land without help. My staff are nothing if not loyal, but I'm still not willing to take any chances.

I keep my eyes focused out my window and bite the inside of my cheek to keep from staring at her again.

The flimsy white dress she has on is thin cotton and doing little to hide the fact that she's naked underneath. The dark dusty nipples which hardened in the cold are almost impossible to look away from, but I manage it some fucking how.

When she stirs in my lap, I have to start thinking about my grandmother to keep my dick from getting hard and traumatizing the woman who has been through enough without a sick fuck like me getting turned on.

I didn't lie when I said I wouldn't hurt her but that doesn't mean her vulnerability doesn't call to me like a siren.

She tenses and relaxes just as quickly but it's too late, I already know she's awake.

I don't call her on it. I let her have a few minutes as we make it down the end of the drive and James parks us right outside the house.

He looks at me in the rearview mirror before his eyes drop to Six and turn sad.

"If you need anything, let me know." I nod as he climbs out to get the door.

He holds it open before heading up the steps to the house and opening that one too.

I maneuver my way out of the car with Six in my arms and hold her against me as I make my way up the steps, passing James on his way back down.

"Get some rest. I'll call you in the morning if I need you, but I think I'll take a few days."

"You got it." He winks, moving back to the car, which he'll park in the huge garage before heading down the trail to the small cabin built for him and his wife. With her gone, I'd offered to have him move into the big house with me, but he refused.

"My woman is in every aspect of this house. Why would I ever want to leave?" he'd questioned, shutting me up.

35

Once inside, I shut the door and set the alarm one-handed before carrying Six into the living room.

I take a deep breath before looking down at her in my arms. Her chest is rising and falling rapidly and although she's doing a pretty good job of hiding it, this woman has to be terrified.

"I'm going to stand you up and then I'm going to take your hood off."

When she doesn't protest, I lower her to her feet.

She sways for a second, so I steady her before letting go.

"You okay?"

"Yes, master."

"Call me Will," I order, not wanting her to call me anything she might have called the others. I grit my teeth at the thought of her with anyone but me, which brings me up short.

What the ever-loving fuck am I thinking? She might, for all intents and purposes, belong to me, but she isn't mine.

"Yes, master," she whispers, making me shake my head. We'll figure it out.

Reaching up, I grab hold of the hood and gently pull it over her head.

Red hair tumbles free as I toss the hood aside. Six keeps her head bowed so I don't see much else.

"Six."

She lifts her head, but not enough for me to get a clear look at her. I close the distance between us and slip a finger under her chin. I tip her head back until stormy gray eyes look up at me.

It's as if the floor shifts beneath my feet. I don't buy into love at first sight, that's not what this is, but lust at first sight is something else altogether. I want to fuck this woman. Christ, I want to do a damn sight more than just fuck her and I can't do any of it because she's off-limits.

I swallow, my mouth feeling as if it's filled with sawdust.

"Welcome to my home."

Jesus. Did I really say that to a girl I just bought?

She doesn't say anything, so I try a question instead.

"Are you hungry?"

She frowns as if she's unsure how to answer. I see something like panic flit across her face for a minute before I smooth my hands up and down her arms.

"I'm starving, so how about we both have something to eat together?"

"I...yes? Master," she stutters.

"It's Will. And good. You stay right here, and I'll rustle us up some food." I hesitate to say the next part, not wanting her to freak out, but she needs to know.

"Don't try to leave. The house alarm is set. You wouldn't get away before I caught you."

Her pretty eyes look at my jaw before she replies. "Yes, master."

With a sigh, I head to the kitchen needing a minute to breathe. This is going to be a lot harder than I thought it would be. Not just because of this whole fucked-up situation but because this woman is beyond stunning. At no point in my planning did I factor any attraction into it.

It's a rookie mistake, but Jesus, it's like someone dipped their fingers into my brain and pulled out a living breathing version of my fantasies. She's young too, but that body tells me she's all woman.

There is no way she disappeared without someone missing

her. Hell, I've just met her and even I'd feel her absence if she were gone.

I push that aside for now and concentrate on the biggest issue, her apparent brainwashing. I'd been prepared for fear. I'd been ready for screaming and crying. But so far, given the circumstances, Six is holding it together remarkably well and that just doesn't sit right with me.

I think about the best way to move forward as I throw together a few sandwiches and a couple of bottles of water.

Truth is, I have no fucking clue what I'm doing. As I walk back into the living room and see Six in the same spot I left her standing, her eyes downcast, I realize that makes two of us.

We've both been thrown in at the deep end and we either have to learn to swim or we'll both drown each other trying to survive.

CHAPTER SEVEN

SIX

I barely breathe, worried I'll somehow even do that wrong. I've already messed everything up, but I honestly never expected to have to make choices. I've never had to pick or choose something before. What if I choose wrong? My heart races with panic. What if this was a test and I've already failed?

I fist my hands, my nails cutting into my palms as I use the snap of pain to center myself.

I feel his presence before I see him, careful to keep my eyes lowered, especially while I'm not sure of the protocol yet.

His footsteps pause and then they move to the left of me.

"Come, let's eat."

I lift my head and see him move to a circular table set with four wooden chairs.

I wait for him to sit before moving closer and kneeling on the floor beside him. This part, luckily, I don't have to think about as it's instinctive. Back straight, head up, chest out, arms on my thighs, palms up.

"Fuck."

I swallow hard before I feel fingers under my jaw tipping my head up once more.

I look at a spot over his shoulder.

He growls. "Look at me, Six. Let me see those eyes."

I tense, then do as he asks, not wanting to disobey a direct order even if I know I'm never supposed to make eye contact.

His dark eyes are angry and I don't know why. What did I do wrong? I run through how I'm sitting. I did everything right. I know I did.

"No more avoiding looking at me. If we are talking I want your eyes on mine," he orders, making me gulp.

"Now why don't you sit on the chair beside me?"

My eyes move over his face, trying to read between the lines but I don't know him well enough to understand him yet. Why would he want me to sit beside him?

He curses again before his thumb slides backward and forward over my jaw in a surprisingly comforting move.

"Okay, Six. I think we need to have a talk about what I expect of you, alright?"

"Yes, master."

"It's Will. I really fucking hate it when you call me master," he snarls, making my eyes widen.

He must read my fear because his face softens.

"It's Will. If that's too weird for you, then I can handle sir, but not master. It makes me think of all the assholes that have come before me and that makes me want to go hunting."

I don't understand all of that but enough to know that the word master infuriates him.

"Say it, Six. Say my name."

"Will, sir."

He shakes his head and chuckles.

"Better, I guess. Now tell me, do you want to sit in the chair beside me or on the floor? I won't force you either way."

I blink and feel that panic again at being given a choice, so I stick with what I know.

"I'm fine here, Will, sir."

His eyes drift closed for a moment and for some odd reason he starts counting under his breath. "Okay, Six. Baby steps."

He stands and walks away before returning with a cushion.

"At least kneel on this so you don't hurt yourself." He offers me his hand as I move. I take it warily and rearrange myself on the cushion.

"Good girl." He smooths his hand over my hair and I instinctively lean into him, resting my head on his thigh.

He freezes for a moment before he continues stroking me gently. His soft touch and repetitive actions relax me.

"Here." He holds out what looks to be some kind of sandwich so I lean forward and take a bite.

I swear my eyes roll into the back of my head. I don't know what this is but it's so much better than any other sandwich I've ever had.

He laughs again. "It's yours. You can take it."

I look at the food as I swallow the bite in my mouth.

I try not to think about when M played this trick on me before. As soon as I touched the food, she took it away and ate it herself. I wasn't allowed to eat or drink anything after that for three days.

Needless to say, I don't reach out for it. The smile slips from his face as he sighs and holds the sandwich to my lips.

"Bite."

I do as he asks and take a bite out of the sandwich, watching as he places it down and takes a bite out of his own. I'm confused about why he is feeding me before himself but so far this man hasn't done anything the way he is supposed to.

Once I finish my mouthful, he holds the sandwich for me to bite again.

He alternates taking a bite of his with feeding me until the plate is empty.

"Here, drink this." He cracks open a bottle of water and holds it to my lips.

I drink it down greedily, far thirstier than I realized. When the bottle is empty, he pulls it away from my lips.

"Do you need more?"

I think if I eat or drink anything else I might be sick.

"No, thank you, Will sir."

"All right. Let's get you freshened up and then I'll give the doctor a call. I'd like you to get checked over."

I don't react to the word doctor outwardly, but inside it takes everything I have to stop my food from making a reappearance.

He stands and offers me his hand. I look at it for a minute before slipping one of mine into his much larger one.

He helps me off the floor and walks me across the room. I keep my eyes down but something, a shadow maybe, draws my attention. I turn my head and freeze solid.

"What? What is it?"

Windows. Lots and lots of windows. In fact, the whole wall is just glass and outside it—nothing but colors.

CHAPTER EIGHT

WILL

She stares out the window in an almost trance-like state with tears tracking down her face. I don't think she even realizes she's crying.

"Six?"

She turns to look at me fully and Jesus Christ, her stormy eyes flash with emotion as the tears continue to streak her cheeks.

"You have windows?" she whispers.

I have never wanted to burn the world to the ground more than I do right now.

"Yeah, baby." The endearment slips out before I can think better of it. "I've got a lot of windows. Go check them out," I tell her softly as she takes a step toward them.

I fist my hands and clench my jaw so hard I feel it click.

She is in her own little world now, drawn to the beauty just beyond her reach. Watching her visceral reaction is almost painful to witness. It's both beautiful and gut-wrenching.

Where has she been? What the fuck happened to this girl?

She reaches out a shaky hand and presses her fingertips to the glass before making a sharp sound that almost splinters my control.

She presses her forehead against the glass as the waning evening light bathes her in an ethereal glow that turns her white shift dress almost transparent.

Her naked silhouette beneath the fabric is enough to make my cock rock hard and doesn't that leave me feeling like a bastard?

The sorrow and reverence pouring off this girl are palpable and yet I have to fight to stop myself from reaching for her, from slipping that dress over her head and driving my cock into her while she weeps. Call me sick but I always did have a thing for a pretty crier.

Giving her a minute, I fire off a text to James for him to get ahold of the doctor and delay him until tomorrow before slipping my cell back in my pocket.

I stare at the woman before me and wonder if I should call someone else. Maybe Jenna or Viddy. Perhaps having another woman around would make her feel safer. Except, aside from the moment when I asked her what she wanted to eat, I'm not getting the terrified vibe from her. Nervous, wary, and way out of her depth—absolutely. But she hasn't cringed away from me once. She hasn't flinched when I've touched her, and she hasn't reacted to protect herself when I've startled her. She doesn't display half of the things I assumed she would. But watching her look at those windows as if she had never seen anything more amazing in her life tells me just how dark her world must have been.

Walking toward her, unable to stop myself, I slide my hands over her shoulders and turn her into me.

I wrap her up in my arms and hold her tight. She is so tense I almost back off, but I don't want her to be averse to my touch. I want to be able to comfort her when she needs it because I have a feeling the next few months are going to be a lot for her to deal with.

She doesn't relax, not even when I rub my hands up and down her back, so I pull back and tip her head up.

"Let's get you cleaned up and changed and then we can go and sit outside. I'll light a fire and we can watch for fireflies."

"Fireflies?" she questions, looking confused.

"Little lightning bugs that produce flashes of light. You'll see. Come on." I take her hand and tug her toward the stairs. She looks over her shoulder at the windows as if she's scared to move.

"I have windows upstairs too."

"You do?" she whispers in awe, making me swallow. She seems so young and innocent at this moment. There are a million things I want to show her, to teach her. But the more she looks at me like that, the more I realize things are about to get a whole lot more complicated.

I keep hold of her hand and look away before I do something stupid like kiss her. I walk her upstairs, intending to take her to the spare room, but hesitate.

I look over my shoulder at her. Her face is pale, her hand is squeezing mine tightly, and yet she isn't fighting me. She's trusting me to lead the way.

Fuck it.

I take her up the next flight of stairs to my room, which happens to be the entire top floor.

"This is my room. I'll show you yours later, but I thought you might like these." I pull her inside, hit the switch next to the lights, and watch as the blinds retract across six huge skylights in the ceiling.

She gasps when she sees and steps forward, stopping when she realizes what she did.

"Go ahead. You're welcome in here. There are only two places in this house that are a no-go and I'll show you which ones they are when I give you the tour."

She stares up at the windows as the last of the sun's rays filter through, washing over her face before her eyes slip closed and she smiles.

For the first time since she arrived, she looks at peace. I watch her silently, almost feeling like an intruder. I'm loath to open my mouth and ruin the moment but I can't bear her wearing the taint of that place any longer. What I can do, though, is give her a million more moments like this one.

"I'm going to grab you a robe, then I want you to jump in the shower, okay?"

She opens her eyes and looks at me, her smile dropping.

"Yes, sir."

I leave her where she is for a minute and head to the bathroom, knowing she'll love it in here too. The bedroom wasn't the only place I'd had fancy windows installed. Directly over the shower is a huge skylight, with another over the claw-foot bathtub.

I make sure there are clean towels and a robe on the back of the door. "Come on." I hold my hand out for her and she takes it less hesitantly this time. At least until she steps into the bathroom and sees the shower.

She looks at me in question.

"Do you want me to show you how to use it?"

Her frown deepens. "Use it?"

"The shower. So you can wash."

She turns back to the shower as understanding dawns. She bites her lip looking at the controls and I can see she's overwhelmed already.

Distracting her for a minute, I point to the skylight.

"Look up. It's like showering outside."

She sucks in a sharp breath when she sees what I'm pointing to before a wide smile spreads across her face.

She reaches down and grabs the hem of her dress and before I can stop her, she tugs the material up and over her head, tossing the now discarded dress on the counter.

And there she is, standing before me, looking like a fucking goddess.

I knew the second I laid my hands on this woman she was going to change my life. I had no idea it would be so quickly. I planned to hold myself back, imagining an invisible barrier between us. That barrier lies in shattered pieces at our feet now. God help us both. She's just sealed her fate because, like Hades, I plan on tying her to me and keeping her locked in my world forever.

CHAPTER NINE

SIX

This place is something out of a fairytale. If I dreamed up somewhere I'd want to live I would never have come up with this. It's so beautiful. There is so much light, it banishes the darkness and makes me feel freer than I ever have before. Even if it's just an illusion, I'll happily give myself over to the mirage.

"Six? Do you want me to help you?"

I turn back to Will and see him watching me with that look in his eyes I've seen so many times on men. For some reason, it doesn't scare me. In a weird way it brings me comfort. I was worried he found me defective in some way and he'd send me back. Watching his eyes drop to my chest before they dip lower, I see he was just better at hiding it than most.

I mimic his movements and let my eyes move over his

muscular body. They freeze when they land on his dick. He's hard, which is good. Hopefully he'll keep me now. But he's big and there is no way it won't hurt me.

"I don't know how it works. It's very different from what I'm used to," I admit quietly. I worry I've said too much. I was born to fuck, not to speak, but Will seems to be different from the trainers. Maybe he is lonely and wants conversation too. I feel that hidden well of hope swelling in anticipation. I force myself to ignore it, not wanting to get ahead of myself. Until he explains what is expected of me and what his rules are, I'm in a very delicate situation. I could make a critical error without knowing it.

"That's okay, I'll teach you whatever you need to know." His voice sounds rougher than before, but I'm not sure why so I just nod and thank him.

He nudges me inside the glass enclosure and points at the buttons, showing me how to make it work. When he shows me how to adjust the temperature to make it warm, I can't help but gasp in delight.

"You have warm water?"

He stops to look at me, his expression clouding for a moment. *Stupid, stupid, Six. You know better.*

"Hey, no, I'm not mad at you. Mad yes. I won't lie about that, but never at you. I'm just trying to get my head around the fact that you've gone so long without showering in warm water that this feels like a luxury to you."

I don't know how to reply but instinctively I know it would be the wrong move to tell him I've never had a hot shower.

"Well, I guess you're going to enjoy this one huh?" He smiles, which makes my stomach tighten.

"Alright, less talking, more washing. Just hit this button

when you're ready. You can use any of the shower gels and shampoos you see. You have a bunch of girly stuff in the room I have set up for you. For now, use whatever your heart desires. I'll just be over here." He points across the room before climbing out and leaving me alone inside the glass walls.

I hit the button and jump when the cold water hits me, making me hiss. I should have known he was lying about the hot water. But just as the thought forms, I feel the water start to warm up.

I feel a smile spread across my face as the tension in my body eases under the warm spray. I glance up and through the window see heavy dark clouds rolling in. I almost pinch myself. It's like dancing in the rain, only the rain is inside.

Tears drip from my eyes, but I don't wipe them away, confident the shower spray will hide the evidence of them.

I'm not sure what's to come or what will happen to me in the future, but I'll deal with it. For this, I can deal with anything.

I don't let my mind wander to the dark thoughts that mock my naivety. Instead, I select a bottle from the wire rack and squirt a blob of orange-scented soap into my hands before lathering up my body. I pause for a second when I hear a groan. When I don't hear anything else, I carry on.

I wash and wash until my skin is pink and tender to touch and only then do I feel clean enough to stop. I don't want to leave. If I could stay under this water forever while it washes away the taint that clings to my skin I would. But I have duties to perform. If I fail, he'll send me back and I can't let that happen.

I shut the water off and turn, jerking hard enough I almost slip.

"Shit. Sorry, Six, I thought you knew I was here."

I did, but I got so caught up in the shower I forgot all about him. That's a rookie mistake that could have ended with me in a whole lot of pain.

"I'm sorry."

He holds open a large fluffy white towel for me to step into.

"Nonsense," he tells me as he wraps it around my body. "You have nothing to be sorry about. How did you enjoy your shower?" he asks, rubbing the soft material over my body.

"Magical," I tell him honestly.

He laughs lightly, making me relax as his hands falter on my breasts.

"You finish off getting dried and I'll find you something to wear. There's a robe on the back of the door that will work for now."

He steps back once I have a grip on the towel and strolls into the bedroom, leaving me confused.

I dry myself as he asked but once that's done, I stand and wait for him with the wet towel in my hands. He didn't tell me to follow him so staying put should be the safest bet.

He returns a few minutes later with a white shirt similar to the one he's wearing. When he doesn't yell at me for not following him, I know I made the right choice. Phew. Perhaps I'm better at reading his cues than I realized.

"We'll get you some clothes, but for now you can borrow anything of mine that you want. I figured this would do for now. Here, let me help."

He holds the shirt open for me, so I drop the towel and step forward. His jaw tightens again but I focus on slipping my arms through the sleeves. I stand before him, watching him as he buttons the shirt slowly from bottom to top, leaving a tingle of awareness across my skin.

"There, perfect. Come on, let's head back downstairs," he tells me almost reluctantly as he takes my hand and tugs me along with him.

He keeps his pace slow enough that I can keep up with him, which I'm grateful for. He is a lot bigger than me. I have no doubt he could drag me if he wanted to, but he seems to be trying to ease me into this gently. Part of me wants to believe he has good intentions, but I'm not stupid enough to fall for a kind smile and gentle hands this early in the game. I've found people have many faces. They can be both cruel and kind, hard and soft, laid back and volatile. Until I get to know him better, I have no choice but to be cautious of the eggshells crunching beneath my feet. One wrong move and the sharp edges will tear me to shreds.

"The wind has picked up so instead of sitting outside, how about a movie instead?"

I want to argue with him. I'd sit outside in the freezing snow if it meant breathing in clean fresh air. But not wanting to rock the boat, I nod in agreement.

"What do you want to watch?"

My eyes widen as I look at him in alarm. This is one test I can't pass. I've never seen a movie. It's not that I don't know what one is. I've even caught fragments passing by the guards' station when they watch one, but as they prefer sports and porn, it wasn't often.

He curses when he must see my panic.

"I wasn't thinking. How about I choose something I think you might like?"

I nod rapidly before he finishes.

"Sit here. I'll be back." He urges me to sit on a huge sofa that swallows me up as I lean back. It's like sitting on a cloud. I run my hand over the soft, gray velvety material as Will disappears for a moment and think back to my room at the compound. My threadbare blanket had felt like such a luxury then. I'd felt grateful for it and even thanked X, who I'd met that day for the first time. Of course, I had to show him how thankful I was with my mouth, but it had been worth it later that night when I wrapped it around me.

I feel sick as I recognize it for what it was—conditioning. I'd been so long without the comforts of a bed or a blanket that when I was given them, I felt I'd been given an amazing gift instead of recognizing they should have been given to me regardless, as kindness from one human to another.

"Here, hold this." Will appears and hands me a bowl, snapping me out of my musings.

He grabs something off the coffee table before sitting beside me and tugging a thick soft black blanket off the sofa behind us.

I choke down the threatening tears at the sumptuous feel of it. So soft and warm. If I'd given a blowjob for the paper-thin blanket at the compound, what would be expected of me for using this?

"Okay, I'm playing it safe and going for *Transformers*. I don't want to trigger anything for you and figure I'll be safe with giant alien robots, right?"

I look up at him in confusion as the television screen bursts to life and the movie begins.

"Trigger anything?" I ask, even though my mind tells me to be quiet.

CHAPTER TEN

WILL

"I don't want to bring up horrible memories for you that you'll have spent time trying to forget," I tell her carefully. I'm guessing *triggers* isn't a term she's familiar with, which makes sense. I'm getting the sickening feeling Six has been held since she was a child.

"I never forget anything," she whispers before turning back to the television. I want to ask her more, but I can see the day has taken its toll. She needs time to let her brain process everything. What better way to do that than with a movie and popcorn?

She quickly becomes engrossed in the movie. Not me. I haven't got a clue what's going on. I haven't been able to take my eyes off the beguiling woman beside me. She's so sweet and almost childlike. There is an innate innocence to her that burns brightly, drawing me in like a moth to a flame. Like the idiot I am, I find it impossible to resist her allure. Even when I know she could be my downfall.

Still, knowing this has disaster written all over it, I don't move away from her. Instead, I press my leg firmly against hers, feeling the heat from her skin seep through the leg of my pants.

She laughs at something and it's such a pure infectious sound, I almost join her. I fight the urge, not wanting to break the moment. She seems peaceful right now.

My eyes move over her and stall on her chest where her hard nipples poke through the material of my shirt.

I close my eyes and bite back a groan. She might look pure and innocent, but Six's body is begging for me to do very wicked things to it.

She must feel my eyes on her because she turns to look at me. "Don't forget the popcorn," I tell her softly.

"Popcorn?"

I bite back a snarl at the shit this woman has been deprived of.

"Here." I lift a kernel to her lips. "Try it. It's what we consider one of the premier movie snacks."

She parts her lips and allows me to slip the piece of popcorn into her mouth.

"It's good. Odd texture, but sweet," she says, surprise evident in her voice.

"Help yourself. There is plenty more where this came from.

"Thank you." An explosion drags her attention back to the television, but I notice the fingers on her left hand twitching. She's not quite as relaxed as I thought.

I slide my hand over hers, stilling her movements before drawing circles with my thumb on the back of her hand.

Her body tenses but I don't stop, wanting her to get used to my touch. I want to desensitize her. I don't think she's afraid of *me* but afraid of not knowing what I want from her. I'd tell her if I had the answer, but right now I'm as lost as she is. I'm big enough and ugly enough to know the difference between right and wrong. I've done a remarkable job skating with ease through the gray area that blurs the two. But now, if I don't fight the impulse, I'll veer wildly of course, and end up somewhere I might not be able to return from.

I don't interrupt her for the rest of the movie, taking joy from watching her reactions. When it's finished, she turns to me with the expression I imagine on a child who has just been told they're going to Disneyland.

"That was amazing. Everything looks so real."

She places the last piece of popcorn in her mouth and licks her lips. My eyes track the movement, imaging what her tongue would feel like licking its way up and down my shaft.

Fuck.

I stand up abruptly, needing to put distance between us before I do something reckless.

"It's getting late and you must be getting tired. How about I give you a quick tour before I show you to your room?"

"I…yes, sir," she answers, standing up beside me.

I want to kick my own ass for making her revert back to her earlier behavior, but I can't without becoming a bigger asshole.

I offer her my hand, which she takes without hesitation.

"Okay, Six, this is the den." I gesture to the area we were

sitting in before walking her around the wall that separates this area from the main area.

"This is the formal sitting area I use if I have guests and whatnot. As you can see, it flows into the dining area and the reading nook over there, near the windows you love so much."

I keep my voice light with a teasing lilt to it.

"Outside is a large deck for grilling and stuff. There is a seating area and a firepit I use a lot, especially in the summer months. Beyond that are the infinity pool and the lake that backs up to the forest.

"There is more seating at the water's edge. It's peaceful down there so you can often find me drinking my morning coffee and planning world domination from down there."

She doesn't ask me any questions. She gazes longingly out the windows into the dark night.

"Come on." I tug her into the kitchen. "This is huge and state of the art and largely unused," I admit with a laugh. "It's not that I can't cook, it's that I'm lazy. By the time I'm finished working, it's just easier to order in. What about you? Can you cook?" I want to kick myself as soon as the words are out. What the fuck is wrong with me?

"No, I've never learned. But I'd like to."

"Then I shall teach you," I reassure her. And I will. One day she will need those skills.

I push open the door at the far end of the kitchen.

"This is the utility room, housing the washer and dryer and shit. I'll show you how to use those once you're settled in."

I point to the door at the far end of the room. "That's one of the no-go areas. I do some work from home, so privacy is key," I explain vaguely. It's not like I can say, *oh by the way there is a dungeon downstairs reminiscent of a medieval torture chamber.*

57

I pull her from the room so she doesn't ask questions and take her up to the first floor. I show her the large family-style bathroom, my office, which is the other no-go zone, and point out the three spare rooms before opening the door on the last one.

"And this room is yours for as long as you're here."

Her grip tightens on my hand a fraction before she loosens it, but whatever I said wipes away the easiness between us, leaving tension in its wake. Perhaps she's worried I've brought her up here to fuck her blind. Although I'll admit the devil on my shoulder would like me to do just that, the angel knows it would break something that could never be fixed if I pushed her too soon.

I watch her take in the room, her expression blank as I point out the attached bathroom and closet.

"You need anything else, you know where my room is." I bend and press a kiss to her forehead, making her jump, before I spin on my heels and do something I'm not familiar with in my everyday life.

I retreat.

CHAPTER ELEVEN

SIX

My skin feels tight, as if it's struggling to keep everything I'm feeling inside me.

I try to keep it contained, but it's getting harder.

Before, I knew the rules. Before, I knew what was expected of me. But here, in this house filled with windows, I don't know what I'm supposed to do, who I'm supposed to be.

Everything is so light, so clean. I feel dirty just standing here. I don't want the stain on my soul to taint this place and strip it of its magic.

I look at the door and bite my lip. I know it's open. Will told me it was. He said I couldn't leave the house, but he never said I couldn't leave the room. I take a step toward it and stop again.

What if this is a test? I remember at one of the earlier facilities they left all the cage doors unlocked when they turned out the lights and left.

I remember the excited whispers and covertly spoken plans they started to form before panic and fear took over and they decided to storm the keep instead of sneaking out.

I stayed back in my corner. I'd already figured out what the others failed to see.

It was on the face of the last guard to leave. His usual stoic expression broke for just a second as the corner of his mouth lifted into a smirk. It was gone as quickly as it arrived, but I'd seen it and I knew it was a test. A test we would all fail.

I tried to make the others listen. I begged them until my voice gave out, but it was no good. I was already unpopular — someone they were wary of because I was treated differently than they were.

I watched them file out, knowing they wouldn't be the same when they returned.

The last person barely made it out the door before the screaming started.

I'd have screamed with them if I'd been able to. Instead, I curled up in a ball and cried so hard I wondered if I might drown in my own tears.

There were twenty-two of us in those cages and twenty-one people who took their chance to run. None of them escaped. Only four came back.

I was right when I said they would never be the same.

The next day, I was given a three-course meal consisting of foods I'd never seen before or since and ordered to eat it.

They made me eat until I was sick while the other four watched. I didn't look at them, but I didn't need to. I could feel their eyes centered on me. A target had been painted on my back.

Their dislike of me turned into hate and loathing. They couldn't do much to me or they'd risk the wrath of the trainers and guards, but that didn't stop the hate-filled whispers or the pinches to my skin as I passed.

The four survivors were punished for trying to leave. They were beaten, starved, and subjected to things I refuse to think about. But that didn't mean the guards weren't pissed at me too.

My cagemates failed to see that I didn't rat them out to the guards. I didn't raise the alarm. I kept my mouth shut beyond begging them to stay, even though I knew it was a trap. My punishment was in the way they turned everyone against me, leaving me more isolated than before.

I shake my head to disperse the memories and lock them back up with the others.

Staring at the door, I wonder if what I'm feeling now is what some of the others felt that day. Staying is the safest of evils but is it worth it? Being a coward has kept me alive but was it really living if I spent my years aging in a windowless cage?

Sometimes the risk and reward are out of balance, like a lottery win I remember someone once talking about. The chances of winning are small but if you never take the risk, you have zero chance of claiming the prize. Small or not, it still means you have a shot.

I swallow and look around the room I'm in.

It's pretty and light, which I think is supposed to be sooth-ing, but it's so unfamiliar I feel like an intruder.

The windows in this room are smaller and higher. I can't

see out of them properly from the floor or the bed. All I see are the branches of a tall tree. Not that I can sleep on the bed, anyway. It's too soft.

I turn back to the door, decision made.

I walk slowly toward it, my heart hammering in my chest, and touch my hand to the knob. I hesitate for a second and contemplate slipping the shirt back on that Will gave me, but I don't want to ruin it. And well, slaves aren't allowed to wear clothes they haven't earned. As of yet, I've earned nothing.

Turning the knob slowly, I gasp when it clicks before I tug it open.

I stand in the doorway for a second, waiting for something to happen. When the house remains quiet, I slowly make my way down the steps.

Despite the house being big, I don't get lost. I know exactly where I'm going.

I can remember the layout of the place like I can remember everything.

It's something I've been able to do forever. I didn't know it was unusual until Ten told me it was. He also told me to keep that to myself and I trusted him enough to do it.

I often wondered as I got older if he thought about that when he killed himself. If he knew he was subjecting me to a lifetime of seeing him swinging lifelessly like that.

My attention drifts from Ten to the moonlight casting shadows across the room as I move closer to the windowed wall.

I walk toward it and only stop when my fingers touch the cool glass.

The rain and wind have stopped, leaving me able to clearly

62

see the full moon high in the sky. It bathes the lake and trees in an eerie glow, making the whole area look majestic.

My intended owner had insisted I understand basic English and math. I'm not sure why and from the two guards I once heard whispering to each other, neither did they. According to them, my role would be limited to the bedroom, so why would I need a working brain?

It's not something I had the answer to, but I wasn't going to complain. Not when I got to read a book for the first time.

It opened up a way to escape even when my body was trapped behind bars.

Later, when everyone else was asleep, I'd replay the words I'd read in my head, remembering each and every detail as I grew imaginary wings and flew to another world filled with endless possiblities.

The moon tonight reminds me of a book I read about men who changed into wolves when the moon was full.

As I slide to the floor and lie down on the cool wood and stare out at the stars, I wonder idly if there might be wolves out there.

Tiny sparks of light flit across the sky in an almost chore-graphed frenzy. I frown unsure of what I'm seeing until I remember Will's words from before. *Fireflies*. Dozens and dozens of Fireflies illuminating the sky like tiny fairies bestowing us with magic. They seem almost otherworldly, fragile yet utterly captivating.

Is this how Will sees me?

I don't know how long I stare into the night, watching their graceful dance before I drift off to sleep, feeling far more relaxed than before.

I might not be free. It could all just be an illusion. That's all magic is without a little faith– an illusion. But I have a window and stars and fireflies and for now, it's enough. It's closer to free than I've ever been before.

CHAPTER TWELVE

WILL

I heard the click of her door when it opened, but I stayed in my seat at the end of the hall, hidden within the shadows.

I wasn't sure what to expect when I left her there. I needed to leave but, for some reason, I couldn't make myself go so I sat and waited. I thought she'd be happy in the room I picked out for her. It's basic but ready for her to put her stamp upon it. It's the room I planned to give her, but now it all feels wrong.

Now I want her in my room with me. I want to be inside her while she gazes up at the stars through those windows she loves so much.

I'd come so close to crossing that arbitrary line, I had to get her away from me. My control was hanging by a thread and I knew if I pushed, she'd have been terrified.

I've managed to corral the animal within for now with a soothing promise that soon she'd be ours, but I'm not sure how long I can hold him back.

As she crept from the room, naked as the day she was born, the animal roared and shoved against the bars I had him locked behind, demanding to be unleashed so he could touch and taste every inch of her. Instead, I remained quiet, keeping my presence a secret as I followed her downstairs. I was half surprised when she didn't head for the door, even knowing I warned her not to. We humans have an innate fight or flight response to most situations, but I'm not sure Six has one.

When she turned the corner into the living area, I knew exactly where she was heading.

I hung back and watched her curl up like a child against the glass and fall asleep.

Once her breathing evens out, I move nearer, sitting in the chair closest to her so I can watch over her.

When I slide my jacket off, I realize there is a chill in the air.

Gently as I can, I cover Six's body with my jacket before walking to the heating panel and adjusting it so it warms the room, including the wooden floor she's lying on.

It takes everything in me to stop myself from picking her up and taking her to bed with me.

It's a fight I know I'll lose eventually.

Tomorrow, that's where she'll be sleeping, even if I have to tie her there myself. But tonight, I know she needs this. This one moment of calm before she has to learn to ride out the storm with me.

I've never felt like a bad person until Six stumbled into my life. Sure, I've done bad things and made bad decisions but nothing that would mark me as evil. Staring at Six's vulnerable form as I picture her running naked through the woods with me chasing after her, I have to admit there is something not entirely good running through my veins.

A dark desire, the one I think of as my animal, likes to toy with its prey, likes to hunt it before catching it and rutting it into a coma.

What could likely be Six's worst nightmare makes my dick weep with need and her possible reluctance only makes it sweeter.

If I do this, there will be no coming back. That morally ambiguous gray line I've been skating will be obliterated and could threaten the ties I have with my friends. Even knowing all that, I can't stop myself from planning ahead.

But first, I need to find out everything I can about the woman. I need to find out what makes her tick, where her soft spots are. She's a shiny new puzzle I want to figure out because once I know how she fits together, I can break her apart and rebuild her.

I don't remember falling asleep but the crick in my neck lets me know that I did.

I blink as the weak early morning sun streams in through the windows and when I open my eyes it's to see Six kneeling by the windows in that submissive pose of hers, watching me.

When she sees I'm awake, she drops her gaze, but I don't stop looking at her.

Her full breasts and rosy nipples have me gripping the arms of the chair so hard I hear it creak. Her red hair slips over her shoulders and hangs around her breasts, almost framing them for me.

Her small waist and flared hips have me itching to grab her.

"Good morning, Six." I greet her softly. "Remember what I said about looking at me?"

Her eyes snap to mine, worry on her face as she waits to see if I'll punish her.

"Good girl. Not that I'm complaining, but where is the shirt I gave you?" I gesture to her body. I'm not lying about having no issue with her walking around naked. I just assumed she would be more comfortable with something to cover her.

"It's in the room, sir. I didn't know I was supposed to sleep in it. I'm sorry," she whispers, her voice wobbling.

"Nothing to worry about. It's your choice now what you do or don't wear. I will leave you some things handy. If you want to wear them, do. If not, that is also fine. The only exception will be if I am expecting company. I'd like for you to be clothed then, okay?"

"Yes, master. I mean, yes, sir." She flushes.

"Do you think for today you could work on calling me Will? When you call me sir, it makes it seem as if I am above you in some way. I'm not. We are both the same. If anything, it is you who has the power. But we'll get to that. I would like us to be friends."

She cocks her head as if trying to process the word.

"Friends?"

I nod and lean back in the chair, spreading my legs as my eyes drop to her chest once more. I don't act coy or try to hide what I'm doing. If it's bothering her, it isn't showing.

"I…" She chews her lip as she decides whether to say what she's thinking.

68

"I'm not sure I know how to be friends with someone," she admits, making me both pissed and sad for her.

"You've never had a friend before?" Christ, where did this woman come from?

She thinks for a moment before a look of sadness crosses her face.

"Once, I think. But he's gone now."

I accept her answer for now without pushing for details. There will be plenty of time for that.

"Why did you sleep here and not in the room I gave you?"

Her eyes widen at the change of topic before she swallows nervously.

"Six, when I ask you a question, I expect you to answer me, but only with the truth. Even if I don't like the answer. I will not punish you for speaking."

"It's too clean, too soft...I...I couldn't sleep."

I motion to the glass. "The windows help?"

"Yes, sir. Will." She catches herself, making me smile.

"Tonight you will move into my room. You'll sleep beneath the stars."

Her mouth opens and she looks at me with awe before something else moves over her face.

"Come here," I order her softly, unable to resist.

Her chest rises and falls rapidly as she crawls toward me on her hands and knees.

Fuck me.

My dick, straining to escape the confines of my boxers, throbs with need.

She stops in front of me, her eyes resting on my shoulder before she remembers my rule about looking me in the eye.

I shouldn't be doing this. It's fucked-up and wrong on so many levels, and yet I can't stop.

I won't stop.

"Closer," I order as I spread my legs wider and she moves to kneel between them.

She looks up at me, waiting for my next instruction with those innocent eyes of hers. The leash holding the animal back snaps.

Reaching down, I unfasten my belt and slip it from the loops of my pants. Tossing it on the floor, I pop my button and lower my zipper.

"Touch me."

Her hands slide over my thighs and I groan just from having her touch me. She moves them up to the waistband of my pants and slips one inside my boxers.

I hiss when she wraps her small hand around my cock. "Pull it out." I lift myself so she can push my pants and boxers down, allowing my cock to spring free.

Gliding her hand up and down my dick, I look at her face as she watches her hands. Her focus is absolute. So much so, the tip of her tongue pokes out the side of her mouth, making a bead of pre-cum ooze from the slit of my dick at the sight of it. Before I can say anything else, she leans forward and swipes it clean with her tongue, making me groan again.

"Jesus, Six."

Lifting her eyes to mine once more, she traces the vein running down the length of my dick with her tongue before swirling it around the sensitive head. She repeats the motion again and again until my legs are shaking and I can't hold back anymore. Sensing that I'm about to lose it, she dips her head and swallows me whole.

"Motherfucker," I grunt, gripping her hair as I hold her in place for a moment. She swallows around me before I ease up enough for her to pull back a touch.

I am not a small guy, therefore I don't have a small dick, but you'd never know with how easy Six makes deep throating me look. She doesn't exhibit any kind of gag reflex.

She sucks and eases back, a string of saliva connecting her lips to my dick before she licks them clean.

It triggers something primal in me. Fuck, I'm only human.

I grip her hair harder and when she slides my cock back between her lips I take control, using my grip on her hair to fuck her face.

Her hands wrap around my thighs as I feel the tingling warning sign in the base of my spine a second before Six starts humming.

And that's my undoing. The vibrations have me erupting down her throat with a growl.

I hold her in place, riding my wave of euphoria before I remember she needs to breathe.

I let go, instantly feeling like an ass when she pulls back and starts sucking in lungsful of air, but she doesn't complain. When my eyes move to the tiny drop of cum at the edge of her mouth that's spilled over, I swipe it with my thumb and offer it to her.

She sucks it into her mouth like she did my cock, cleaning the pearly drop with her tongue.

"Now it's my turn."

CHAPTER THIRTEEN

SIX

J'm so focused on the dampness I can feel between my legs that it takes me a minute to realize he spoke.

What does he mean, *my turn*?

He doesn't explain it to me with words, but with actions. He stands up and shucks off his pants before unbuttoning his shirt and pulling it free, leaving him in just his boxers.

I stay kneeling on the floor, not sure what I'm supposed to do next.

Will doesn't have that same problem. He scoops me up and carries me to the table, sitting me on the edge of it.

"Lie back."

I do as he asks.

"Bend your knees, then let them drop open."

I hesitate for a moment but do what he wants. This time I can't look at his face. Not that it matters. He only has eyes for my pussy.

"Good girl. Use your hands to hold yourself open for me."

With a gulp, I do what he wants, wondering if he can hear the galloping of my heart.

Dipping his head, he takes a deep breath, his nose brushing over me as he groans.

"You smell delicious." And then without further ado, he runs his tongue over my clit, making me jump.

Good god.

"You're so wet. You get off on sucking my cock, huh?"

"Will?" I call his name nervously, not sure what the hell is going on. Nobody taught me this damn lesson because even without a memory like mine there is no way I'd forget.

"You taste so fucking good," he murmurs against me before his tongue swirls over me once more. Then he's licking and sucking and doing something else. Hell, I don't know what he's doing, but I don't ever want him to stop.

Something coils and twists inside me, something not unpleasant but unfamiliar enough to make me panic.

"I can't. Something's happening." I gasp as he presses his tongue inside me.

"You gonna come, Six? Don't be scared. Let go. I'll catch you."

I don't think he means literally let go but I do anyway, releasing my legs so I can grab handfuls of his hair and hold him to me.

He sucks me hard and something inside of me explodes, making white dots dance behind my eyes as a wave of intense pleasure washes over me.

He drinks me down, not stopping for a second until I'm too sensitive for him to continue.

Pulling back, his chin still wet with my juices, he grins and it makes my breath catch in my throat.

"Oh yeah, Six. We're going to be the best of friends."

I sit on the end of the bed and wait for the doctor Will is talking with to come up.

I burrow into the softness of the robe Will helped me into before he told me what to expect.

It's not the first time I'll be seeing a doctor. I've seen more doctors than I care to admit. I just hate the whole process. I'm not even sure why at this point. Each of the instructors was overly sexual toward me. It was part of the training so it's to be expected, but I could tell in their own ways every one of them was affected by me in one way or another.

Not that I wanted their interest, but in a world where emotions were meant to be stomped out, I found myself fascinated at the responses I could draw from these otherwise in-control people.

I suspect it's one of the reasons Madam M hated me so much. With her pale skin, she was awful trying to hide the flush whenever she was aroused. Not that she ever touched me. She just got off watching and directing me.

Doctors are a different breed altogether. They are cold and clinical, or at least the ones I've encountered. They were given free rein to touch me whenever and wherever they needed to. For some reason, it was their cold indifference that made me feel like I was nothing more than a useful toy.

Logically, I know my reasoning is flawed, but it didn't change the way their icy hands somehow seemed to penetrate beneath my skin to my heart.

Now here I am in a room bathed in sunshine and still I feel the chill as I wait for the doctor to arrive.

When the door opens, I see Will standing beside a man who must be only a few years older than Will. His hair has more silver threaded through it and he doesn't have the muscular physique that Will does but he is still what I would imagine women would think is attractive, at least if he wasn't standing beside Will.

"Six, this is Dr. Livingston. He is here to give you a full checkup, just to make sure you're in good health and don't need anything, okay?"

"Yes…Will." I catch myself before calling him sir.

"I'll leave you to it. Take your time."

He pulls the door closed behind him, leaving me with the doctor and the coldness I hate so much.

"Hello, Six. As Will said, my name is Dr. Livingston, but you can call me John. What I'm going to do is take some blood, check your blood pressure, and things like that before I examine you, alright?"

"Yes, doctor," I whisper, not comfortable calling him John even if he is being nice to me.

"How old are you, Six?"

"I turned eighteen yesterday." It's why I'm here and not back at the compound, but I don't say that to him, not sure how much Will has told him about me.

"Really? Well, happy birthday for yesterday." He smiles but I can't find it in me to return it. A birthday to me is not something to celebrate. Not where I came from, anyway. All it meant was another year off the countdown that started the day I was sold.

"I'll admit, I thought you were a little older than that. You look very grown-up." His eyes move over me and suddenly something else pierces the cold indifference I'm wearing. Fear. This man isn't acting how he is supposed to. Or maybe doctors are just different outside of the compound.

As nervous as Will makes me, I wish he had stayed.

I don't talk again. The doctor does enough of that himself, chattering away about things I don't know anything about as he removes the blood pressure cuff from my arm.

"All that looks good. Now this is the fun part," he jokes, or at least I think he's joking. I look toward the door, hoping Will walks back through it. But, of course, he doesn't.

The doctor doesn't miss where I'm looking though, and his grin seems less friendly than before.

"Will is a very busy man. He knows what's happening here. He told us to take our time after all. Now remove the robe and lie back on the bed, please."

I swallow and stand, feeling my body shake, even though the room is quite warm.

I hear his sharp intake of breath as I lie down in the center of the bed.

"Scoot further to the end, please."

I move and do as he asks as he approaches the bedside.

I turn my head to look at the ceiling, ignoring the tent in his pants.

I never thought I'd wish for cold indifference. Nobody out here acts like they are supposed to. It hurts my head because if they are acting differently, all my training was for nothing.

"I'm going to palpate your breasts and check for lumps." His voice has a husky tone to it now, which I try to shut out.

His cold hands cup my breast, making me jump.

"Settle down. That's a good girl." His words are slick and practiced and make me feel like bugs are crawling over my skin.

He tugs on my nipple hard, making me bite my lip as tears spring to my eyes.

"Hmm…your nipples are hard. Seems you enjoy the stimulation," he mutters to himself before moving toward the end of the bed.

"Spread your legs nice and wide for me. I'm going to make sure everything feels okay."

I do as he asks. Turning to look up and out the window, I see two blackbirds sitting on a branch high up in a tree. They don't make a sound as they watch my tears fall and for some reason, that makes me cry even harder.

I wish they were bigger. Big enough that they could fly me away from here.

I hear the snick of a bottle opening before a wet finger touches my clit.

I jump again, but a hand presses against my belly, holding me in place.

He moves his finger backward and forward over my clit, rubbing me hard until it starts to feel tender.

"Yes, I knew you'd get wet. Sluts like you always do."

I'm not wet, not even close.

A stuttering breath escapes me as I bite my lip to keep from screaming. I don't want to be sent back so I need to keep quiet, but the second his fat finger tries to push inside me, I lose my mind and kick him in the face before scrambling off the bed.

"You little fucking bitch," he snarls before reaching for me and grabbing my hair. He yanks me hard, which makes me scream in pain as my neck is wrenched back.

That's when the door crashes open.

The look on Will's face as he takes in the scene makes me cower, but it's not me he's pissed at.

In seconds he has the doctor pinned to the wall with his hand around his throat, his feet barely touching the floor.

"What happened?" Will snarls.

"The little whore attacked me," the doctor chokes out.

"I'm not talking to you." Will slams the doctor against the wall once more, his head cracking against it with a thud.

Turning his eyes on me, he scans my body before they rest on my tear-stained face.

"Tell me what happened, Six."

I wrap my arms around myself feeling so very very cold as I sit on the edge of the bed shaking.

"He made me lie on the bed so he could examine me. I...I didn't want him to, but I know the rules," I whisper.

"Six." My eyes snap back to Will's.

"He felt my chest then pulled my nipples hard. It hurt, but I didn't shout," I tell him, needing him to know that I tried to be good.

Will blinks, processing my words before banging the doctor against the wall once more, ignoring his protests.

"What else?"

"He put some liquid on his hands then...he rubbed me down there. It started to get painful, and I wanted him to stop but..." I shake my head again.

"I tried to be good, Will, I promise. But then he said he

knew I'd get wet, sluts like me always do, and then he pushed his finger inside me." I shiver at the look on Will's face.

"I just wanted him to stop. I didn't mean to kick him. I just wanted him to stop touching me."

"It was a regular fucking exam. That's what I'm supposed to do, especially when we don't know what kind of fucking disease you might have from all the men you've fucked," the doctor shouts, making Will turn his head slowly to look at him.

And that's when the doctor's face goes an alarming shade of white and the seriousness of the situation finally sinks in.

CHAPTER FOURTEEN

WILL

*T*he fear on Six's face makes every protective instinct I have rise to the surface.

This is my fault. I should have brought in a woman doctor but I only have male doctors on my payroll, something I plan to fix immediately.

"You called my woman a slut?" I hiss. She's a fucking victim of trafficking and this man calls her a slut. I don't care if she did or didn't overreact to —

My thoughts cut off when I see his hands. His bare hands.

"Where are your gloves?" I question in a deceptively calm voice.

He stares at me for a moment, his mouth opening and closing as he tries to think of something to say. As the color in his face bleeds to white, I see the truth in his eyes.

He thought he could do what he wanted to Six, given her history, and nothing would come of it. Whether he thinks she's expendable or he assumes she wouldn't say anything matters not.

"You came into my house and hurt my woman?" I ask him quietly, my grip tightening to the point that he can't answer, so I loosen it a little.

"Will, she's just a whore. You told me that yourself," he chokes out before I pull back my arm and punch him in the face.

"She is not a whore." How the fuck he hears *victim of trafficking* and processes that as *whore* is beyond me.

I hit him again when he opens his mouth. His teeth split the skin on my knuckles open, but I don't let it stop me.

I punch him over and over again. When I drop him to the floor, I kick him in the head before stomping on his face until there is nothing left but a bloody pulp.

I'm breathing heavily by the time I realize he's dead. I kick him again for the fuck of it. "Pussy." I spit on him.

Turning to Six, I find her in that fucking submissive pose with tears running down her face.

"Fuck."

I approach her as if she's a wounded animal before crouching down in front of her. Sliding a finger under her jaw, I tilt her head back. Little blood splatters cover her cheek and forehead, standing out starkly against her pale skin. It looks wrong on her. Like someone has taken a statue of an angel and desecrated it, but the sight of her scared eyes looking into mine feels like a bullet to the heart.

Before I can say anything, she speaks first. It's barely more than a whisper, so I almost don't catch it.

"Please don't send me back. I'll be good, I promise."

I frown as it clicks that she's not scared of me, she's scared I'm going to return her. I scoop her up into my arms, carry her out of the room, and take her up to mine.

Banging my door open, I carry her into my bathroom and place her gently on her feet before turning on the shower.

She watches me as I strip out of my bloody shoes and clothes until I'm as naked as she is. When I reach out and tug her to me, she comes willingly, her hands landing on my chest as she looks up at me.

"You're not going anywhere. You're mine, Six, and there isn't a single person on this planet that will take you from me."

"You promise?" she whispers, her eyes staring into mine as she seeks the truth.

"I promise."

I can't take it anymore. With a groan, I slam my lips over hers. The adrenaline coursing through me prevents me from being soft and gentle like she deserves.

I pick her up as she opens her mouth to me. My dick presses against her pussy as she wraps her legs around me, making her whimper.

I break the kiss when I realize that it's a whimper of pain, not pleasure.

I walk to the counter and sit her on the edge of it before bending down in front of her.

"Open for me, Six."

She bites her lips before lifting her legs and opening them.

Her clit looks red and puffy and as I run my blood-smeared finger gently over it, she hisses.

"Sorry, sweetheart." I press a kiss to where she is tender before picking her up again.

"Let's get cleaned up and then I have some salve that should help."

When she doesn't answer, I stand and cup her cheek, making sure her pretty eyes are on mine.

"I'm sorry I scared you. I won't let anyone hurt you or disrespect you, but I swear to you I will never lay my hands on you in anger."

Tentatively she reaches up and echoes my actions, sliding her small hand across my jaw, the scruff from not shaving today scraping against her palm as I turn into it.

"Trust me," I urge her, knowing I'm asking for a lot, even if I did just kill a man for her.

"Okay, Will," she says softly before touching her thumb to my lips.

I lick the pad, making her gasp.

"You're killing me," I groan, picking her up and carrying her into the shower with me.

I stand her behind me, keeping the spray off her while I wash the doctor's blood from my body. I reach for the shower gel and pour some into my hands.

"I'm going to wash you. My hands are going to clean away the echoes of hands that came before me. When we step out it will be the beginning of us. There is nobody else in this, Six. Our pasts can't hurt us unless we let them. All that matters is you and me. Understand?"

"No," she replies with a confused frown.

"Don't worry, you will."

I start by rubbing the soap over her shoulders and back before moving to her chest. I glide my hands around her breasts, wanting nothing more than to suck one of her rosy nipples into my mouth. Not yet. Not while she is still raw from the dead man on the floor downstairs.

As gently as I can, I clean between her legs before moving her into the spray so she can rinse the soap away.

Once that's done, I squirt shampoo into my palm and massage it into her wet hair, feeling her relax beneath my fingertips. I let her rinse and I repeat the process with the conditioner.

Once we are both as clean as we're going to get, I wrap a towel around my waist and another one around Six before taking her into my room.

I'm not planning on leaving the house today. I yank on a pair of faded jeans that have a tear in the knee but are soft from being washed so often.

I don't bother with a shirt, but I do grab one for Six, who watches me walk toward her. Tugging her towel free, I help her slip it on before buttoning it up and pulling her hair free.

"Come sit and I'll braid it for you, or your shirt will end up soaked."

She looks at me with a thousand questions in her eyes, but she doesn't ask any. Instead, she lets me comb and braid her hair without a word until I've finished. Only then does she turn to look at me and speak.

"Nobody has ever taken care of me before," she tells me softly, her eyes moving over my face. "Thank you."

CHAPTER FIFTEEN

WILL

I leave Six out on the deck wrapped in a huge blanket with a book in her lap. I'd dragged her out here, knowing it would calm her, bypassing the chair I sat in earlier as she sucked my dick.

Her face lit up with the unencumbered view, but all I could think about was the feel of her lips wrapped around my shaft as I came down her throat.

When I handed her a random book from the bookcase, she looked at me as if I'd just handed her the moon. I aim to make her look at me at least once a day with that same expression of bliss on her face. I really want to see it when I'm moving inside her.

I'm just finishing making a mug of cocoa when James strolls in with Fisher behind him.

"It's too early for dead bodies," James grumbles, moving to the fridge and grabbing a beer.

"But not too early for beer?"

Fisher adds his two cents. "You wake up to pretty lips around your cock, then coffee is fine. But you wake up to a murder scene? Well, coffee just isn't going to cut it."

Fisher is ten years younger than me and a giant pain in my ass. He came to work for my father when he was eighteen and cocky. He lasted a week before my father fired him. I saw potential in the man though. It wasn't often that people stood up to the old man. Ten years later, he's still a cocky asshole, but he's also family. Loyalty is something worth more than gold in this world and these two have it in spades.

"So, what did the good doctor do to deserve his face looking like ground beef?" James asks, taking a swig of his beer.

"He assaulted Six."

James's beer pauses in front of his lips. "He did what?" he snarls before slamming the beer on the counter and storming upstairs.

Fisher laughs. "Should I stop him?"

I shrug. "It's not like the man can get any more dead."

"True. How do you want to handle this?"

"Nobody knew he was coming out here. I'm his dirty little secret. I pay him cash under the table so he doesn't have to give any to the taxman. He has an ex-wife, no kids. The only people that might miss him are his patients."

"Home invasion?"

"Nah, I don't want anyone digging around before I've had a chance to make sure the dickhead didn't leave anything lying around he shouldn't have."

86

"Want me to go search his place?"

"Yeah. I also want any computer equipment he might have. Don't make it obvious. Replace it with a dummy one if you need to. I'll have Beckett break into his practice and check his files tonight. Once that's done, I'll have James stage it so Dr. Dickhead and his shiny little sports car end up in an unfortunate accident."

"That'll work." Fisher nods as James stomps back into the kitchen with a smear of blood on his chin.

"You have a little…" Fisher waves to James's chin.

James wipes the area, missing the blood completely and making me snort.

"Gone?"

Fisher shakes his head. "Nevermind. I'm gonna head out. You have the doctor's keys? I might as well drive his car. It won't raise the alarm that way if someone sees it parked in his driveway."

"In his jacket on the chair there." I point to the navy blazer over the back of the chair.

Fisher checks the pockets and when he finds what he's after, heads for the door.

"I'll check in later and let you know what I find."

"So, is it gone?" James tips his head up so I can see his chin, making me grin.

"Almost," I tell him, but his eyes are aimed over my shoulder.

I turn and find Six standing there with her hands behind her back and her head bowed slightly.

I walk toward her and lift her chin. "Everything alright?"

She murmurs something that I don't catch so I dip my head. Her lips moving against my ear make my dick twitch.

"I need to use the toilet."

I smile and take her hand, pulling her to the bathroom.

"I'll wait outside for you."

I figured giving her the tour yesterday would have made things easier, but I need to remember it will take a while before she is comfortable to just wander around.

I hear the flush and the sound of water running before Six pulls the door open.

"You can use any of the bathrooms in the house. This one though is your closest while you're down here. You don't need to ask me next time, alright?"

She nods, fiddling with the hem of her shirt.

"Okay, Will."

"Good girl. Now head back outside. I am making you something I think you'll like."

She looks flummoxed, making me wonder when the last time was someone did something nice for her. The whole thing makes my chest ache.

We split off at the kitchen where I find James has poured the cocoa into a mug and placed it on a tray with some cookies.

I grin at the memories it evokes. Claire was always baking me cookies and trying to fatten me up. I was a skinny kid, not growing into my body until I turned sixteen.

"Want to come out so I can introduce you?"

"Damn right I want to meet the woman who has you in knots."

"I'm not in knots."

"There is a bloodstained asshat upstairs that would likely think differently if his brain wasn't like soup right now."

I huff but I don't deny it any further. What's the point? She does have me in knots. Why deny it?

"Just be careful. You have no idea what she has been through or the damage it's done. Nobody walks through the fires of hell without getting burned along the way."

"You think I don't know that?"

"Do you? I mean, do you really know what you're getting yourself into? I'm not saying you should send her back, but you don't have to keep her. And don't tell me that's not what you're planning. I recognize that look in your eye. It's the same one you had when you found that damn stray cat you insisted on keeping. And what did it do to repay you?"

I feel the scar on my wrist, remembering the cat going crazy and tearing the skin when I was maybe twelve years old.

"This is different, James."

"Is it? From where I'm standing you've opened up your home to another stray and have no idea if she's feral or not."

I grip the counter and glare at him.

"I'm a big fucking boy. If Six needs to score her nails into my skin to feel better, so be it. You want to know why I don't just fix her up and send her on her way?"

"It's what you were supposed to do. Gain her trust and set her free."

"That was before I met her. That was before I realized I couldn't patch her up and send her home because she doesn't have one. She has nobody, James. Not a single fucking person to take her back."

"You don't know that."

"I do. Trust me." She hasn't asked for anyone, not a single name has passed her lips.

"Why does it have to be you?"

"Why shouldn't it be me?" I snarl.

He sighs, shaking his head. "I just don't want to see you

hurt. You're all I've got. I'm not trying to be a dick. If she's what you want then I'm sure I'll end up just as captivated by her as you are. But don't ask me not to worry about you. I don't know how to do that."

How do you stay mad at that?

"You're a pain in my ass," I growl before grabbing the tray of cookies and cocoa.

"Yeah, well it takes one to know one," he grumbles, following me out to the sitting room.

"What are you, five?"

He chuckles behind me, but my eyes are all for the woman I can see through the glass as she looks across to the lake. As if sensing me, she turns her head and watches me approach, her eyes never leaving mine as I push the door open and head toward her.

"Hey." I place the tray on the table and lift the mug, handing it to her.

"I thought you might like some cocoa."

She looks down at the mug in her hands with a frown before talking a small sip.

The look on her face makes both James and me laugh.

"Six, this is James. If ever I'm not around, James can help you out with anything you might need. He is one of my very special friends and as such, I'd like you to treat him how you treat me—"

The ringing of my cell cuts me off.

I almost ignore it but think better of it when I see it's Viddy.

"I've gotta take this. I'll be right back."

I turn and jog inside, heading up to my office before answering.

"Viddy. How's it going, beautiful?"

"Don't ask. No seriously, don't ask unless it's over multiple bottles of tequila."

"That good, huh?"

"You have no idea." She sighs. "There was a shootout in the park today."

"What? Was anyone hurt?"

"It was a clusterfuck, Will. Lily was there."

I suck in a sharp breath even though I know she's okay. There is no way Viddy would have been so calm otherwise.

"Jesus fuck. Cash must be losing his fucking mind."

"Oh, it gets better. Layla was shot protecting Lily and a little boy around the same age. The boy's mom was killed, executed in fact, and we suspect it's because she was mistaken for Layla herself. A whole lot of shit has come to light, which has me questioning the picture we have of this woman. I need you to dig into Layla a little more for me. Not the usual route that my guys are going through but using your contacts. I want to talk to someone who knew her, someone who met her, spoke to her for longer than five minutes. Because from where I'm standing, Layla is nothing more than a ghost."

"I'll see what I can do. I always figured there was more to the story. I'm well aware of what it's like to be tarred with someone else's brush because of your association with them." My father was the biggest prick on the planet. He made so many shady deals, all so he could stuff his wallet and blow it on his smorgasbord of mistresses.

I'm far from an angel myself, but unlike my father, I have limits. Lines I won't cross. Like trading in flesh. Not that he made a habit of it. The guns he traded were more than enough to line his pockets. But in this business, you come across all kinds of criminals. In a bid to be everyone's friend, my father had no issue trading in goods once in a while instead of money.

It was using my father's old contacts that I was able to get in with the traffickers that sold Six. Now I'd need to delve into the stench of the underworld again, this time looking for answers.

"I'll ask around and get back to you. If you can think of anything else, V, just let me know."

"Will do." She hangs up, leaving me looking out the window, wondering briefly about the choices I've made that brought me here.

With a sigh, I get to my feet and head back downstairs, hoping James has been able to put Six at ease. When I round the corner and see Six on her knees between James's thighs, tears dripping from her chin, I lose my fucking mind.

CHAPTER SIXTEEN

SIX

"*He is one of my very special friends...I'd like you to treat him how you treat me...*"

I don't know how long I sit there as the words echo in my mind before I robotically place the cup on the table.

James sits in the chair to the far left of me. I drop to my knees and slowly crawl toward him. His mouth moves but I don't hear a word he's saying. I kneel in front of him and slide my hands up his thighs on autopilot. My cheeks feel wet and my vision blurs as I reach for his belt.

His hand closes over mine, halting my movements as a loud angry voice cuts through the air.

"What the fuck?"

I turn my head to look at Will and see his face tight with anger. I turn to look at James. When I see his cheeks wet and his eyes glassy, I frown, looking back and forth between the two.

Did I do something wrong?

"She...I don't even know what happened. One minute you were talking and the next she was on her knees. I tried to make her stop but she was somewhere else altogether, Will. She couldn't hear a word I was saying and I was reluctant to touch her in case it made it worse."

"Six!" Will snaps, stalking closer to me. He wraps his hand around my arm and pulls me up.

He doesn't hurt me but his hand touching mine when I feel so raw makes me feel like I might shatter at any moment.

"What happened?" he asks me as James says his name like a warning.

When I don't answer, he shakes me. Again, not enough to hurt but it still scares me. I don't know what I did wrong so I don't know what punishment to expect.

"Answer me!" he roars. I whimper as James jumps up and grabs Will.

"That's enough. You're scaring her," James snarls at him.

A look of fleeting horror crosses Will's face before he releases me so quickly, I stumble back.

Turning away, he grabs the closest thing, which happens to be the mug on the table. He picks it up and with an anguished sound, he throws it at the window.

An alarm blares, making birds take off in flight from nearby trees.

As James tries to calm him down, I turn toward the woods and I run. I don't know what I'm doing or where I'm going but I'm too scared to stay and find out what my punishment will be. Will is so much bigger than me. He could hurt me. Or he could kill me.

Visions of Two's pretty face with her vacant eyes flash in my head. For a moment I wonder if she chose to go out that way, recognizing as Ten did years before that sometimes the only freedom a slave can have is death itself.

I should want to die. There are a million ways out here I could do it. But even after all this time, I still have a fire that burns within me. One that wants to live. I've always wanted to see the world in color just as soon as I found my way out of the dark.

I cry out as something sharp tears into my bare foot, but I don't let it slow me down. It's just pain. Pain means I'm alive and right now that's enough.

I run as fast as my legs can carry me, which granted isn't all that far. I might have a small lean figure but that was due to the strict diet I was placed on when I was a child. That kept my weight within the desired levels apparently, although I have no idea who came up with the desired levels. M, more than likely. She always did have horrible things to say about the bigger girls who were held at the facility.

Diet aside, I'm incredibly unfit. I've never exercised before and walking is as strenuous as things ever got for me. Once I read a book about the importance of exercise and decided to recreate some of the moves in my room. Apparently, I was too distracting to the guards.

I made them sinners, and sinners had to be punished.

I've read the Bible and couldn't find the part where it said *thou shall fire a bullet into a guard's head*, but not even God's rules applied in a place like that.

Out of breath and knowing I'm being so loud I'd be easy to track, I decide hiding would be my best option.

I look around the densely populated woods and find a large downed tree. Making my way over to it, I see it's plenty big enough to hide me. I lie next to it and press as closely as I can to the wood before covering myself with the fallen autumn leaves.

It's cold and damp and for a moment I'm back in the cells. Not the one I just left but the one where Ten lived and died. I feel my heart rate pick up.

I try to fight back the panic but it's difficult when my emotions are already so out of whack. I try to lock them down but it's getting harder and harder to do. The only thing keeping me grounded is the throbbing pain in my foot.

I squeeze my eyes shut and count in my head, trying to keep myself focused on the numbers. The snapping of a branch next to me has me freezing solid before hands are hauling me up.

I don't think, I react. I fight and struggle with everything I have but I'm not a fighter and the man holding me could probably overpower me with one finger.

He doesn't hit me, though. He wraps his arms around me tightly, leaving me unable to move before his lips whisper against my ear.

"Stop fighting me, firefly. I like it when you run because it means I get to hunt you. But if you don't want me to bend you over this log and shove my cock deep inside you, then you need to stop rubbing your ass against me."

His words wash over me and I still for a moment before the first sob rips from my body.

CHAPTER SEVENTEEN

WILL

I tuck her head under my chin and carry her bridal style back toward the house.

I don't say another word, not trusting myself not to say something else fucking stupid.

I wasn't lying though. I have an odd kink that makes me more fucked-up than she is. I like to chase pretty girls and pin them down while they fight. There is a feral part of me that thrives on the chase, no matter how hard I try to suppress it. The difference between me and a monster is willing victims— people who happily play my game for the night before hurrying home to their boring lives with a wild memory of a night they got to go crazy.

I have a whole lot of fail-safes in place—forms for written

consent, NDAs, and contracts in some cases. But once the night is over, the women leave.

It keeps me sated for a while, but like anything you starve yourself of, I wind up craving it more.

I've always been a little off, not finding things sexually simulating as my peers of the same age did. I questioned my sexuality, but it seemed I had little interest in either sex. Until my father sent me for therapy after my mother's death.

I was pissed and looked for ways to get back at him for making me go. We both knew my mom was dead because she couldn't live with my father's inability to keep his dick in his pants.

Dr. Jane Johnson provided me with the perfect means for revenge. But what started as a way to give my dad the finger became so much more.

Turns out, Dr. Johnson had a rape fantasy. She liked to be chased and forced to submit against her will, but only by a person she trusted. I had no clue how that worked. How could someone trust a person who would do that? This led to her describing the world of consensual non-consensual sex.

After she explained, I understood why trust was so impor-tant. In a situation like that, a person handed themselves over to someone else and asked them to ignore words. To block out the screams of *no* and *stop* and instead read body language. I learned to take cues from her reactions to me, what she liked, what she wasn't as keen on, and what made her drip like a fucking faucet.

But Dr. Johnson made a mistake. She became complacent working with teen boys whose fathers didn't really give a fuck about them or were never there to notice something was wrong with them. It's what her patients had in common. Except one.

By the time she was fired and jailed for sharing her brand of crazy with the wrong fifteen-year-old boy, it had been too late. I liked what I'd learned and going to vanilla sex after that left me wanting more.

I used professionals but their reactions rang false. Bored housewives with husbands that never noticed them made the ideal candidates. One night of debauchery before they went back to the monotony of their marriage meant they got their rocks off and guaranteed their silence. Their husbands remained oblivious to their infidelities.

I spent years figuring out the aspects I liked the best, finding I leaned more toward primal play. It gave me the freedom to devolve to my baser instincts of hunting, fucking, and fighting.

It had been enough until Six.

Now with the tiny weeping woman in my arms, I couldn't think about ever touching another woman again. I know with absolute clarity that Six is it for me. She ended up in my path for a reason, whether that be fate or serendipity. Who knows? But I refuse to give her back.

The problem with that though, is how could Six cope with the kind of sex I liked after experiencing everything she had?

To keep this woman, I'd have to suppress that part of me. I could. For her, it would be worth it. That's at least what I'd been telling myself since the moment I decided she was mine.

But then she ran and I haven't been able to get my cock to go down since.

"Is she okay?" James's worried voice breaks me out of my thoughts.

"No, but she will be."

His eyes drift down to her feet and he curses. "She's bleeding. I'll go grab the first aid kit."

He disappears inside and I hesitate to follow him. Instead, I carry her down to two large lawn chairs that sit right on the water's edge. I drop onto one of them and pull Six tighter into me, rocking her slightly as she cries.

Once she calms, I pull back and look down at her. I hate that she looks at me scared, but I'd be lying if I said her tears don't turn me on. There is no way she doesn't know this because my cock is hard as stone beneath her shapely ass.

"I think we need to talk, firefly."

She tips her head, her red-rimmed eyes staring into mine, a solitary tear running down her cheek.

"Tell me why you ran."

She hesitates before answering. "I'm scared."

"Of me?"

"Of everything," she whispers. "I'm scared of living, scared of dying. I don't know who I'm supposed to be."

"That's easy, you're supposed to be mine."

She shakes her head, grief etched into her features. "But I wasn't, though, not really. Two was supposed to be yours, but she died in the back of the van, so I changed out the hoods." She hiccups, making me freeze.

I remember the hood with the number two on it.

"Wait, Six isn't your name, it's your number?" It might not be the most important part of what she's saying but it's fucked-up enough for me to want to start smashing shit again.

"It's the only name I've ever had. It's mine now. The others?" She blows out her breath as she sits straighter, her hand gripping the front of my shirt.

"All the others have been replaced. They either died or

were sold or just disappeared only for someone else to arrive with the same number. But not me. Six was the only gift I've ever been given and it's mine now."

I can't say I understand but she's adamant and who am I to take this away from her?

"What was your name before? Who were you before you were stolen?"

She blinks, confused again. "I wasn't stolen. I was born in a cage. I was never anything but a slave, Will. It's all I've known. I've never been anyone else. I'm just Six."

CHAPTER EIGHTEEN

SIX

My words must shock him into silence because his mouth moves but nothing comes out before he snaps it closed.

He looks like he wants to be sick, so I lean away, but he pulls me closer once more. I'm not sure why he's not punishing me. I ran away. That kind of thing usually gets a girl like me killed. Maybe this is a trick and he'll kill me later when I'm not so prepared for it. I'm too tired to care right now.

Right or wrong, I like it here in the cradle of Will's arms. He smells good and he's warm and... I'm just so sick of being cold.

"Okay, Six, we'll come back to that," Will says through gritted teeth, smoothing his hand down my back.

"Tell me about Two and why you think she should have been mine instead of you."

"We were being delivered together. They gave us something to make us sleep, but I was the only one to wake up. I was checking on her, you know, but when I saw she was gone, I took the opportunity presented to me and switched the hoods."

"How did you know the driver wouldn't check and why risk it? There was no guarantee that I wouldn't be as bad, if not worse, than the person who bought you."

She shakes her head. "I don't know. It was almost as if a voice was urging me to make the swap, which sounds silly I know, but what did I really have to lose? You were a gamble, yes, but I already knew my master was a bad man, so it was a risk I was willing to take."

"Wait, you know who bought you? If you know him, he'll have known it wasn't you the second he gets a look at Two."

"The driver—R—he could identify us but not if the hood stayed on until after delivery. I've never met my master. I'm sure he was told the basics of what I looked like and Two was a similar weight and height and had the same hair color. I hoped it would be enough for us to pass as each other."

He searches my eyes as a noise behind us makes me jump.

"It's just James with the first aid supplies."

I feel myself shutting down as shame has me folding in on myself.

"Hey, it's okay," James says softly as he bends down to inspect my foot.

"I'm sorry," I whisper to him. I'm still not completely sure what I did wrong, but I know it was bad. I made Will so mad and made James cry.

"I don't understand the rules yet. I won't mess up again," I vow. Instead of making him happy, he curses.

"Will," he hisses.

I look up at Will whose eyes flitter down at me, filled with an emotion I'm not sure I've encountered before.

"The only rules are that you can't leave and that nobody touches you but me. I will never be okay with sharing you, Six, so you don't ever have to worry about that."

"You said he was your special friend and that I should treat him like I treat you," I remind him.

A light flashes in his eyes, making him curse.

"I meant to treat him as family," he says softly, rubbing his hand up and down my arm.

"But...I don't know how to do that. I've never had a family before."

I hiss as James prods my foot. He apologizes but I stare at Will, who is stuck on what I just said. I'm not sure what his family was like, but no matter how fucked-up it could have been, he still had people who anchored him to the world.

He smooths his hand over my hair almost absently. I'm not sure at this point if he's trying to soothe me or himself.

"Well, things are gonna be different now, Six. We'll show you how to be a family. Don't let it worry you. We'll start with baby steps. My parents are both dead, but James is like a father to me, more so than my own ever was. If you have any questions, you can always go to him and he won't judge you for them. He sure as shit won't punish you."

I'm not sure how to react. I was expecting anger and threats, but they are both being so nice to me. I don't know if I can trust it though, no matter how much I want to.

"I…um…okay," I whisper, hoping he can't read how anxious I am.

"You can trust him, pretty girl. Will is the best man I know." James winks. "And you can trust me too. That I can promise you."

CHAPTER NINETEEN

WILL

She looks at James, who nods and smiles softly at her. It's only because I know him as well as I do that I notice the simmering anger beneath the veneer of his smile.

"My wife Claire would kick my ass for hurting you, but I need to pour some of this solution onto your foot to stop it from getting infected," he tells her, keeping his voice light, not betraying any of the anger he's feeling.

"It's okay."

He doesn't wait for her to change her mind. He cleans her up and apart from her body tensing, she shows no outward sign of her discomfort.

"There. Good as new."

"Thank you," she replies softly. She chews her lip as if she wants to ask something but isn't sure.

"What is it, pretty girl?"

"You said you have a wife. Can I meet her?"

Pain flashes over James's face for a moment before he taps Six's leg. "I lost my Claire, unfortunately. But I can tell you, she'd have loved you."

"Why? I'm nobody. I've brought nothing but chaos. One man is dead because of me and—"

I place my thumb over her lips, silencing her.

It's James that answers. "Because you make my boy happy." He leans closer, his face inches from Six's. "And you are not nobody. Don't ever let me hear you say that again. You are somebody to me, somebody to Will. As for that...dickface asshat, I refuse to call him a man because real men don't terrorize women. He is the reason he's dead. And he's lucky it was Will dealing with him and not me. I'd have put him through a wood chipper for scaring you."

"Christ. She's going to think we're crazy enough as it is without you flashing your psychotic tendencies at her," I bite off.

We both freeze when Six laughs, our eyes finding each other's as a silent promise passes between us to protect and keep Six safe at all costs.

"No more running away, okay? There are big bad things in those woods that would eat you up if they caught you," James warns but his eyes don't leave mine as they fill with mirth.

I'll kill him and shove him in his precious wood chipper. Let's see how funny the fucker finds that.

"I'm sorry. I won't run," she promises.

I hold her tighter as James stands with the first aid kit in his hand. "Good. Now I'm going to go and leave you to it. The clean-up crew texted me to say they are on their way."

In other words, keep Six out of the way.

"No worries. I think I'm going to run Six a bath and we'll watch a movie upstairs."

"I'll fix some more cocoa for you and send up some food. Go. I'll message you if there is any issue."

"Thanks, James." I stand and scoop Six up into my arms and carry her up to my—no—*our* room.

Without James acting as a buffer between us, we seem at a loss for words all of a sudden. The consequences of our actions weigh on us both.

Once I reach our room, I sit her on the edge of the bed and move to the bathroom. I put the plug in the tub and turn on the water. I pick up a bottle of something floral-smelling and pour a liberal amount into the bath.

I'm not even sure where this came from. I'm not the kind of guy that buys bath shit, especially since I rarely use it myself. Spinning the bottle around, I search for the label and smirk when I see the logo for Megan's boutique. It doesn't surprise me. Megan is the old lady to the presidents of the Chaos Demons motorcycle club, but she's also the owner of a fancy boutique that specializes in stuff like this. I don't know her as well as Viddy. But as Viddy's best friend, it's not a stretch to guess the women took pity on me.

I stay in the bathroom while the water runs, buying myself a few minutes to regroup. What happened downstairs was my fault. I overreacted to a triggered response and blew shit way out of proportion. But seeing her on her knees before James flipped a switch in me I never knew I had.

If she had done anything other than run, I could have salvaged the blossoming buds of our relationship. It's easier to leash the beast when he doesn't have the scent of his prey in his blood. But run she did, and now nothing I do will hold back the hunger inside me.

I grip the edge of the tub and take a deep breath, willing my cock to go down. It's impossible when all I can remember is the sight of her tears, the feel of her pounding heart, and the terror etched on her face.

I'm a sick fuck. My first instinct hadn't been to comfort her but to flip her onto her hands and knees and slide my cock inside her. It's only the knowledge that she was hurt that held me back.

I squeeze the tub edge harder, feeling my knuckles crack. Jesus, I need therapy. But look how well that worked out the first time. Hell, this time around they would lock me up and throw away the key.

Turning off the water, I stand and make a decision. I'm not strong enough to fight the beast within but perhaps my beautiful broken girl is strong enough to tame it. I guess it's time to find out.

I strip off my clothes and stalk back to the bedroom. I pause in the doorway when I realize Six has fallen asleep, curled in a protective ball.

Walking toward her, I stop for a moment, consider my actions, then shrug off my reservations. It's far easier to give in than to fight all the time.

Carefully, so as not to wake her, I move Six so she is lying on her back across the bottom of the bed. Reaching up, I unbutton the shirt she's wearing and spread it wide, exposing her body to me.

I've never laid my eyes on a more exquisite sight in my life.

Unable to help myself, I dip my head and flick the nub of one of her nipples with my tongue as my hand shifts to wrap around my cock. I stroke my hard length as I pull back and look my fill. Reaching out, I move her legs so she is wide open.

I swallow down a groan at the sight of her pretty pussy spread out before me and move my hand back to my dick.

I fuck my fist harder this time, imagining it's her pussy clamped tightly around me. It doesn't take long before I'm shooting ropes of cum over Six's exposed pussy and stomach.

Once I'm spent, I lightly run my fingers over her clit, coating my fingertips in my cum before slipping them inside her. I'm a bastard. I don't know if she is on birth control, but I can't make myself pull them free.

I thrust my fingers in and out of her slowly before gathering more of my cum and pushing it inside her. I'm so mesmerized by my actions it takes me a while to realize her breathing has changed and her eyes are wide open and watching me.

CHAPTER TWENTY

SIX

*T*he adrenaline wore off, making me crash, but it wasn't long before something dragged me back to the surface.

Heat pools low in my stomach as my body hums, electrified. I open my eyes and see Will standing over me, his eyes fixed between my legs.

That's when I realize he's touching me. My eyes flutter as fire begins to lick over my skin. I don't know what he's doing but I like it. It sweeps away my worries and fears and makes me feel alive and very needy.

When his fingers slip inside me, I almost groan. I hold it back, not wanting to break the spell cast over us. That's when he looks up and sees me watching him.

I worry for a moment he'll stop, but he doesn't. Now that

he knows I'm not going to fight him, he pushes harder, moves faster. The heat continues to rise until I'm boiling from the inside out.

"Squeeze my fingers, firefly. Make your greedy pussy suck in my cum."

My back arches as the heat sparks a fire I can't contain. I explode, all the pieces of me scattering before reforming.

"Fucking spectacular," Will growls before picking me up and carrying me to the bathroom.

He stands me on wobbly legs beside the bath.

"Your foot okay for a minute?"

"Yes," I answer, unable to unscramble my brain enough to get out any more words.

Reaching up, he slides the shirt from my shoulders and lets it drop to my wrists. He tugs each of my hands free from the cuffs and lets the shirt drop to the tiled floor before lifting me with ease and lowering me into the warm water.

I hiss when pain lances through my foot, but it's manageable. Especially when the warm water seeps into my bones, making me feel almost as liquid as the water I'm sitting in.

"I've never had a bath before." At least, not that I can remember.

He scowls. "Move forward a little."

I do as he asks and jolt when Will climbs into the warm water behind me. He pulls me back against his firm chest and wraps his arms around me before taking a deep breath.

I copy him, taking a deep breath of my own, using it to help calm my nerves.

"There are things I need to tell you." His gravelly voice washes over me. "Things that will make you look at me differently. Things that will make you want to run again."

"If I run, will you chase me?"

"Every fucking time." His voice whips over my skin.

"Then what does it matter? I won't look at you differently. I'm trained, remember? I know the rules. I can be everything you need," I soothe, knowing it's both the honest truth and a fucked-up lie.

He growls before biting my neck, his hands sliding around to cup my breasts.

"I don't want you to be anything other than who you are. You shouldn't have to drop into a pose or hide your reactions from me."

"But that is who I am. Right or wrong, Will, I don't know any other way to be."

"You called me Will." His voice is gruff as he tweaks my nipples.

"I...I...you told me to, I thought."

"I did. I'm not mad, I'm happy. I like the sound of my name coming from your lips. I'll like it even more when you're screaming it as I fuck you."

I gasp and feel myself get wet at his words. I still don't understand my body's reactions to him. I've heard worse, seen worse. I thought I'd grown so numb to it I'd never be able to feel anything anymore. I could fake my responses so well that nobody would know, but it's not a skill I've needed to use with Will.

Isn't it funny how I've been taught by the apparent best, and yet I've learned more about myself in a couple of days than I ever did in my last eighteen years?

"Tell me why you think I'll run."

He pauses for a moment before his fingers trail over my breasts and nipples, making me squirm.

"That's just it, Six. I want you to run, but only so I can catch you."

I frown, not sure I understand what he's getting at. "Can you explain it a little more?"

"When you ran today, you were scared, yeah? Your fear turned me on. So much so, I'm not sure my dick has truly gone down since I found you. It took everything I had not to push you to your knees in the dirt and fuck you."

I swallow hard at the images his words evoke. "Do you want to hurt me?"

"No, Six. I might get off on your fear but not on your pain."

"But if I know you're not going to hurt me, why would I be scared?"

"It's the nature of being hunted. Plus, once I feed the beast, I won't be able to hold back. I won't be able to be gentle with you. I'll mark you up and cover you in my cum, branding you as if we were animals instead of humans."

"Okay," I reply, my voice shakier this time. I doubt I'd be scared but I could fake it.

"I know what you're thinking, Six. But your fear isn't something you could fake. I would never physically hurt you to get it, but once the hunt begins, I'd employ every other weapon in my arsenal to bring that fear to the surface."

"Like what?"

"If I told you, it would stop the fear. I'd need you to be one-hundred-percent sure before agreeing to it. Once the hunt begins, I'll ignore the word no, even if you scream it in my face."

Okay, yeah, that scares me a little. "But what if something goes wrong, or I get hurt and you don't stop and—"

He pinches my nipple, cutting off my words.

"It's my job to read your body. That's the key to all of it. You have to trust me enough to rip you apart and piece you back together again."

I've never given my trust to anyone before. Never had it broken beyond repair, leaving me guarding it like a dragon does its hoard. He has given me no reason not to trust him, so I don't have any reservations about handing it over. But I'm smart enough to know that if he breaks it, it will forever damage something between us.

"Tell me what you're thinking."

"I can give you my trust. You've done more to earn it than anyone else in my life but..." My voice drifts off, wondering if I even have the right to ask.

"What is it?"

"We haven't had sex yet. Will you want to, you know, do it first or not?"

"I'm not sure I'd last that long. I'm finding it really fucking hard keeping my hands off you."

He nuzzles my neck as my eyes slip shut. I'm up for giving him what he wants, but I'm already scared about how much it might hurt my first time. From what people have told me, it's awful.

"Relax, firefly. You said you'd trust me."

"It's not that. I'm just nervous about how much it's going to hurt. Everyone told me the first time is the worst and I'm prepared as much as I can be but —"

I snap my mouth shut when I feel his body go rock solid behind me, making me wonder what I said or did wrong.

"Explain," he snaps.

Well, if it's fear he wanted, mission accomplished.

CHAPTER TWENTY-ONE

WILL

$\mathcal{I}$ must have heard her wrong. There is no way Six spent all this time in captivity and is still a virgin. No fucking way am I that lucky. No way is she.

"I'm sorry," she whispers, and I realize I've freaked her out.

I maneuver her until she is facing me, her legs straddling mine.

"I'm not mad, baby. Not even close. I just want to make sure I'm understanding you correctly. Are you telling me you're a virgin?"

"I've had medical exams...fingers...um..." She dips her head but not before I see the flush of red across her cheeks.

I tilt her chin up so she is forced to look at me. "You ever have a cock inside you, Six? And not the plastic kind. An honest to god flesh and blood cock throbbing within you?"

She shakes her head. "No, sir." Her eyes widen at her slip, but I let it go knowing she's flustered. That, and I'm still trying to absorb the shock.

"How is that even possible?" I choke out, my dick impossibly hard once more.

"My owner wanted to be the one to take it," she whispers before a soft smile plays on her lips. "I like that he didn't get that from me, that I get to give it to you."

"God, Six, you are making it so hard to be good."

"Who says you need to be? I'm tired of always being the good girl. Show me how to be bad."

And who am I to argue with that?

"You sure? Because I'm already addicted after one taste. I can only imagine how much stronger the craving will be when I've been inside you."

She nods nervously, but I can see the curiosity in her eyes.

"This is a big ass bath, but I think your first time should be in a bed, don't you?"

She bites her lip, hesitant to answer.

"There is no right or wrong answer here, but you only get one first time. I get one shot to make it everything you hoped it could be."

"I like the water," she tells me softly. "The bath, the lake, the rain. It feels clean and new and..."

I press my thumb over her lips.

"Then the bath it is."

The tip of her tongue licks the pad of my thumb, making me groan. She's making it really difficult to think.

"We need to talk about taking precautions so you don't get pregnant."

I like the idea of one day fucking a baby into her, but not yet. I want her to myself for a while.

"We all got screened at the compound regularly, even me, despite the fact that I hadn't, you know…" Her voice trails off as she blushes.

"That's good, Six. Real good."

"And um, I have something inside me that stops me from getting pregnant. I've had one since I started my periods. It has to be changed every five years but this one is only a year old," she rambles, looking worried that I might have a change of heart.

She's out of her goddamn mind if she thinks for a second that's going to happen.

"You're okay with me taking you without a condom?"

Holy crap, it must be Christmas and I missed the memo.

She frowns. "I am yours to—"

I cut her off with a stern look. "You're mine to protect. I never want you to do something that will put you at risk just to please someone else. Now I can tell you, I'm clean. I was recently screened too and I never fuck someone ungloved. But with you, I find I don't want anything between us."

"I don't want anything between us either. I…I trust you."

She doesn't, but she will.

"Stand up for me, Six. I want to look at you."

She does so without hesitation. The water cascading down her body is more erotic than any porn video I've ever watched.

I have an insatiable urge to lick every inch of her, but I'll cut to the chase this time. I'm too close to the edge to drag this out.

"You are so fucking beautiful."

She bites that damn lip again, drawing attention to her

mouth, reminding me how fucking exquisite it was to slide my cock between her lips.

"Lift your leg and place it on the ledge here. You can hold on to me if you need to."

She does as I ask, opening herself up to me.

"I feel like I've died and gone to heaven," I tell her, looking up at her flushed face as I lean forward and swipe over her clit with the tip of my tongue.

Her hands fly to my head. She grips my hair and I grin. I blow lightly against her, feeling her shiver before I suck her clit. She moans and grips my hair tighter.

Knowing I'm giving her something no one else has, makes me want to prove something to her. The woman gives phenomenal head. It's only fair I return the favor.

I lick, flick, and suck her clit before slipping a finger inside her. She's tight as fuck, something that makes my dick throb in anticipation.

"So wet, so delicious. You like that, huh?"

She makes a noise I'm taking as a yes as I continue to work her into a frenzy. When she starts to tremble, and I worry her legs will give out, I pull back.

Fisting my cock, I slide my hand up and down, my eyes on the wetness coating her thighs.

"Come sit on my cock, Six. Slide your pretty pussy down him nice and slow."

Eagerness has replaced her nerves, her gray eyes staring at me with an excited smile on her face. She maneuvers herself so she's standing over me with her feet on either side of my legs before she gets to her knees.

I hold my cock steady so she can position herself over me. I have to grit my teeth when I feel her heat on the tip as her hands move to the edge of the tub to balance herself.

I slide my hands to her ass and guide her as she slowly lowers herself all the way down until her ass is flush with my balls.

"Holy fuck, Six. Holy fuck."

She grimaces as she holds herself steady, her pussy strangling my dick.

"You okay?"

She nods. "It's better now. It didn't really hurt. I just feel really full. You're so big." She gasps as I flex inside her.

"I need you to move, Six," I spit out through gritted teeth as I fight the urge to thrust into her.

Cautiously at first, she uses her arms to lift herself, my dick sliding almost all the way out before she slides back down faster and harder than before.

I spit out a few choice curse words and invent a few more as I fight the urge to come right there and then.

"That's it, Six. Fuck me. Take what you need."

My grip on her ass tightens as she bounces faster, finding a groove and speed that makes her gasp and me see fucking stars.

I move my hands to her tits, cupping them before tweaking her nipples, tugging on them when she groans in appreciation.

"Six," I warn her. I'm not going to last.

She throws her head back, her movements becoming erratic.

I take control, gripping her hips as I move her the way I like.

"More," she begs. My greedy girl.

I thrust up into her hard and feel her tighten around me.

Dipping my head, I suck a nipple into my mouth before biting down lightly.

She screams and comes, her pussy rippling around me, making it impossible for me to hold out any longer.

With one final thrust, I bury myself inside her and come with a moan. I release her hips so we can both collapse backward.

We lie there for a second recovering when she lifts her head and smiles at me.

"I think I might like sex."

I pull her to me and burst out laughing.

CHAPTER TWENTY-TWO

SIX

*H*e made me wait a whole freaking month, more than long enough for my foot to heal and any tenderness in other areas too.

He hadn't stopped touching me, but he refused to have sex with me after the first time. At first, I was worried I had done something wrong. Then I realized, with a huge amount of frustration, he was building the anticipation. Despite my grumbles, it had worked. My excitement almost eclipsed my nerves.

I wait for the signal and take off at a fast pace, my aim to put as much distance between us as possible. My heart pounds in my chest but not from fear, from exhilaration.

I focus on where I step, not wanting to fall at the first hurdle and hurt myself. I've only been going for about ten minutes when I have to slow my pace. If this is going to become a regular thing, I need to start building my stamina.

Pausing for a minute to catch my breath, I strain my ears and listen to pick up any foreign sounds that don't belong. The forest is quiet.

I continue weaving my way about so I'm not going in an obvious straight line. I'm not sure how he'll be tracking me, but I don't want to make it too easy.

It's chilly out now. My hands and tip of my nose are cold, but thanks to the clothes Will provided, the rest of me is warm. The only difficulty I have is how restricted I feel wearing them. I'm not sure how long I keep going before I need to rest. I look around for a hiding spot and find a large tree that's twice as wide as me. I move behind it and sit, trying to slow my breathing, which is far too loud right now. I may as well wear a beacon saying *here I am*.

Eventually my heartbeat returns to normal and I relax a touch. As long as I'm quiet he won't find me.

As time wears on, wariness sets in. What if he's given up and left me here? Or gotten lost? God, what if he's hurt? I feel the first tendrils of panic take hold. I fight them back knowing it's my imagination playing tricks on me.

Deciding I should keep moving, if only to distract my wayward thoughts, I get to my feet and continue to climb. The hill isn't overly steep, but my legs feel like jelly by the time I reach the crest.

I stumble near a tall oak tree and reach out to catch myself. I'm shoved against the trunk, the bark rough and abrasive against my cheek as I cry out.

"Boo," Will snarls against my ear. He reaches down and

pops open the button on my fly before yanking the zipper down.

"I'll admit, I thought it would take me longer to find you. But I guess I overestimated you. I should have known better than to expect more from a slave."

My heart thuds again, this time with pain caused by the sharp slice his words inflict on me.

"I'm sorry. I promise next time I'll do better."

He laughs and it's a cold hard sound that makes me feel weak and brittle.

"You think there is gonna be a next time? It's hardly fucking worth it now, is it?"

He yanks my jeans and panties down, the frigid air as cold against my skin as his attitude.

"I ask one thing of you and you couldn't even get that fucking right. Pathetic."

He shoves two fingers inside me, making me screech and buck against him.

"Look at that. You're soaked for me. What a surprise. Well at least one of us is enjoying themselves."

He thrusts his fingers into me over and over as I grip the tree for support.

"If I'd known you didn't have a clue how to please a man, I'd have thrown you back," he whispers against my ear, twisting the knife deeper as tears score my cheeks. I messed-up. I didn't mean to, but he doesn't need to be so mean. I shove against him, needing to be away from this horrible version of the man I was coming to care for. He yanks my hair with one hand and fumbles with his belt with the other.

"Oh no, you've had your fun. Now it's time for me to have mine."

I feel his cockhead at my pussy and panic, not wanting him anywhere near me. I scream for him to let me go as I buck and fight. As I push back, his cock slips a little inside me. He takes advantage by thrusting the rest of the way in.

I start to fight in earnest when I feel him pause for a moment and press his lips against the skin of my neck. It only lasts about ten seconds but it's enough to remind me this is all an act. He promised me he wouldn't physically hurt me, but he said nothing about mentally. I knew he would have to draw the fear out of me somehow, but I never realized he would be so vicious.

I stop fighting as hard, not wanting to hurt either one of us. He's bigger than me, stronger than me, and right now I'm completely at his mercy.

I don't know why I feel a rush of heat between my legs at that, but I do. I know Will does too when he starts hammering into me harder and harder.

"Such a dirty girl, letting me fuck her like this."

A sob escapes me, but it does nothing to stop the heat blossoming inside me. I shouldn't like it, and I'm not sure I do, but my body knows what it's doing and takes control while my mind plays catchup.

"I should get you on your knees and fuck that pretty little mouth of yours, let you cry all over my cock before I come all over your face."

Yanking my head back with the hold he has on my hair, he licks away the tear on my cheek. He shoves himself so far inside me I swear I can feel him in my womb. I feel the exact moment he comes, filling me with a growl. His hand drops to my clit and starts rubbing it hard.

My toes curl, my back arches, and I come with a choked whisper, losing my breath and the ability to hold myself up.

And just like that my Will is back, turning me gently and wiping my tears with the pads of his thumbs. His eyes move over my face, taking everything in.

"You okay?"

Am I? Not really. Not even close. I'm not one-hundred-percent sure why. While I was scared, I still knew with certainty he wouldn't hurt me, but I let his words get into my head. They left me feeling raw and vulnerable.

Next time I'll know what to expect, but for now I've had enough. "I want to go home," I whisper.

CHAPTER TWENTY-THREE

WILL

$\mathcal{I}$ watch her sleep, scared if I take my eyes off her, she'll slip away. I fucked up. No, that doesn't begin to describe what I did. And now this woman I'm already obsessed with can't look me in the eye. She glimpsed the monster and now that she knows who I really am, she'll want to go.

I thought I was reading her body right, but fuck, I never took her history into account.

"So fucking stupid." I shove my hands into my hair as she stirs.

"Will?" she calls, a tremor in her voice.

"I'm here." I flick the lamp on and move to sit beside her.

"Please don't be mad anymore."

"I'm not mad at you, Six. Jesus. I'm mad at myself. I fucked up. I'm not sure how I'll ever get you to forgive me."

"No, Will. You told me what to expect. I just...it was more than I thought it would be."

"I should have—" She places a shaky hand over my mouth and shakes her head.

"No. I don't think anything you said would have helped. I needed to experience it to fully understand it, or at least try to. It's the only way to know if I can handle it."

"And can you? Handle it, I mean? I don't want you to have survived all these years just for me to break you."

"I'm stronger than you know. I think we need to talk more about it. Maybe have some subjects you don't touch, just in case."

I reach for her and drag her onto my lap, tilting her head back so I can stare into her eyes. She's so fucking brave. She's right. I'm underestimating her but I also overestimated myself.

"I fucked up. I've never done this with someone who likely has PTSD. I would never choose someone who suffered from it to participate, yet I was so caught up in my selfish needs it never even occurred to me. I promised to keep you safe and yet you were at risk because of me. I could have triggered an episode. Jesus fuck," I curse when I realize just how bad it could have been.

"Hey, I'm okay." She reaches up and cups my face. Her movements are unsure, like she isn't used to physically giving comfort, but her innate need to comfort me overrides her fear.

"If you had triggered me, I think you'd have noticed. Especially after what happened with James."

I sigh. Maybe she's right but it doesn't absolve the guilt.

"Let's just take it off the table. I don't need it, and you are far more important than my fucked-up urges.

"No, stop that. I know you think you're some kind of monster, but you're far from it. I know monsters, Will. They didn't live under my bed, they tore me from it. You are nothing like them. If you were, you'd have told me nothing. You'd have just tossed me into those woods and told me to run. You have done nothing but look after me and protect me since I arrived here. Are those the actions of a monster?"

I press my forehead against hers.

"I liked the taste of your tears on my tongue when I fucked you, Six. Your fear made me come harder than I've ever come before. You still think I'm not a monster?"

"Yes, because if I told you I never wanted to do that again, you wouldn't make me, would you?"

I don't answer because she's right. The whole point of this, the one thing that separates me from a rapist, is consent. The lines might blur after. Fuck knows in a court of law I'd be screwed if I didn't have signed contracts and permissions. No means no after all. No matter when it's given.

"This isn't fair to you, Six. You deserve so much better than this." I should back off, offer her a role as housekeeper as I planned all along.

Her hands slip to my thighs where her nails dig into the material of my pants.

"I was wet," she whispers, making me swallow at the memory of what it felt like to slide inside her.

"I was turned on. I came. I know despite what people say—that people's bodies can betray them when they are being raped. They can get wet and orgasm while still one hundred percent not wanting to be violated. This wasn't that. I fought you, but not because I didn't want you to fuck me. Because I didn't want you to speak. Your words echoed too many of my own dark thoughts. I was mad and sad, but I was turned on, Will. My body didn't betray itself."

"You were scared, Six." I point out, even though it might have been the aim of the game.

"I was scared that I liked you and you became someone else. I was scared because I figured that meant I couldn't trust myself and if I don't have that, Will, what do I have?"

My pulse thunders beneath my skin as I take in her words.

"I've always had to be in control, even when I'm forced to submit. Every move I make, every word I say is thought out and precise. It's a mask I have spent a long time perfecting so that nobody would know that their conditioning wasn't quite as flawless with me as they thought. If they knew I was still me inside and not the caricature version they tried to make me they would have corrected me. They would have found a way to beat me down until I was an empty shell ready for my next command."

A tear slips free. I catch it with my thumb and suck it into my mouth, tasting her sorrow for myself.

"I'm tired, Will. Tired of being strong. Some days I feel like one tiny touch will shatter me and then you come along and suddenly I don't need to be the strong one anymore."

Another tear, followed by another as she lifts her wet eyes to mine once more. She's so fucking captivating I can't look away.

"When we were out there and you had me pinned against the tree like that you took all my control and smashed it into a million pieces. I didn't need to be strong or wear my mask. You controlled every aspect even when I came. It was utterly terrifying, but it was also the first time I've felt truly free."

I pull away and stand, kicking off my shoes before getting back on the bed, this time with my head on the pillows. The dark circles under Six's eyes are a reminder that her sleep isn't as restful as it needs to be.

"Come lie with me."

I hold my arm open to her. She hesitates for a moment before crawling up the bed to me and laying her head upon my chest.

She throws one of her legs over mine so I slide my hand over her thigh and use it to anchor her in place.

"Okay, Six. We'll figure it out. I can live without it, remember that. What I can't live without is you. Not now that I know."

"Now you know what?"

"You're not ready to hear it yet, but I'll tell you soon. Sleep. We'll talk more tomorrow."

I can sense she wants to protest but she bites her tongue, still used to keeping her words to herself. Normally anything that reminded me of her captivity would piss me off, but it works in my favor right now because I need to think.

All the things she said, I need to consider if they are the words of a person who is desperate not to get sent away or if they are from a woman who has finally found her way home.

CHAPTER TWENTY-FOUR

SIX

I know I'm alone before I open my eyes. I stare at the ceiling, feeling lost and unsure about what happens next. I meant what I said last night. I might not have the answers yet, but I'm more than happy to figure things out along the way. I can't bear for Will to think he's a monster.

I climb from the bed and head to the bathroom, taking care of business before having a quick shower.

I look up out of the window at the gray sky and wonder if it's going to rain.

Too cold to dance in it, according to Will, but there is still something soothing about curling up with a book as the rain lashes against the windows. With that thought in mind, I hurry to get dry and make my way back into the bedroom.

I tug the closet open and look at all the things on the left that Will purchased for me before turning to Will's side and slipping a black shirt from its hanger. I feel bad knowing he spent money on me that largely goes to waste, but I'm still adjusting to wearing anything that constricts me.

I tug the shirt on and button it up. It falls to mid-thigh and covers everything in case Will isn't alone. I use the elastic on my wrist to tug my hair into a messy bun and head out to find Will.

The smell of food catches my attention the second my feet hit the staircase, so I head that way. I pause in the doorway where I find Will at the breakfast bar drinking coffee while James, his back to me, cooks something on the stove.

Will must sense me. He turns and holds his arm open for me.

I don't need a second invitation. I step into the safety of his embrace and take the juice he offers me from the spot in front of him.

"Morning, firefly. How are you feeling?" he asks me softly, for my ears only.

"I'm okay. Are you?" I brush a strand of hair from his forehead as I wait for his answer, marveling that I can touch him whenever I like, without repercussions. For someone who has been starved of skin contact beyond training sessions, it feels heavenly.

"I am now. Eat and then we'll talk, okay?" His eyes move over my face before he presses a kiss to my lips.

I think he intended it to be a quick peck, but I open up to him instinctively. We both fall into the void, oblivious to James cooking or Fisher entering. Until Fisher whistles, making me freeze. Will pulls away and sighs before tugging me onto his lap.

I look up and see Fisher and James watching us with smirks on their faces, making me blush a dozen shades of pink.

"You lucky bastard. I should have known better than to stop you before you got to the good part," Fisher tells Will, who growls at him. James steps closer and clips him across the head.

"Think it, don't say it," James scolds, making me giggle.

"Sorry, Six," Fisher apologizes, but his wicked grin tells me he's not sorry at all.

"I'm not sure I believe you."

"Smart and beautiful, a deadly combination. Speaking of... he turns to Will after snagging an apple from the fruit bowl and taking a huge bite.

"The good doctor's funeral was today. Police have officially closed his case after it was ruled an accidental death."

"Good."

"You want some breakfast, Six? Eggs, bacon, and pancakes sound good?" James interrupts, changing the subject.

"I've only had eggs before, but I'll try anything once."

Will's grip on my hips tightens. I feel him harden beneath me, making me realize my words could be taken in a completely different way.

"No bacon?" Fisher whimpers with his hands over his heart. "That is a fucking travesty."

His words make me laugh again.

"Well prepare to have your mind blown, pretty girl." James winks as he plates up enough food to feed three of me and slides it in front of me with a knife and fork.

Eyes wide, I look at Will for help. His lazy grin has me rubbing my thighs together, a move that doesn't escape his attention.

"I'll finish off what you can't. I'll eat anything you offer me." He winks.

Jesus, when did it get so hot in here?

"And on that note, I need to go take a shower and spend some time with Rosy Palm. James, save me a plate," Fisher orders before disappearing upstairs.

"Rosy Palm?"

"Five fingers. You know what? Never mind." Will shakes his head.

I shrug. "Does Fisher live here too?" I know James has a property behind us somewhere, but I'm not sure about Fisher. He's not around much so I never thought about it, but showering isn't something you just do anywhere, is it? Sometimes not knowing simple things like this confuses me. I can read a book and absorb the information in a click of my fingers, but social cues and sarcasm are still things I struggle with.

"One of the guest rooms upstairs has a bunch of mine and Fisher's clothes just in case, but Fisher rarely crashes here. He has an apartment in the city. He hates how quiet it gets out here," James answers.

"I get that. I love it during the day but sometimes the silence can be deafening at nighttime. There is nothing to drown out my dreams."

"I understand that, pretty girl. More than you'll ever know."

I glimpse a look of sorrow in his eyes before he hides it. Yes, I think, he understands all too well how much the silence likes to welcome in the ghosts.

"So, what do you two have planned today?" James asks, taking a bite of food from his own plate. "I don't think the rain is going to let up anytime soon."

I look at Will to see if he has any plans, but he shakes his head, leaving it up to me. I struggle to make choices, having spent a lifetime without any. Will has slowly been leaving me to make more of them.

Instead of panicking, I take a second to think. What do I want to do today? I close my eyes and think over my options.

"I want to read near the windows so I can watch the rain," I answer softly and wait for a rebuttal like it's a test I might fail. Logically I know Will isn't like that, but I was conditioned to think one way for eighteen years. It will take more than a few weeks to adjust to the vast changes in my life. When he doesn't tell me it's a stupid idea, I open my eyes and see him watching me with a soft look in his eyes.

"Sounds good to me. We could have a lazy day and then settle in front of a movie later."

I nod. It sounds heavenly. I drop my eyes to my plate, disappointed that my food is all gone. Everything here tastes so damn good.

"Everything okay?" James asks. I look at him and see him watching me with a frown. Taking a risk, I open my mouth before I can second guess myself.

"Can you teach me how to cook?" My voice is barely above a whisper, but I know they both hear me.

"I would be honored, Six. My Claire left me a bunch of recipes that sit idly on a shelf just waiting to be shared with someone who would love them as much as she did."

"Hey, I—" James looks at Will, cutting him off with a look.

"I love you, Will. You know that. I am insanely proud of the man you have become. I've always believed you could do anything you put your mind to, but I'm sorry to say that cooking is not one of them."

136

Laugher bursts out of me, surprising us all. I distinctly remember Will telling me he could cook when I first arrived. But now that I think about it, almost all our food has been delivered.

"I resent that, old man. Maybe I just need a better teacher."

"You could burn water," James deadpans.

"Fine, be like that. But I have a sneaky suspicion that you're intimidated by my potential. Don't worry, your secret is safe with me."

"How you don't have to stoop when you walk is beyond me, you big-headed bastard," James grumbles, turning to the sink.

I look up at Will and grin, seeing his mirth reflected back at me.

It's moments like this that make everything I've been through worth it. I survived hell and I didn't do it so I could get revenge but so I could savor the taste of each slice of normality I could find.

CHAPTER TWENTY-FIVE

WILL

Six read to me as I lay with my head in her lap. Her hand played absently with my hair as she lost herself in the words. I studied her while she was distracted. I cataloged every freckle, the bow shape of her lips, the slope of her nose. I burned them into my memory as our perfect lazy day became a moment in time I'll always remember. A moment of calm in the chaos of our lives.

Sipping my coffee, I can't help but smile at James's loud laughter followed by Six's giggle as he attempts to show her how to cook, despite the late hour.

I don't stray far. I want to give them a moment alone, knowing it's important for Six to form bonds with people other than me, even if I'd love nothing more than to keep her to myself.

She has quickly become important to me in a way I never could have seen coming. That might scare most men, but not me. In Claire and James, I had the perfect example of what love could bring to the table. I never shied from it. I waited patiently, almost convinced I'd never find that one person made just for me. And there she was, in the most unlikely of places. It matters little where she came from, only that she's here now and I intend to keep it that way.

Should I be concerned at the speed at which she had sunk beneath my skin? Perhaps if she had been anyone else I would be on guard, but Six is an exception to the rule. A woman in every way, but there is a guileless innocence to her too. One that can only come from a woman who never got to be a child. She was born with a purpose and locked away in her tower, much like a fairytale. Only I'm no white knight. If I had been, I would never have been in a position to save her.

My cell rings, distracting me from my thoughts. A glance at the screen shows it's Jude.

I frown, not used to getting a call from this particular brother, although it's not unheard of.

"Hey, Jude. What's up?"

"Cash's woman has been taken. We're trying to locate her. Any help you can give us will be appreciated. I'm tapping my old informants. Viddy and Kai are on their way over to help with the physical search right now, but we need a starting point."

"Fuck. Alright, I'll make some calls and see if I can find anything. I'll keep you posted."

"Thanks, man." He hangs up as I head up to my office, taking the stairs two at a time.

I fire up my laptop and ignore everything else as I dive into the dark web, looking for a proverbial needle in a haystack.

I'm just about to give up and try another avenue when a notification pings for the secure email I used when purchasing Six. I open it and log into the website using my security details. I almost throw up when I see what pops up on my screen.

I slam the lid closed and grab the laptop before heading down the stairs and into the kitchen.

"I've gotta go. Cash needs me."

"I'll drive you," James offers as Six looks at me worriedly. Unfortunately, I don't have time to comfort her right now.

"No, stay here with Six and call Fisher in too. I'll be back as soon as I can."

"You'll be okay," I reassure Six, knowing she'll be internally freaking out about me leaving her alone here with James and Fisher. She shows me her inner strength though, when she stands tall and presses a kiss to my cheek.

"I'll be fine. Just come back to me in one piece, okay?"

"I promise."

I don't hang around any longer, knowing time is of the essence right now. I catch the keys James throws me and hurry out to the car, tossing the laptop on the passenger seat as I climb in and buckle up. I tear out of the driveway and head toward Cash's place, breaking dozens of speeding laws in the process.

I don't know how long it takes me to get there. I drive on autopilot as I wrack my brain, trying to figure out what our next move should be. I keep coming up blank. The signal for the video is bouncing around all over the place so I can't get a lock on it.

I grab the laptop and climb out of the car, not bothering to shut the door.

I spot Viddy's SUV and a dozen other cars, but I don't pay them much attention as I head inside, ignoring the dozens of guns now pointed at my head.

I don't waste time. I open the laptop, type a few keys, and turn it for Cash to see. I've only ever seen him look this wrecked when he woke up in the hospital after he was shot to find out his daughter had been kidnapped. Luckily both he and Lily were okay but I'm not sure Layla will be gifted the same outcome. Cash has likely figured this out himself as his face pales further.

"What the fuck is that?" Stuart, one of Cash's security team, croaks out.

"It's streaming live on the dark web. I got an encrypted notification and when I opened it, it was to this and the count-down clock."

The image is of Layla gagged and strapped naked to a bed in a dark room somewhere, tears streaming down her face. Her horror and fear are so potent, every man and woman in this room can taste it.

Comments floating up the side of the screen make lewd and vulgar suggestions of what to do to her. Each payment confir-mation brings with it a new wave of sickening suggestions.

"He's going to rape her and stream it live," Viddy whispers, just as horrified as the rest of us.

"Worse, this site…it has a specialty." I swallow hard, feeling nausea swim in my gut.

"What the fuck is worse than this?" Viddy snaps.

But Cash has already figured it out. He physically recoils from the image on the screen as if it burns him.

"He's making a snuff movie. He's going to kill her," he chokes out, revealing the sickening truth to the room, which erupts at his words.

CHAPTER TWENTY-SIX

SIX

I watched a movie with Fisher and James as the hours rolled by, but I couldn't tell you what happened if my life depended on it.

It's late, or early, depending on how you look at it. Most people would be asleep in their beds but I'm too on edge to rest. I've tried to remain calm. The cracks in the facade are beginning to show. The room feels like it's closing in on me as fear starts to wrap itself around my heart. What if he gets hurt? Or worse, what if he's dead? I never knew I needed anyone until Will pushed his way into my life. And now, I don't think I can survive without him.

"He'll be okay, Six. This is what Will does. Only now he has you at home to come back to. He won't take any risks that might jeopardize him waking up beside you," Fisher says, making me jump.

I turn to look at him, fighting back my threatening tears.

"I know. It's just…"

"Hard. It's hard to let someone you care about put themselves in dangerous situations. But that's who he is, Six. He couldn't change now even if he wanted to. It's in his blood. You have to trust that he knows what he's doing."

I nod and blow out a breath. Logically I get that, but fear trumps logic every time.

"Why don't you go on up to bed and get some rest? You look exhausted. I promise I'll come wake you if I get any news," James offers.

I want to tell him he's crazy if he thinks for a second I'll be able to sleep, but when I look at him I realize he's giving me an out. He knows I need to be alone to regroup and let my guard down, something I can't do in front of these two, not yet at least.

I nod and climb to my feet.

"Thank you." I hesitate when I move to the stairs.

"I promise, Six, if he calls, I'll wake you."

I offer him an awkward smile and retreat. I make it all the way upstairs to our room before the tears fall.

I crawl onto the bed and look up at the stars. The rain disappeared earlier, leaving clear skies, which made the temperature drop dramatically. Frost has begun to appear as the weather went from one extreme to another.

I start counting. It's something I've done over the years to give my brain something to focus on when everything is spiraling out of control.

I reach one hundred before my racing heart starts to slow, but I don't stop counting. The distraction keeps me from dwelling on how alone I feel right now. Will has this whole other life separate from me. I don't begrudge him that one little bit. It's just...when we are together, it's like we are the only two people in the world. Now that he's with the other people who care about him, I feel very small and alone, which is kind of pathetic.

A small growl slips out as my anger replaces my fear, not at Will but at myself.

I stomp to the bathroom, strip out my clothes, and toss them on the floor before climbing into the shower.

The water is so cold it's jarring but I don't get out of its punishing spray. I dip my head and hold my breath as it starts to heat, using the shock of the frigid temperature to snap my brain from its harrowing thoughts.

I need to get a grip. I can't break down every time he leaves, but it's hard not to fall back on old habits. I've had so many people leave me over the years. Even though it wasn't their fault most of the time, it didn't lessen the blow. Most people never returned and those that did were never the same.

I tip my head back and let the water wash everything away —my tears, my anger, my pain. I shut everything down and build a brick wall around my tender heart.

I don't know how long I stand under the unrelenting water. When hands land on my hips, I scream and whirl around, my heart in my throat. I see Will standing behind me, his face looking ravaged with pain. And just like that, the wall crumbles to dust.

It takes me a second to realize he's fully clothed. Sensing

he's not up to answering any questions right now, I look after him like he has done for me a dozen times over.

I reach up and open the three buttons at the top of his long-sleeved T-shirt before slipping my hands to the hem. Slowly I raise it and wait as he lifts his arms. He bends so I can help pull it free before tossing it into the corner.

He looks down at me, water dripping from his nose and chin, but his desolate look has been replaced by one filled with heat.

I reach for the button on his jeans and pop it open before tugging the zipper down. I slip my hands inside the fabric and slide his jeans down over his ass and hips, bending to drag them down his legs. I stay on my knees while he kicks them away, leaving his naked body on display before me.

I look up at him and his heated gaze makes my nipples pebble and my stomach cramp with need, but this isn't about me. This is about giving Will something to focus on because I never want to see that look on his face again.

I reach for his hard dick and stroke it up and down with my hand as he locks his legs. With my free hand, I cup his balls and feel him tense in anticipation as I dip forward and suck the tip of his dick into my mouth. I lave the end with my tongue before taking him deeper.

His hands slide into my hair and grip it tightly. The small bite of pain makes my pussy throb. Taking him as deep as I can, I relish his guttural groan, humming around him as I continue to stroke his balls.

I work his cock with my mouth, keeping my movements slow and steady, driving him crazy until the threads of caution snap and he takes control. His grip tightens as he thrusts into my mouth harder and faster. It's a strange moment between us in which he takes what he needs from me, but I hold the power. Kneeling before him doesn't make me feel weak, it makes me feel like a goddess. Will is a formidable man and to make him lose control like that makes me feel pretty damn good.

"Fuck, firefly," he hisses. I expect him to come so I brace myself, ready to swallow him down. Instead, he pulls himself free and reaches for me, lifting and spinning me around to bend over the bench on the far side of the shower.

I barely have time to hold on before he's surging inside me. I scream at the intrusion. I might be dripping wet, but his dick is big enough to stretch me to my limits.

He pauses for a second, giving me a chance to tell him to stop. That's the last thing I want so I thrust my ass back into him.

Taking that for the green light it is, his fingers dig into my hips as he grabs hold of me and starts fucking me like he hates me. I love it.

His thrusts are brutal and I know I'll have finger-tipped bruises tomorrow. It will be worth it. The intensity of the moment, the act of wild abandon, is so at odds with Will's usual calmness that I feel as if we are caught in a storm, both of us tossed around and out of control before *boom*! In a moment of absolute clarity we come together, then crash back down to earth in a wrecked heap.

It takes me a moment to collect myself, my breathing as ragged as Will's. I straighten up before turning into him when he pulls me tightly to his chest. We stand like that for a moment, soaking each other in before I feel his fingers on my jaw.

I look up at him as he speaks. "Thank you." His voice is hoarse, as if he's trying to swallow his emotions, but I don't need him to do that for me. In this house, he should just get to be Will. Not the suit-wearing, fear-inducing millionaire arms dealer, but the man he is beneath the veneer. The Will that is just mine.

CHAPTER TWENTY-SEVEN

WILL

I wake before Six, but I don't move to get up. After the horror of last night, I can't find it in me to move away from her. Watching Cash's agony made me realize that despite our god-like reputations, we are all just mortal men who can bleed. Nothing strikes a more devastating blow than attacking us through the very heart of what makes us who we are—our women.

I tighten my arm around Six when she mumbles in her sleep. She settles once more, but every time I close my eyes, all I see is Cash's horrified eyes and Layla's tear-stained cheeks.

For the first time since Six came here, I question if it's the right decision. Being with a man like me will always mean she has a target on her. People will use her to get to me. In a way, I can't fault them for their logic. Six is my Achilles heel. The weak point in my defenses because I know there isn't anything I won't do or anything I won't give up to keep her safe. So why can't I set her free? There is no denying she'd be safer as far from me as possible.

Layla is lying in a hospital bed right now because of the actions of a dangerous man. Not even Cash with all his security and bodyguards could keep her safe.

But Six isn't Layla. She was never free or safe. She never made a bad choice that led her to a monster. She was born in the belly of the beast and shaped into the woman she is. It's only because of her will of steel that she is as selfless and kind as she is. She is living proof that even people in hell can be blessed with a miracle. Because that's what Six is to me. A miracle. There is no way she should have survived, no way she should have become this perfect creature that's the embodiment of every fantasy I've ever had. She's temptation and salvation all weaved together in an irresistible package. If it's a test to measure my integrity, I'll fail every time. No matter what, I can't bring myself to let her go.

She deserves better, there is no getting around that, but I can't keep walking this path without her. I've become apathetic to it all. The monotony of life wore on me until Six knocked me on my ass.

"Will?"

I look down at a sleepy Six as she wakes and reaches for me.

"I'm right here, Six."

It takes her brain a second to realize she's in my arms. When she does, she relaxes.

"Is everything okay?" she asks me tentatively.

I sigh and pull her tighter to me, wishing I could keep this from touching her. But hiding this facet of my life would only leave her open to danger she would be oblivious to. Better to know the risks and take precautions than walk through life with your head in the clouds.

"Last night, my friend's woman was kidnapped."

"Oh my god. Is she okay?"

"She's in hospital. It was touch and go for a while but according to the text I got a little while ago, she's gonna pull through." Viddy had also let me know she'd sprung Cash from the cell he spent the night in after he lost his ever-loving mind. The whole thing was a clusterfuck, but everyone survived. That's all that matters right now.

"Is that something that happens a lot in your world?" She doesn't sound scared. Wary, more than anything else.

"When you live and work on the wrong side of the tracks, you inevitably attract danger. But these were unique cases."

"Cases as in more than one?"

Yeah, I was never going to slip that one past her. Six is far too clever for that.

"Layla, Cash's woman, was married to a very bad man. He kidnapped another friend of mine—Jenna—and Cash's little girl. I won't go into details, but they were both returned safe and sound. Layla's husband was killed but her connection to him made her a target. She was kidnapped due to that connection, not because of anything Cash or any of the rest of us did."

I can see her thinking the whole thing over before she speaks. I brace myself, ready for a fight. If she tells me she wants to leave, she'll find out exactly what kind of man I am.

"Sounds to me like Jenna and Layla were lucky. Normal men and women would never have had the skills or connections to get them back safely. Sometimes the only way to fight the darkness is to rely on the people who know how to navigate it. Not everyone who lives on the wrong side of the tracks is bad. Sometimes they just like the view better from over there." She smiles and I realize she's teasing me.

I roll us until I have her pinned on her back.

"Fuck, I love you."

She freezes, looking like a deer caught in a car's headlights. "I...I..."

I press my mouth to hers and drink her in. I kiss her until she's boneless beneath me before pulling back.

"I don't expect you to say it back. I know it's early days. But, firefly, I'm not a little boy trying to get in your pants, I'm a man and I know what I want, what I feel. I don't need to hear those words from you, not until you're ready, but you need to hear them from me. You deserve to hear them whispered to you every day.

"I've never had anyone love me before," she whispers, breaking my heart.

"Now you do. And I promise, if you let me, I'll love you so damn hard you'll never feel unloved again."

I kiss her again and shiver when she drags her nails down my back, my dick thickening against her.

"I want you to chase me."

I pause and pull back, frowning.

"I want to try again, Will. And yes, it's for you. But it's for me too. I haven't been able to stop thinking about it."

"I don't know, Six. We haven't really talked about what happened last time and what—" She presses her fingers to my lips.

"If we talk about it too much, it will soothe my fears and take away the very essence of what we're doing. Last time you played on one of my worst fears and yet you didn't trigger me. I think knowing that gives me baseline knowledge I can handle pretty much anything you throw at me. All I ask, just to be sure, is that you don't use the threat of sending me back. That's my line, I think." Her breath picks up, letting me know this is a genuine fear of hers.

"I can promise you this, right here and now, that I will never send you back. This is your home and even if you wanted to leave, I wouldn't let you. That makes me a fucking dick, but I don't care. I'm keeping you, Six. And nothing you can say or do will change that."

CHAPTER TWENTY-EIGHT

SIX

*I*t's milder today than it has been and according to the forecast, this is expected to continue for at least another week. Normally the weather wouldn't bother me but as I try to move stealthily through the woods, I'm not too proud to admit this whole running and hiding thing is much easier without worrying about frostbite.

I've spent time in these woods since Will last fucked me here, anticipating the next time we would play. As a result, I'm more familiar with the layout. I head in the direction opposite the last time. I take the easiest route, looking to put as much distance between us as possible before veering off course to hide. I pause and listen but when I'm met with nothing but silence, I carry on.

The slight breeze blows at my knee-length skirt as I climb

over a downed log and move deeper into the denser part of the forest. A skirt seems like an odd thing to wear for our hunt-capture game, but Will wanted to take advantage of the warmer temperature. Who am I to argue?

Flat-heeled thigh-high leather boots protect my legs but will provide Will with easy access when he catches me. Especially when I'm not wearing any panties.

A thick sheepskin-lined jacket with nothing more than a front-fastening sports bra beneath keeps me warm but is supple enough not to restrict my movements.

If I had to guess, I'd say this outfit was bought for this specific purpose, even though I wasn't sure I'd ever convince Will to give this another shot.

I love how protective he is of me, but I don't need protecting from him and I sure as hell don't want him to change. The man I'm becoming desperately attached to would fade and become someone else. That's the last thing I want.

It might not be the same thing, but it reminds me of Ten and how the boy I cared for faded away until I was left only with a ghost and a pocketful of regrets.

I'm not sure how long I've been out here but the position of the sun has changed and the light seems to be fading, leading me to believe it's been a while.

I've kept my pace steady and I haven't tired as much as last time. But now that I'm thinking about it, my feet ache and I need something to eat and drink.

Looking around for somewhere to hide, I frown when it looks like I've stumbled into a clearing. I must have been more lost in my head than I thought or I'd have avoided this part.

A scorch mark in the grass with a set of logs forming a

hexagon around it makes me think of a campfire. But I can't picture Will camping. I see a picnic bench and —

A stick snaps behind me and I run for cover at a dead sprint, toward the woods. I don't bother to look around to see how close he is, knowing it will only slow me down.

I run hard and as fast as I can, wincing when a low branch whips across my cheek. I don't slow down until I physically can't go any farther. I listen for him, but my breathing is too loud to hear anything, so I give up.

This time, I see the perfect spot to hide — a large overhanging tree with a couple of low branches. I climb onto the first branch. When I know that it's solid, I move up to the next, repeating the process until I'm up far enough not to be spotted immediately.

I settle back against the trunk of the tree, the wide branch more than spacious enough for my butt and legs to stretch out on. Carefully tugging off my small pack, I pull out the bottle of water and sandwich Will insisted I take with me.

At the time, I couldn't anticipate needing it. I was sure I would have been found already. It looks like Will was right, I muse as I devour the sandwich in a few bites. As I'm swallowing the last bite, it occurs to me that Will was a little too adamant about me needing it.

I drink the water down quickly, pondering what that could mean. Has he given me that much of a head start or is this all part of his mind games? I'm determined not to fail this time. I'm not going to fight the fear. I'll embrace it. But it's hard to know how I'll truly react until he finds me.

Once I'm finished, I shove everything back into the pack and rest for a while, my legs aching now I'm sitting down. The urge to nap is strong, but I'd probably fall out of the tree and break my neck.

I wait a little longer, resting while I can because I have no idea when I'll get the chance again. It might be safe enough here now, but Will would find me if I didn't keep moving. With a sigh, I slowly make my way back down the tree, cursing when the skirt catches on a stick. I manage to pull it free without losing my balance, but still slice my hand on the sharp bark.

Walking through the forest in a skirt is one thing, but climbing a tree in it is another thing altogether.

I freeze when I hear the distinct sound of voices. I don't move, clinging to the tree, hoping beyond hope that being pressed against the trunk will give me some kind of chameleon blending powers.

Holding my breath for as long as I can, I open my mouth and breathe out slowly so as not to give away my whereabouts. How had he gotten so close without me realizing and who the heck was he talking to? I'm guessing he has his cell phone on speaker, but does that mean he's told whoever he's talking to about what we're doing?

My skin flushes hot over that. It's not that I'm ashamed, but I thought it was something just for us.

Deciding to risk it, I move as quietly as I can down the remaining two branches until my feet touch solid ground. As soon as they do, I move behind the wide solid trunk.

As the voices get closer, I realize Will isn't talking on the phone. The voice is too clear, too close. There is no slowing my wildly galloping heart now. Not as my brain tries to figure out a perfectly logical reason Will has someone with him. Maybe he thinks I got lost or something. Perhaps I've been gone longer than I realized and he's worried.

I'm about to step around the tree and reveal myself when their conversation flows over me.

"Are you sure about this? Because you can't take it back afterward."

I recognize the second voice as Fisher's, but the usual joviality is missing from his tone. His voice is as cold and serious as I've ever heard it.

"I'm sure. But it's only this one time. Six is mine. You get this one free pass and that's it. You still want in?"

"A chance to fuck Six's tight pussy without getting shanked? Damn fucking straight I'm game."

"Well, then may the best man win."

"So, if I find her first, I get to fuck her?"

"The winner takes the prize," Will agrees. Holy fuck, I think my heart stops for a minute.

"Six know this?"

"Six is on my playground now. She gave me her limits. She said nothing about sharing her."

"I thought you didn't share."

"I don't plan on losing."

Fisher laughs at that. "You forget who you're talking to, Will. I'm the best damn hunter within a hundred miles of here and you know it."

"We'll see. Run along now before I change my mind."

I hold my breath when I sense movement closer to me. If they are as close as I think, they'll hear my traitorous heart attempting to burst out of my chest.

Nobody finds me but I don't trust myself to move as I try to process what just happened. Will told me that day with James he would never share me. So why now? Is he that confident he'll find me first? Maybe he won't really let Fisher touch me. Maybe this is all a trick. Except Will doesn't go back on his word.

For the first time since I left the house, fear and uncertainty begin to swirl. Knowing Will is out looking for me brought me a sense of breathless anticipation. Knowing Fisher is looking for me makes me want to run home.

That's not a bad idea. If they are expecting me to keep going, maybe the safest place is back at the beginning.

Without a better idea, I wait a few more minutes, take a deep breath and step around the tree. When nobody jumps out and attacks me, I retrace my earlier steps and head back the way I came.

After ten minutes or so, I start to relax. Right around the time a body plows into me, knocking me to the ground.

A rough scream rips out of me, more from shock than anything else. My front is pushed into the dirt and a body presses down over me.

"Will?" my shaky voice asks as hands shove my skirt up over my ass. He doesn't answer. I try to turn but a hand shoves the hood of my jacket over my head before pressing a palm into the side of my face, holding me in place.

I kick my legs out as fear swamps me, making my breathing ragged and my limbs heavy. I'm in too vulnerable a position and he's too strong.

"Will?" I shout again when fingers probe my slick pussy. A hard cock shoves its way brutally inside me.

I scream at the invasion, but I'm helpless to do anything other than take each savage thrust. Tears run down my face and pool in the dirt beneath me as my body wars with my head.

I try to apply logic to the situation but every thought is too fragmented, splintering and falling to pieces before I can grasp onto it.

Will or Fisher, Will or Fisher? I don't know, can't find a calm space in my head to try and figure it out. I scream in both frustration and shame as my orgasm twists and yanks at me, even as I try to fight it.

I can't be sure it's Will. I don't know if I'll get punished or if I should fight harder. I don't know what to do.

On that thought, I give in to the helplessness of it all and let go. My body relaxes as I capitulate to the man on top of me. When he senses my surrender, he roars out his release.

I feel him coat my insides and that tells me who it is.

"Will," I whisper. This time it's not a question but a statement of fact. He would never let Fisher fuck me without a condom.

Pulling out of me, he flips me over. His dark eyes glare down at me as he shoves three fingers inside me, making me moan.

"Clever girl. Did you like me fucking you? You were soaked long before I came inside you. Oh, perhaps you got wet thinking it was Fisher's cock inside you." He snarls as he leans over me. "Nobody's cock but mine will ever fuck this pussy. Nobody comes inside you but me."

He thrusts his fingers back into me and with his free hand flicks my clit hard. The grip I had on my sanity slips as I fall into the abyss with a whimper of his name on my lips.

CHAPTER TWENTY-NINE

WILL

I sit staring out at the lake. The cup of coffee in my hand has long gone cold, but I don't move to put it down.

Fucking Six in the woods had been spectacular. I'd found a way to scare her without tripping her triggers. Both of us had come home, eager to pick up where we'd left off after taking a shower to wash away the remnants of the forest floor. That was when I'd noticed a slice across her palm that looked like it needed a stitch or two.

Pissed at myself once more, it was only Six's whispered reassurances that she'd cut it herself climbing a damn tree, of all things, that had calmed me down.

Deciding to kill two birds with one stone, Six agreed to let me take her to the hospital to get it fixed up so I could also pop in and see Cash and Layla.

She was hesitant to leave her sanctuary but after a deep breath, she agreed.

Of course, she wasn't as happy with me when she realized I'd be leaving her with James and Fisher while I went to see Cash. Not because she was being left out of things but because she was too embarrassed to look Fisher in the eye. I'll give the man his dues. He gave me a shit-eating grin, but he wiped it clear before Six could see it, sensing not to push her too hard. Especially when we would be taking her out of her comfort zone.

I kissed her stupid—her words not mine—and left her with the guys while I went to find Cash. As much as I wanted him to meet my girl, I couldn't do it yet. Not like this when Layla was so hurt.

What I hadn't expected when I'd pushed open the door to Layla's room was to catch the tail end of his conversation with the doctor as she moved to leave.

I step aside and let her pass, glaring at Cash.

"What are you doing here?" he asks when he spots me.

"You're fucking married?"

"Shh...keep your voice down. Layla needs her rest."

He stands and signals for us both to sit in the chairs in the corner of Layla's room.

"You married Layla?" I repeat. "When?"

"A while ago. I wanted unfiltered access to Layla and her life."

"You already had that with her living with you." I point out.

A look of guilt flickers over his face before it's replaced

with something else. He dips his head quickly, but I've already seen it. I'd already figured out he cared for her, but…

"Cash…just how long have you been in love with… your wife?"

He looks up at me and swallows. "Since the night I carved my knife into her skin and she looked at me with peace in her eyes instead of panic."

I jump to my feet and start pacing, "You did that to her face? She said it was her husband."

"He told her he was going on a business trip. When I dragged her from her bed, she guessed he returned early. Afterward, when she realized he had been dead at the time, she assumed it was one of his men or one of his so-called friends. Apparently kidnap and torture were a regular occurrence."

"Christ, Cash." How the hell is she supposed to get past something like that?

"Layla knows. It's fucked-up, but the truth came out before all this went down. It was rough, but we were just turning a corner when this happened and now it's like I'm back to square one."

"You're lucky you have a square left to stand on at all," I grunt before sighing. "You did the work once. If she means as much to you as you say she does, then you'll work twice as hard to keep her."

"When did you get so fucking sage in your old age?"

I rub my hand over my face, not feeling very fucking wise at all. I have a former slave downstairs getting stitched up, one I like to hunt and mount like an animal. I'd be pretty fucking hypocritical to condemn Cash for his actions when mine are just as messed up.

"Since I accidentally ended up with a slave I didn't want and now I can't get rid of." I wince saying it out loud.

"Shit. How's that going for you?"

"Let's just say it's taken on an unexpected turn." Understatement of the century there.

He looks at me for a minute before grinning. "You like her. God, you're fucked."

"You know what, Cash? You're a dick." I huff, but I don't deny it.

"Well, apparently, we both are. So, what are you going to do then? I'm guessing the whole you-letting-her-go scenario is looking less likely."

"Oh, that's easy. I'm going to make her fall in love with me." If I had to guess, I'd say she's halfway there. She's just scared.

He laughs loudly, the noise rousing Layla from her sleep, which I take as my cue to leave. Standing, I head to the door, gently squeezing Layla's foot before heading out, pulling the door closed behind me.

Maybe we are both fucked-up. Hell, there is no maybe about it. But as I look through the window at Cash's hand cradling Layla's, there is no denying, as broken as we are, we have an uncanny ability of finding women equally broken. Maybe that's the key. All our beautiful broken pieces fit together perfectly.

I whisper a tune as I make my way down to Six, hoping we won't have to wait too long. When I find her, she's already been stitched up and is listening to the nurse tell her how to look after the cut.

I look at James, who nods to let me know everything went smoothly. I had been worried about Six being around so many other people. It's a lot for someone to deal with at the best of times, let alone someone who has spent most of her life isolated.

She must sense me standing there because she turns toward me and offers me a smile. She has no idea how in awe of her I am. That's okay. I plan on taking her home and showing her exactly what I think of her.

You know what they say about best-laid plans? I had no idea a few hours later that one phone call would change our lives again.

CHAPTER THIRTY

SIX

"*L*ayla is dead."

Those are the last words he spoke to me after hanging up his cell phone.

I watch him as he stares aimlessly at the lake, unsure how to help him. A shroud of helplessness cloaks him, as if the weight of the world is on his shoulders. I know none of this is his fault, but the man takes every strike against his pseudo-family as a personal attack that he alone should have prevented.

I take a tentative step toward him and pause for a moment, wondering if it would be best to leave him alone. But then I remember the desolation I felt after Ten was gone and figure being alone is the last thing he needs.

I slip my arms around his shoulders and lean my head

against him. He doesn't turn to me, but he doesn't make me leave either. He lifts his hands and holds my arms around him in place.

"I'm so sorry, Will." If I could take his pain away I would. I understand him feeling helpless even if what I feel is a fraction of what he does.

"If I'd just found that site quicker. Maybe things would have turned out differently."

"It's only because of you that they found her at all. You can't beat yourself up for this, Will. You did everything you could. Sometimes the stones are already cast and nothing you do can change destiny's course."

"I didn't really know her, but her story..." He swallows and pulls me around the chair he's sitting on so I can climb onto his lap.

"Her story is a harrowing one. If anyone deserved happiness it was Layla. I hope to fuck her next life is more forgiving than this one."

"I wish I could have met her." I have a feeling we would have had more in common than most. "It sounds like she was a strong woman. I'd have been proud to call her my friend."

He nods, offering me a small smile before it falls away.

"I don't know how to help Cash through this. He loved her, you know? I don't think even he realized the depths of his feelings until she was gone. How do you come back from that? He lost the mother of his daughter and now his wife. How the fuck do you find the strength to get up in the morning when your reason for living is gone?"

I cup his jaw, pressing my lips to his before answering. "He gets up because he loves his daughter. I only know him through the stories you've told me, but the man you've told me about would never hurt his little girl by leaving her. He won't break her heart like that. I feel it as surely as I know you won't break mine.

"All he can do is get up, put one foot in front of the other, and keep going until the pain lessens. It will never go away. His heart will never heal completely. How can it when a piece of it is missing? But for Lily, he won't give up, he won't lay down, and he won't forget. You just have to prepare yourself for the fact that the Cash who emerges from his grief might not be the same man he used to be."

"You sound like you're talking from experience."

Now it's my turn to swallow hard as memories flash behind my eyes. "Once upon a time, there was a boy."

Will tenses beneath me, but he doesn't interrupt me.

"I was so young. It feels like a lifetime ago. He was the closest thing I ever had to a friend. I never put a label on it before because friendship never felt like the right fit. We were too young for it to be anything romantic, but we were tied to each other in a way that goes far beyond the usual bonds of friendship. So much so that the day I lost him, I swear I felt that bond snap. I never felt truly alone until then. Like a balloon that had slipped free from a child's hand, floating aimlessly without an anchor to pull it back."

He runs his fingers through my hair in a soothing gesture as I breathe through the ever-present pain.

"I understood even back then all the reasons why he did what he did. I forgave him a long time ago, but it doesn't mean I can forget the fact that he left me behind.

"He had reached his limit. He knew he couldn't handle one more day in the hands of those monsters. But instead of taking me with him, he left me to the very people he liberated himself from. So yeah, I understood, but fuck it hurt. It still does, like a cut that scabs but never heals completely. That's why I know Cash won't do anything stupid. He loves Lily too much to become a festering wound."

"I'm sorry, Six. What happened to...the boy?" Will asks softly but I can tell by his tone he has already put the pieces together.

"I was so excited to have a blanket. I hated being cold all the time. I still remember feeling euphoric as I huddled beneath the thin scratchy fabric that night. I was too young to understand that there was perhaps a reason why we had been denied blankets before." I swallow again, feeling my stomach swirl with nausea.

"When I woke up, Ten was hanging from the bars of his cell. The blanket I'd cried grateful tears for wrapped tightly around his neck," I whisper, pain clear in my voice even after all this time.

"Fuck," Will hisses, pulling me tightly to him, tucking my head under his chin as he rocks me gently. Offering me comfort while I soak his T-shirt with tears for the boy I lost and the ache that he never had the chance to grow into a man.

We sit in silence for a while, safe in the sanctuary of each other's arms until a cough draws our attention to the man behind us.

"Hey, I thought you could both do with a hot drink to warm you up." James smiles sadly at us as he hands us both a drink — coffee for Will and hot chocolate for me.

"Thank you, James."

James winks at me before looking at Will with concerned eyes.

"Viddy called me. Guess you left your cell inside. She just

wanted to let you know that Layla's funeral will be next week. Apparently she had a pretty specific will, one that took care of almost every detail, which I guess is a kind of blessing. It's one less thing for Cash to have to worry about."

"That's sad," I whisper before I can think better of it.

"Lots of people make wills, especially those who have children," James points out.

I nod. "I know, but somehow I don't think that was Layla's reasoning for having one." Call it women's intuition if you like, but something about the whole thing just makes me feel as if...

"She knew she was going to die, perhaps not when she did, but she knew she wouldn't get the happily ever afters gifted to those around her. Some people just aren't that lucky." My heart aches for a woman I never met.

James's hand clamps down lightly on my shoulder.

"She might not have had the ending she deserved, but for a little while at least, she got to experience the kind of crazy love some people only dream about. I had that with Claire, so I have to believe that given the choice, even knowing how things would end, Layla wouldn't change a thing."

I'm not sure I agree with that, but I understand what he's saying. Love can be that single flame in a dark room. A tiny spark can cause an inferno. I feel that hissing and crackling between Will and me. It's only fear that lets me hold it at bay because if I give in and let go what's to stop us from both going up in flames?

CHAPTER THIRTY-ONE

SIX

I float, staring up at the sky, watching the stars weave their magic upon the world.

So much has changed. Once upon a time, I thought the closest I would ever get to the stars would be when I died and my soul soared above the earth saying its final bittersweet goodbye.

Now, floating in the shallow end of the pool underneath them, I barely remember the girl I was before.

There are times, though, when a painful memory slices my insides. It digs its way out, expelling itself from my body until I'm gasping for breath on my knees with vomit dripping from my lips.

Those are the moments I wish I could go back. Not as the younger version of me but as the spectral version I am right now. I'd hold that little girl so tight, love her so hard, and fight every single day for a chance to see her smile.

I'd do it in a heartbeat even though back then I never knew I was broken. I didn't know how to read the signs, didn't understand what the cracks in my skin or the bruises on my heart meant. I had no point of reference, nothing to compare it to. I knew there was life outside the compound, but I had no idea what that encompassed.

I escaped a cage only to make myself a prisoner of my emotions. It was inevitable that the door I hid them behind would eventually splinter and fall, but that doesn't mean I was ready.

How do you process something so unfamiliar that you can't recognize it for what it is?

Love, desire, passion, lust, anticipation were all foreign concepts to me. On paper, I knew what they were, but I'd never experienced them for myself and I'd only ever seen the darkest version of those emotions twisted in others.

It's not that I don't want to love. I just don't know how to. Nobody ever showed me before and I'm terrified that somehow I'll get it wrong. What if I don't recognize it until I see it on the face of the next woman wrapped in Will's arms?

I've survived everything this life has thrown at me, even on the days I didn't want to, but I won't survive losing him. My tattered heart might be defective, but it's still mine to give freely. And I choose to give it to Will.

I think I knew I would the second he killed that doctor for hurting me. I wish I knew how it's all supposed to work. What do I say and do? Is there—

I jolt when I sense someone behind me. I slip under the water and surface again with a splutter.

"It's me, firefly," Will's voice whispers in my ear, making goosebumps break out all over my chilled skin as his hands move to my hips.

"You know you shouldn't be out here alone. Not until you're more confident in the water," he admonishes softly.

I turn in his arms, rest my head against his chest, and let him pull me out deeper, trusting him to keep us both afloat.

"I was miles away. I didn't even hear you get in the water. I promise I was staying where my feet could reach the ground."

I pull back and look at his face illuminated by the moon, his dark eyes ringed with shadows, and the look of defeat he's wearing has me reaching up to cup his jaw.

"Are you okay?"

"Fuck no, but I will be. Seeing Cash like that...it's hard. It's as if a part of him died with Layla. He's still here, still walking and talking and doing everything he needs to for his daughter but there is no light in him anymore. He's just going through the motions."

"I'd give anything to be him right now," I whisper without thinking.

"How can you say that? He's half the man he used to be. The pain that emanates from him makes me question how he can even hold himself up."

"He loved her, and she loved him. Do you know what a privilege that is? Some people can only dream of experiencing that. Not everyone is destined to meet their soulmate, Will. Some people wander the earth, always feeling like something is missing but never finding the one person who can fill that void. Cash hurts now, but I bet if you asked him if he could go back and make it so they never met, he'd eviscerate you.

"He wouldn't trade a second of it. Not all love is soft and

pretty. Sometimes love is brutal and savage, ripping you apart at the seams, but the pain has to be worth it."

"How do you know?"

"Because the absence of love hurts even more," I whisper.

He cups my face and presses his mouth to mine, swiping the water from my lip before his tongue demands entrance.

I melt into him, gripping his shoulders as his hands move to cup my ass and pull me to him. I wrap my legs around his hips and realize he's naked too when his hard hot cock presses against me.

"When I'm with you, it's like the whole world disappears," I whisper against his lips as he reaches down and nestles his cock at my entrance.

"Funny, because when I'm with you, you are the whole world. Nothing else seems to matter."

He slides inside me, making us both groan.

"If I could love anyone, it would be you," I admit, throwing my head back as he kisses up the column of my throat.

"I can teach you how to love. Even without the words, I vow you won't go a day without seeing it, without feeling it." He thrusts harder inside me, his grip on my ass tightening.

"I want to brand my name into your skin. I want to fill you up until your belly swells with my babies. I want to grow old with you and sit on that very deck while we watch our grand-children play," he murmurs against my ear as I spiral closer to the finish line.

"I want to watch you walk toward me dressed in nothing but white lace and diamonds before I pledge to honor, love, and cherish you for an eternity."

He sucks on a spot at the base of my throat that tips me

over the edge. I whimper and tighten around him as he hammers into me harder and harder before spilling inside me.

"You think you don't know what love is, firefly, but you do. It's inside you just waiting for you to let your guard down long enough for it to burst free."

"I'm scared."

"I know. So am I, which is why it won't happen overnight. But someday..."

I cup his face and press my lips gently to his before whispering, "Someday."

CHAPTER THIRTY-TWO

WILL

*L*ife inevitably carried on. Although I was still struggling with how to help Cash, who had pulled away from us all, I had kept my promise to Six. Every day I carved out time just for her as I threw myself headfirst into teaching her about love. What it's like to receive it and what it's like to give it. Although she still hadn't said the words out loud, I feel the tangible threads linking us together.

"As much as I don't want to move, I'm starving," I admit, trailing my fingers over Six's hip.

"I could eat." She grins up at me.

"Hmm…" I press a kiss against her forehead before sitting up.

"I'll grill steaks and get the firepit going so we can sit outside."

"Sounds good. Should we invite the guys?"

I smile at her as I reach for the oars. As much as I'd love her all to myself, she's been carefully building bonds with James and Fisher. She needs that. It helps her feel safe here and gives me peace of mind when I have to leave her for work.

I'm here more often than I'm not, but I can't always be here to protect her. When I'm not, I need to know she'll trust the team with her life.

"Sure. James will be home now. Not sure about Fisher though. That would depend on if he met anyone with tits or a dick today. He takes it as a personal challenge, I think, to show the world the length of his dick, one victim at a time."

She laughs, her whole face lighting up. "Well, he hasn't shown it to me."

"Probably because it's his favorite appendage and would cry like a little bitch if I cut it off."

"You're so mean."

"I'll show you mean." I hook the oars and reach for her.

She squeals as I pull her onto my lap and tickle her.

"Stop, stop." She laughs as she squirms. Her legging-clad ass grinds in my lap, making my dick hard in seconds.

I thrust up against her before biting down on her earlobe. "Now look at what you did."

She moans as I reach up and tweak her nipples through the thick fabric of the hoodie she's wearing.

"I think you caused this. You should fix it."

"I really should," she agrees breathlessly.

"On your knees, firefly."

She scrambles off my lap, making the little boat wobble as she positions herself in front of me. I climb to my feet and look down into those stormy eyes of hers as I reach for my belt buckle.

A loud crack reverberates around us, making birds take flight just as pain explodes in my leg and I lose my balance, toppling into the water. I sink under as the pain and shock throw off everything else until I feel hands grabbing at my hair, trying to pull it out at its roots.

I surface with a gasp to find Six screaming my name as she desperately tries to pull me back into the boat.

Another crack and the splintering of wood just inches from my head has me grabbing Six's wrist and yanking her toward me. The boat tips as Six's balance falters and I use the momentum to tip the boat over completely and drag Six underneath it with me.

She coughs and splutters as she presses close, her arms around my neck, her racing heart pressed against mine.

"What's happening?"

"Sniper. We need to get out of here. We're closer to the forest than we are the house and from the position of the shooter, I say we have no choice but to swim for the bank and make a loop around the property."

"I...Okay. Just tell me which way to go."

"Just follow my lead and stay close enough that you can grab me, okay? Are you strong enough to do this?"

She's new to swimming and although she can do enough to get by, the distance to the shore is farther than she likely realizes. Not to mention the clothes she has on will slow her down.

"I can do it," she whispers, her teeth chattering.

With no other option, I nod and press a kiss to her cold lips.

"I need you to stay with me. I need you to tell me you love

me, and you can't do that if you don't make it to the other side with me."

She sobs but nods her head frantically. "I promise."

"Take a deep breath and stay under the water for as long as you can. When you need air, surface quietly and quickly before sinking back under. Don't do it though until you absolutely have to."

"Okay. I can do this," she whispers. I'm not sure if she is trying to reassure me or herself.

I hold her hand. "Ready?"

She nods. We both take a deep breath and sink under. I tug her with me, easing us out from under the boat and into the direction of the shore, hoping I didn't get turned around in the chaos.

My leg burns like a motherfucker, and I have a funny feeling that the cold water numbing my body is the only thing stopping me from keeling over. I let go of her hand when we're free, needing both hands to swim, especially now I have a bum leg.

I feel her beside me but that doesn't stop me from reaching out now and then just to make sure. I feel her begin to surface for air and even though I could go longer, I surface with her.

We both suck in air and sink back under, thankfully without incident. I pray the gunman is long gone now his shots have been fired, but something is telling me that would be far too easy.

I sense Six slowing down so I reach for her, tugging her along as best I can.

My foot hits something, making me suck in a lungful of water as pain radiates up my leg. I surface and gulp in air as I choke, thankful we've made it to the little corner of the cove that is shielded with trees.

I drag her along until we reach the sandy ground where we both collapse.

"We need to keep moving," I choke out as Six climbs to her feet.

I try to follow suit, but my leg won't hold me. "Fuck."

Six whizzes around to face me, her eyes widening with horror when she sees the blood pouring from my leg.

"Will!" She drops to her knees, her hands hovering over me as if she doesn't know where to touch.

"You need to run, Six."

"I'm not leaving you," she snaps, whipping off her sodden hoodie and pressing it against my thigh.

I hiss at the pain, knowing I won't be going anywhere.

"Yes, you are, Six. I can't run and you can't stay here. It's not safe."

She ignores me, reaching for my belt and snapping the buckle open before tugging it free from the loops of my jeans. I watch in fascination as she ignores the tears running down her face and wraps the belt around my thigh just above where the bullet hit me.

She pulls the makeshift tourniquet tight, making me see stars. "Come on, let me help you."

She shoves her shoulder under mine and helps me up. I lean on her and drag my leg as we make our way to the trees. I'm dripping with sweat by the time we make it, despite my clothes being soaked and the temperatures being frigid.

I stumble and she catches me. When I stumble again, I fall, almost taking her with me.

"I can't, Six. I'm done."

"No. I can help you." She reaches for me again, but I shrug her off, my head spinning as I lean back against the tree behind me.

She drops to her knees, her freezing hands cupping my cheeks. "Please get up. Please," she begs.

I grip her wrists and tug her until I can press my lips to her before pulling back. "You need to run. Get help. Follow the stream. It loops around the lake and will take you to the back of James's property. You need to trip the alarm and get James."

"Will," she whispers with so much despair that it makes my heart bleed.

"You have to, Six. It's the only way, baby." I press her hand to my heart, feeling it thud under her touch. "I love you. I love you so fucking much," I tell her, my voice wavering. I swallow, trying to hide it.

I don't want her to know that I'm not going to make it. She'd lie down beside me and stay and I can't have that. I need her to live. Nothing else matters.

"I love you too. I'm sorry it took me so long to say it. I didn't understand it before, but I do now." She sobs.

"Promise me, promise me if I go, you'll hang on. You can't leave me, not now, not ever."

I run my fingers over her cheek, wiping her tears away. I do the only thing I can. I lie to her. "I'll be fine. Go."

CHAPTER THIRTY-THREE

SIX

*a*fter hiding Will as well as I could, I head in the direction of the stream, remembering his words.

I know these woods. I can do this. I have to do this. I can't lose Will. I won't survive without him. I ignore the cold numbing my body and focus on running as quietly as I can. Who knew the games Will and I played would prepare me for something like this?

I stop for a moment and listen, but I can't hear anything. It doesn't mean I'm alone. I know that, but the longer I go without hearing a gunshot or the telltale snap of twigs from being followed, allows hope to blossom inside me.

If the shooter ran, thinking he did what he set out to do, then all I need is to find James and everything will be okay.

The cold has seeped into my bones, reminding me of nights

spent in a cell many moons ago. I have come so far since then and I don't mean geographically. I never realized how small I had to make myself to survive within the bars of my cage until Will saved me.

Six months ago, I'd have fallen apart, but I'm stronger now. I won't let my fear rule me. I trudge across the stream and crawl on my hands and knees up the steep embankment on the other side.

I keep moving, knowing Will doesn't have time to spare. Each step that takes me farther away from him is a fight against every instinct I have, but I keep pushing on. Just when I think I can't make it one more step, the back of James's cottage comes into view.

The sight of it somehow fuels me with a boost of energy, which pushes me harder. By the time I reach his door, I'm stumbling. But I made it. That's all that matters.

I try the handle and find it open and push my way in.

"James. Help me, Will's hurt," I shout. Moving through his house looking for him, I come up empty.

"Fuck!" I panic, not knowing what to do without him.

A bleep from the kitchen counter has my eyes whipping over to see a cell phone plugged into the wall charging. I run around the counter to grab it and skid in something wet on the floor, falling on my ass.

That's when I find James, lying in a pool of blood.

"Oh my god." I crawl over him and see his eyes flicker open.

"James," my voice cracks. I don't know what to do. There is so much blood. It's coming out of multiple wounds on his body. I don't have enough hands to stop the flow, but I try anyway, pressing against the one closest to his heart.

My hair falls over us both as I look into his eyes. Eyes that tell me what I already know.

"Please don't. He needs you," I whisper, trying to push the blood back into his body somehow as my hands grow slick with it.

He smiles, blood leaking from the corner of his mouth as he lifts a shaky hand to my cheek. "Love him and let him love you back," he whispers.

I can't hold back my howl at how hopeless and futile it all is. Everyone is dying, every person I care about is leaving me alone.

His hand falls as his gaze takes on an unfocused look.

"Claire? Oh, how I missed you," he murmurs, the rise and fall of his chest slowing down as his eyes drift close.

"Please, God, someone help me!" I scream in vain as James's chest stops moving, a small smile fixed on his face as he takes his last breath.

I press my head to his chest and scream until my throat is raw before crawling through the blood and reaching up to the counter, yanking the cell from the wall.

It's different from Will's cell and I can barely use that one. When I can't open it, I realize it needs James's fingerprint. Moving back toward the man, I lift his hand and rub his fingers over my wet pants to get the blood off. It takes me three tries before the cell opens and I see the little phone icon.

I press it and it brings up the last number called. I hit it and hold the phone to my ear.

It rings and rings and when nobody answers I want to scream and throw the damn thing until it suddenly connects.

"This better be good. Jackie has a mouth like a vacuum and—

"Fisher?" My voice breaks.

"Six? What's wrong?"

"Will's been shot, and James is dead and I don't know what to do." I start crying again, feeling so fucking useless.

"Where are you?" His voice thunders over the line.

"I'm with James in his kitchen but I need to go back to Will. I had to leave him in the woods."

"No, you find somewhere to hide, and you wait for me, do you understand? Will would want you safe, Six."

"I...I can't leave him out there alone."

"He won't be on his own for long. I'm on my way, Six. I promise and I'm bringing friends. Go hide, please. If you won't do it for me, do it for Will."

"Okay," I whisper.

"Good girl. I'm on my way." He hangs up and I look around for somewhere to hide but the only place I can truly hide is the forest.

Placing a kiss against James's forehead, I grab a knife from the counter and head toward the door, grabbing the wind-breaker hanging beside it. I shove the knife in the pocket before slipping my arms into the coat and tugging it around me.

My hands are shaking too much for me to close the zipper, but at least it's warm and dry. I make it back to the edge of the woods when I hear the sound of a gun firing once more.

"Will," I gasp, running toward the sound.

I don't care if I get shot, nothing matters anymore but getting to Will. I run as hard as I can, ignoring the tree branches whipping my face and the wet pants chafing my skin.

I trip over a tree root and fall hard, slicing open my palms and biting my tongue hard enough for my mouth to pool with blood.

When my hair is wrenched back, almost snapping my neck in the process, I remember there are worse things than being shot.

"Stupid fucking bitch. Did you think we'd just forget about you?" He laughs but it's anything but pleasant.

"After all the effort we went to, and you threw it away by letting that motherfucker touch you."

He lets me go just so he can rear back and kick me. The force of it throws me on my back, knocking the wind out of me before he straddles me.

I've seen this man before. He looks different but I'd recognize those eyes anywhere.

"Can't be too pissed though, seems the boss doesn't mind if I fuck you now you're damaged goods." R snarls at me. His beard is gone and his usual bald head is covered in greasy dark hair which is long enough for me to pull if I can just reach it.

"Fuck you." I shove and try to flip him off but he's too strong.

"Oh, that's exactly what I intend to do."

He pins my arms at my sides with his knees as he tugs my jacket open. Panic wells up inside me, making me struggle, which is when my fingertips graze over the bulge in my coat pocket. Closing my eyes, I turn my head and look away, letting my body go lax beneath him.

"Aww, baby don't give in just yet, I like it when they fight. Just ask your mama. Oh, that's right, you can't." He laughs before licking the side of my face.

As he leans over me, I slip my hand in my pocket and grab the hilt of the knife. I fight the urge to yank it out now and take a swipe at him, but I bide my time, knowing I'll get one shot before he incapacitates me.

"You don't know anything about my mother." I seethe, gritting my teeth when he reaches down and grabs my breast hard.

"Is that right? Well, little girl, I beg to differ. See, your mom wasn't as sweet and innocent as you seem to think. She was a whore long before we turned you into one. There wasn't much she wouldn't do with the right motivation. She had no problem popping a few holes in some condoms before fucking the targets we gave her. When you were conceived, we were thrilled."

I grip the knife hard and slowly ease it out of my pocket.

"Of course, you don't know who your father is, but we do. One little DNA test and you suddenly became a bargaining chip. If I'd have known you were going to run and fuck the first man you met, I'd have taken my shot at your cherry, consequences be damned."

"You're lying. Why should I believe anything you tell me?" I snap, hoping to keep him distracted enough that he doesn't know what I'm doing.

"Better a liar than a whore.

"Your father has systematically worked to bring us down over the years, taking out key players and messing shit up. You were supposed to be our ace in the hole but you fucked everything up. I'm only sorry I waited until now. Your little fuckbuddy might like his fruit ripe for the picking but me, I like it young and fresh."

In other words, he likes kids. Somehow knowing that makes this ten times easier.

"Know how I like my fruit? Sliced."

I twist and yank my arm free while he is off guard and

punch him in the throat. There isn't much weight behind it, not from this angle. But it's enough for him to rear back. I swing the knife and stab it into his chest. I pull it out and stab him again, remembering that movie Will and I watched where the bad guy refused to stay dead.

I stab and stab until my arms feel weak and R topples to the side of me. I lie there for a minute, my rapid breathing sawing in and out of me, my whole body covered in blood.

Once I feel I have the strength to move, I shove him the rest of the way off me and scramble to my knees.

That's when I hear the sound of a gun cocking.

I lift my head and come face to face with the barrel of a gun. I don't stop to think. I know I'm dead if I don't try so I throw myself at the person holding the gun. They are faster than me, smashing the handle of the gun down on my head faster than I can say lights out.

When I come around later, I find myself in the middle of my worst nightmare.

CHAPTER THIRTY-FOUR

WILL

A gunshot has me jumping. My eyes fly open as my fear for Six swamps me, overriding the pain in my leg and how damn cold I am.

I tense at the footsteps running toward me, which in turn makes me hiss. I close my eyes and wait for the next bullet to hit me.

"Fuck man, you okay?" My eyes open at Fisher's voice.

"Just peachy." I cough as I try to sit up straighter.

"Woah, hold on. Let me check you out."

"No, I need to get to Six."

"Six is fine. She's hiding out at James's place…"

I look up at him and see his face has paled. "What is it?"

"It's James. He's dead."

His words hit me harder than any bullet could have and

causes me far more pain. James had been the one constant in my life and more of a father to me than mine ever was.

"How?"

"I don't know. Six found him. She called me so I told her to hide and I'd rally the troops. Speaking of..."

I see movement out of the corner of my eye and turn my head as both Reid brothers appear from nowhere.

"More money than God and you've only got one fucking boat?" Kai curses, making me shake my head.

"We couldn't get across the lake. We had to come around the long way. I hate to agree with Kai, but you need another boat. Carrying you out of here is gonna be as fun as jerking off with sandpaper."

"Let me look first," Fisher tells them, not intimidated by the two men at all.

Using his knife, he cuts the material around the belt tourniquet and tugs it, giving him a better view of the wound.

"Shit. You don't do things by half, do you? I don't think an artery was hit, purely because you're not dead, but I'm not willing to remove the belt and take the risk. It probably saved your life."

"That was all Six."

"Well, let's get you out of here and patched up, then you can show her your gratitude."

Kai bends beside me, catching my eye. "This is going to hurt like a motherfucker, but Viddy will cut off my dick if I let you die. I really like my dick."

"I'm feeling the love, Kai."

"You should. I'm a lovable guy."

"Ignore him. He'll shut up eventually," Jude offers from the other side of me.

"He is right about this hurting though. If you have to puke, aim for him. But know this—even if you pass out and we have to carry you every step of the way, we will."

I nod with gratitude, which is right around the time they hoist me up and I pass the fuck out.

When I come around, I'm lying on the ground staring up at the sky and wondering if I imagined the whole thing.

Fisher leans over me. "Hey, sleeping beauty. You hanging in there?"

"Seems that way. Where are we?"

"Almost back now. You're heavier than you look."

"Take me to James's."

"No can do," Jude says, shoving his cell in his pocket. "That was Viddy. She says her medical team is two minutes out. She also found your girl. She's back at the house, covered in blood and clearly in shock, but seems otherwise uninjured. Viddy will get her checked over too, just to be sure."

"Thank fuck," I grit out.

"The shooter is dead. We'll deal with him after you've been seen to," Jude finishes.

"Help me stand and I'll take some of my weight." I need to see Six with my own two eyes and make sure she's okay.

Fisher helps me up as I brace myself on my good leg. The world spins on its axis for a second and I almost face plant until Kai catches me.

"Ohh fuck."

I open my eyes slowly, feeling so fucking tired. I focus on Fisher, following his eyes to where he's looking, and see the large pool of blood where I was just sitting.

"Fuck," Jude hisses from beside.

"Sorry, Will, we've gotta go now." Jude and Kai grab me up as blackness encroaches and everything starts to fade away.

I can make out the worried tone in their voices, but it's not enough to stop me from slipping into unconsciousness once more.

CHAPTER THIRTY-FIVE

VIDDY

$\mathcal{J}$ watch her, taking in her hunched body as she sips the warm tea quietly. She's not who I would have pictured Will choosing for a partner in a million years, but opposites attract. I should know that.

She looks terrified and right now there isn't a damn thing I can do about it.

"Are you up to telling me more about what happened? The more details you can give me, big or small, the more I can piece things together."

"I...I...just don't understand what's happening," she whispers before breaking down and crying.

Shit. I'm not going to get anything from her like this.

"Okay, don't worry. We have plenty of time for that. Why

don't you head upstairs and take a shower? Clean up, lie down, and I'll find something for you to eat."

"I...I...okay." She finally agrees before standing and swaying a little.

I reach out, wrap my arm around her, and help her toward the stairs. She takes her time, seemingly in a world of her own, which makes my concern for her grow.

I don't know much about shock, but I do know that for Six, the lights might be on but there is definitely nobody home.

I take her to Will's room and walk her inside, making sure she is steady before stepping back.

I ponder telling her about the phone call I placed while making the tea. She'd probably snap out of it if I told her Will was alive and on his way back, but I don't want to get her hopes up only to tear them apart again. Jude said he wasn't looking good and he's not one to exaggerate.

"Will you be alright by yourself for a minute?"

She nods slowly before answering, "I'm going to shower, then sleep. I just need to close my eyes for a little while, please. It's all too much. The blood, the death, I can't —

"Shh...I get it. You don't need to explain. Take as long as you need. I'll be downstairs if you need me."

It's hard to remember sometimes that not everybody can live in our world. The blood and carnage I see daily are so entrenched that I can't remember my life without it. But not everyone feeds on the darkness as we do. What's home to us is a nightmare to others. I'm not sure how this will play out if Will survives. She looks like she wants nothing more than to run far away.

"Okay, I'll leave you to it."

I leave her standing in the middle of the room and pull the

door closed behind me. I'm not good at comforting weepy females. Killing them, sure. But offering them comfort? Not so much. In that respect, I'm as lost as she is.

I head down the stairs to the kitchen just as my cell rings again.

"Yeah?"

"Ambulance is en route. I know you have a team coming, Red, but he needs surgery and that's if he makes it to the hospital on time," Jude tells me.

"Shit. Okay, I'll let Baker and Danny know. They are on the lookout for the medical team. Where are you?"

"Almost at the far end of the dock."

"Take a left when you get there and bypass the house. It's quicker to get to the gate that way. I'll have one of the guys head up to meet you."

"Got it. You doing okay?"

"Ask me later." I hang up, not wanting to think about losing a man I've come to love and care about.

I call Danny and fill him in, relieved as fuck that I didn't say anything to Six. The best thing she can do is rest. Hopefully when she wakes, I'll have some answers for her.

I pace around the kitchen, feeling fucking useless. I can't call Cash. He's still mourning the loss of Layla and this might be the straw that breaks the camel's back. I can't call Wyatt now that Jenna is on bed rest. They had both been shocked to find out Jenna was pregnant, but that didn't mean they weren't happy. I just wish they had an easier go of it.

With horrendous sickness and bouts of bleeding, Wyatt's already worried about Jenna losing the baby. I don't want to add any more stress to his plate.

I spin at the sound of someone running down the hall and

pull my gun. When Jude's face appears, I toss it on the counter and run to him.

He catches me like he always does, picking me up and holding me tightly to him. We stand there for a minute, breathing each other in before he gently lowers me to my feet.

"Tell me what happened."

"Will is en route to the hospital with Fisher. Danny has gone with them for extra protection. The medical team turned up as they were leaving so the doctor is riding on board with Will while the rest are being rerouted back to the hospital. Baker and Kai are heading up to James's place. What about the guy who attacked Six?"

"Dead when I found her trying to bury him. She's been virtually catatonic since. I don't know what happened to her or what she saw but it's a lot for any normal person to deal with."

"Where is she? Perhaps I can talk to her?"

I rub my hand up his chest. "I know your inner cop wants to fix things, but right now she needs a minute. She's taking a shower and then she's gonna rest. Hopefully she'll sleep until we have news on Will." I look into his eyes and swallow, not sure I want to know the answer to what I'm about to ask.

I ask him anyway. "Do you think he's gonna make it, Jude?"

His hands slide over my hips, holding me tightly to him. "I just don't know. He was hanging in there but moving him might have caused more damage." His eyes close as he presses his forehead against mine.

"He better wake up. I have a million questions I need to ask him before I kick his ass. A slave, Jude? Really?"

"Don't look at me. I was as much in the dark as you were. But you know Will. He wouldn't hurt her."

"No, of course he wouldn't," I agree. But looking around Will's house, I'm all too aware of just how much he likes to collect pretty things.

CHAPTER THIRTY-SIX

WILL

J'm old. Most days it's not an issue, beyond not being able to drink like I used to, but right now I'm feeling my age and more.

Getting shot hurts like a motherfucker, but it's never been as close a call as this time. I like to think my pain threshold is pretty good, but whatever damage that bullet did feels like the equivalent of getting a blowjob from a piranha.

"Quit moaning. You're turning me on, big boy."

I crack my eyes open and see Fisher grinning at me. "Fuck you."

"You're not my type. I like my men with a little less brawn and a little more brain."

I snort. He's full of shit. He likes his men with a functional dick and mommy or daddy issues. The opposite of how he likes his women.

"As enlightening as this whole conversation is, we have questions before the police show up with some of their own. You know its hospital policy to report gunshot victims, regardless of the circumstances." I turn at the sound of Danny's voice and see him at the end of the bed.

"I'm not staying, so if they have questions, they better hurry the fuck up or they can wait."

"They are on their way up. Anything you need to tell me before they get here so I can let Viddy know?"

"I don't want them on my property so I'm about to lie my ass off. I'll tell you the rest when they've gone."

Danny opens his mouth to say something else, but closes it again when the door opens and two police officers stroll right in.

Good thing my dick wasn't out.

"Gentlemen. We'd like to speak to Mr. Harris alone, please," the younger of the two police officers announces with a cocky smirk. God save me, I've been in the game too long to be intimidated by a kid with a baby face and a chip on his shoulder. Hell, I likely killed someone before he'd been little more than a cumshot in his mom's pussy.

"They can stay. I've already told them what I know, which is fuck all. I woke up next to the lake in the park with a gunshot wound to my leg and no idea how I got there. I flagged down a passerby and called my man Fisher here, then I passed out."

"You don't remember how you wound up with a bullet in your leg?" He rolls his eyes, so I ignore him. I look at the older guy, who I vaguely recognize. Must be one of the ones in Viddy's pocket.

"Not a clue. I'm a businessman that works closely with the military. Most of what I know is classified but naturally that makes me a target too. This isn't the first time I've been shot. It likely won't be the last. It's a risk I take to make sure our soldiers have everything they need on the frontline. You can be sure though, if and when I remember, you'll be the first to know. I want this person locked up as much as you do. Trust me."

The puffed-up peacock chest of the young cop deflates at my words before he turns to Fisher.

The older cop grabs his shoulder. "That's enough for now. Mr. Harris has to be exhausted. Please come down to the station when you're feeling better and hopefully by then we'll have a suspect in custody."

"But—" the younger one protests, shutting up when the older one levels him with a glare.

"Feel better soon, Mr. Harris." He tips his head before ushering them both out of the room.

I wait until the door is closed and Danny gives me the all-clear to let me know they've gone before speaking. "I need clothes."

"You need to rest," Danny fires back as I ignore him and sit up with a groan.

"For fuck's sake, Will. You nearly died."

I glare at him. "I know, I was there. But I need to see Six. She must be going out of her mind."

"Viddy texted to say she thinks she's in shock. But she managed to get her to take a shower and rest, which is exactly what you should be doing. You are no good to her dead."

"I like you, Danny, so know when I say this, I mean it. You can either help me or I will shoot you and climb over your still-warm body to get to her. You have no idea what's going on in Six's head. She doesn't know you, any of you. There are three people she trusts. Two of us are here and one is dead, so tell me, what will it be?"

"Viddy's gonna fucking kill me," he mutters before yanking the door open.

"I'll find you some scrubs to wear and a doctor so I can let him know you're signing yourself out against medical advice. I'll call the doctor that came with us and tell him to call you later so he can come check on you. If you don't answer I will drive to your house, knock you out, and carry you back my fucking self."

He slams the door behind him, making it rattle in its frame.

"It's so hard for me to understand why you don't have more friends," Fisher deadpans.

"Fisher, it's Six. There is nothing I won't do for her."

He sighs before nodding. "I know. I want to get back to her too. It's just going back means accepting that James is gone and I'm not sure I'm ready. That man was like a father to me."

"He was to the both of us. But Fisher, you have me and Six. I know you work for me, but I've always looked at you as an annoying little brother who I sporadically want to kill. And Six? Well, she needs a brother who is as protective and loyal as you."

Swallowing hard, he squeezes my arm quickly before dropping it. "I'll help you watch over her. Nothing will fucking happen to her on my watch."

"I know. Thank you."

"That's what families do, right?"

CHAPTER THIRTY-SEVEN

SIX

*T*he fear and panic weigh me down. I know I should fight it but no matter how hard I swim, I can't break the surface. Instead, I lie here drowning in a sea of terror as my voice screams in my head for me to get up.

The cold seeps into my bones as I wrap my arms around myself, trying to draw comfort from my own embrace. I've been alone most of my life, even when I was in a room with multiple caged people. We were still very much separate from each other. I never knew any other way. After all, how can you miss something you never had? Then Will came along and showed me a whole world I never knew existed. Not knowing if he's gone, not knowing if he is dead or alive is what's killing me the most.

His presence has been like a soothing balm to my soul.

Without him, the old fears and worries feel fresh and new. But the worst one, the one that's made my legs buckle and brought me to my knees, is what if he was never real? What if I dreamed him up and I'm still locked away in a cage somewhere?

I shiver and open my eyes but it's so dark I can't see or feel anything. It's like my past and present have collided and I can't seem to figure out which way is up.

How did I end up here? I can't remember anything beyond those woods.

I don't know how much time has passed, how long I've just been lying here, but I don't have the energy to sit up, let alone crawl to the door.

My head is pounding to the same rapid beat of my heart and my body is wracked with shivers. I feel numbness enveloping me and I welcome it. I don't want to cry anymore. I don't want to feel anymore. If Will is dead because of me, I don't want to be here without him. I'll lie here hoping that when I open my eyes, he's lying beside me once more.

I must cry myself to sleep because when I open my eyes next, they feel puffy and sore and my cheeks feel tight. The room is still pitch-black. I hold back a sob when I realize it's not just a horrible dream. I refuse to let my panic bring me to my knees again. I'm not that same girl who had nothing left to lose.

I'm more than just the number they gave me. I am Will's firefly. And if there were ever a time he would want me to be strong, it would be now.

I hear it again, the sound that must have woken me. A

muffled voice speaks too quietly for me to make out the words, but close enough for me to realize someone is either talking to themselves or on a cell phone.

I open my mouth to call for them, but stop. It's not a voice I'm unfamiliar with, so why can't I place it?

I climb to my feet, wincing when the room spins around me. I touch my fingers to my forehead and when they come away damp, I realize it's not because my hair got wet in the lake. It's because I'm bleeding.

But how?

I wince as I think back, forcing myself to remember James, who was butchered on his kitchen floor. I swallow bile and let my thoughts drift with an odd sort of detachment, as if they are someone else's memories, not mine.

The man in the woods. Being pinned. The knife.

Each image pops into my brain before swiftly moving on to the next. I can't believe I forgot. I never forget anything. I touch my forehead again and remember the gun, the pain, and then nothing but dark.

There was a second person in the woods. I couldn't see their face because of the hood they were wearing, but I remember the crack of the butt of the gun smacking into my head. I don't remember the part between passing out and waking up here.

The talking stops and it's completely silent for a moment, so much so I strain my ears to discern if I'm alone once more. The sound of the door opening has me scrambling away in the dark. In my haste, I trip and fall, catching my elbow painfully on the unforgiving floor.

"Now, now, Six. Is that any way to say hello?" the voice snaps into the dark, making me suck in a sharp breath.

I blink back tears and bite my lip to keep from whimpering, despite the pain. As dark as it is, I'm safer down here on the floor than trying to stumble my way around, risking serious injury. I'm not sure I'd survive another blow to the head right now, especially as I'm not sure if any of this is real or if I'm hallucinating.

"I can hear you breathing," the voice mocks in a sing-song tone. I try to put the pieces together, but they don't fit. None of this makes sense.

"Fine. Be like that." I hear scraping before they speak again.

"As you won't be making it out of this room alive, let me tell you a story. Once upon a time, there was a beautiful girl. She lived with her mom and dad and big sister until tragedy struck and the two sisters ended up as orphans.

"Death made them closer than if they had been twins, until one day everything changed. See, Melly was so fucking smart she ended up working a job she loved even though it took her away from me. Did it hurt? Sure, but I was so fucking proud. Then all of a sudden, the sister I knew and loved was gone. I thought the worst. You do, you know? Even though things like kidnapping and trafficking were things that happened to other people. Not shit that happened to two orphan girls who had already lost so much.

"It took me a long time to find the trail and follow it to Melly, but I was too late. By the time I tracked her down, she was already dead."

I don't move, enraptured with her story despite myself. At least her talking buys me time for someone to find me, right?

"Lucky for me, my sister's handler found me and told me exactly who was responsible for her death. He recruited me, trained me, and gave me the tools to get my revenge. I look just enough like my sister did to entice, but not enough to raise questions."

She sounds so proud of herself, but her voice soon drops to a hissed whisper filled with hatred.

"Do you know what it's like having to fuck the man responsible for your sister's death? To have to fake an orgasm while he whispered her name?"

I don't answer, not wanting to give my location away.

"I got the last laugh, though when I found out I was pregnant, just like I hoped. Leverage is a wonderful thing and I had all the time in the world for my plans to come to fruition."

She stops talking for a minute, the room falling into an eerie silence. A bright light flicks on, momentarily blinding me, so I close my eyes against the pain. The feel of a gun pressing against my cheekbone soon has them shooting open.

"Stand up slowly."

I do as she asks, my body stiff from the cold. I take in the concrete walls but not much else, not willing to turn my head and risk getting it blown off.

"Strip."

With shaky hands, I slowly comply as she continues her story.

"That baby was going to be my golden ticket. But you had to go and blow everything."

"I don't understand. I didn't do anything. All I—" my words are cut off by a punch to the stomach, making the air whoosh out of me.

"I thought you learned your place better than that. No worries. I'm more than willing to correct your behavior. Did I tell you to stop undressing?"

I shrug off my jacket and fumble for the hem of my T-shirt, only half focusing on what she's saying as I swallow the urge to vomit. I don't understand how she thinks I had any part to play in this crazy story of hers. I haven't seen anyone since—

Two. Two was her daughter. Holy crap, what kind of sick parent does that to their own child?

"Ah, I can see the cogs turning. Looks like you figured everything out. You always were a precocious child."

"I didn't kill Two, I swear it. She was already dead. I just took her place."

She reaches over and grasps my face in a tight grip, making me wince. "I don't give a fuck about Two."

"But I thought she was your daughter?"

She bursts out laughing in my face before tapping the gun against my temple. "Sorry daughter dearest, but that title is all yours."

I freeze in shock. "No, my mom died."

"She wasn't your fucking mother. She was just another slave. I threw you to her when you were born, knowing you'd need some kind of nurturing. No point raising a kid that will off themselves at the earliest convenience like that pathetic boy. What was his designation again? Oh, that's right, Ten."

"No. I don't believe you." That's impossible.

"Like I care."

"I was sold—"

"You were mine, but I had to keep a certain low profile so none of the guards or designations killed you in a bid to piss me off."

I close my eyes, trying to apply her words as a filter to my life, but I can't. There is no rhyme or reason for it.

"If what you're saying is true, then why? Why keep the guards from touching me if you don't care about me at all?"

She grins maniacally at me, pointing to my jeans with the gun as a reminder that I've stopped undressing again.

"I had no use for a child and your father would never have been drawn in if he suspected you of being underage, but that doesn't mean he doesn't like them young. As soon as you turned eighteen, you were fair game. Cohen had already planted a club slut in their ranks before he died, all I had to do was get you to her and she'd have brought you into the fold.

"Motorcycle clubs love their sluts. A warm wet hole for a cumshot is all they need. And who better to take your cherry than your dear old daddy and your bastard brothers? I had you set to be delivered. All I had to do was get rid of his bitch and her kid."

I stare at her, feeling hatred well inside me. The fact that she's telling me all this is proof that I'm not leaving this room alive.

My anger bolsters my strength, pushing my fear aside as I stand in nothing more than a pair of lace panties before a woman who has done nothing but subjugate me, humiliate me, and use me for her own personal needs.

"Fuck you. I'm glad your sister is dead. She'd be so fucking ashamed of you. You're nothing but a sad pathetic asshole. You're sick and twisted. The things you did to me are bad enough but what you did to the others? No wonder she left you. I bet she figured out what a psychopath you were and said good riddance."

She slaps me in the face hard enough for me to lose my balance, but I don't let it deter me. I sweep my leg out as I fall and take her with me, watching with glee as she topples over and bounces her head off the concrete floor.

She drops the gun. I scramble for it, snatching it up and running for the door. I yank on it, but it doesn't budge.

Laughter has me whirling around and aiming the gun at her.

"It locks from the outside and the whole place is completely soundproof."

Fuck. What the hell is this place anyway?

She climbs to her feet, ignoring the blood running down her face as she steps toward me.

I scream at the top of my lungs, hoping she's lying and someone will hear me, but I know they won't. I shouted enough when I first woke that if anyone was coming for me, they'd have found me by now.

She grins. "Scream all you want. I always did like the sound. Especially when you were screaming my name. Yes, Mistress M. Please, Mistress M. Oh the sweet, sweet begging got me off every time. I'm not going to lie, it got me wet knowing you had no clue that M stands for mommy," she mocks like the sick freak she is.

I've always loathed this woman. I knew instinctively she was the most dangerous of the trainers despite her being a woman. I must have sensed the evil in her all along.

The gun shakes as I hold it, but she doesn't stop her slow steps toward me.

"Nobody is coming for you. Everyone you care about is dead. It's not what I planned, but it will be enough for now. When I don't check in with X, your father will receive an email. He'll find out about his baby girl and all the things I made her do. I was even kind enough to prepare some photos, just in case." She laughs, her whole face lighting with glee.

"You bitch."

"Aww, poor baby. You thought I'd let you go? I had a tracker planted in you when you were a day old so I would always know where you were. When you didn't arrive when you were supposed to, I tracked you here. I could have taken you at any moment. Hell, I watched you getting fucked in the mud only yards from where I'd been camping."

I think back, to the scorched ground at the campsite the day Will chased me, and shiver.

"I'll admit it was hot. I got myself off watching." She gloats, making my finger twitch on the gun trigger.

"I've been watching you this whole time. I've searched every inch of this place, biding my time and waiting to take you. I only let you stay when I figured out who the man fucking you is. I thought I could turn him, but something has come up and unfortunately for you, that's pushed my timeline up a little. Seems your fucking father has been dabbling in things he shouldn't again. Luckily, finding this room turned out to be a bonus I couldn't pass up.

She shakes her head and grins. "This isn't what I wanted or planned, but that's life. Sometimes you have to roll with the punches. You have to admit, it's kind of poetic that you die in a dank dark basement similar to the one you were born in."

She's so close now that if she reaches out, she'll be able to grab the gun, a thought that strikes us both at the same time.

I pull the trigger, saying a silent thanks when it fires. I don't know the first thing about guns. Though my aim is off, it still clips her in the shoulder, making her scream with rage as she staggers back.

How she is still on her feet, I don't know. When she charges me, I shoot again. This time my aim is true, hitting her in the stomach.

She drops to the floor, her wide eyes blinking up at the ceiling in shock.

I feel tears run down my face, but I don't move the gun away. She grins that fucking grin that makes me cringe, whispering something, so I step closer.

"There were two bullets, one for each of us." She smirks before coughing, blood spraying from her mouth.

"Now you really will die alone." She gasps, the wet sound the last words she utters before I fall to my knees and wail.

CHAPTER THIRTY-EIGHT

WILL

I'm man enough to admit that leaving the hospital early might not have been one of my best ideas. My leg throbs like a motherfucker and if I make it home before I throw up it will be a miracle.

I lean back against the seat and close my eyes, willing my stomach to settle. I'm glad Fisher went ahead. If I'd known how long we'd wait for the doctor I'd have snuck out. The only reason I stayed was for the prescriptions. No way do I want an infection just to end up back in that place.

"You doing okay back there? You've gone pretty fucking pale. I knew this was a bad idea. If you throw up in my car, you're paying to get it cleaned," Danny complains from the front seat, but I don't have the energy to answer him.

I just need my bed and my woman. I don't give a shit about

anything else right now. I keep my eyes closed in a bid to keep my shit together as we make the long trek home.

I must drift off. Danny's voice snaps me out of my nap. "You need help?"

Probably, but I'm a stubborn motherfucker. "I'll be fine with the crutches." Hopefully. They want me to keep my weight off my leg, at least until the stitches heal.

"I'll grab them. Hold on."

He climbs out and moves to the trunk, fetching the crutches and walking them around to me. He pulls the door open and holds the crutches ready as I maneuver myself out of the car and grab them from him.

"Thanks, man. I owe you."

"Oh, don't worry, I'm keeping a tab."

I chuckle at the asshole despite myself.

He keeps his pace slow, staying right beside me just in case. We both look up when the door swings open and Viddy hurries down the steps toward me. I brace myself for a hug, but she stops just in front of me, her face void of emotion.

"Will." Her tone says it all.

"I know you're pissed, V, but things between Six and me are between us. I'm not hurting her or holding her against her will." At least not anymore.

"It's not that. It's Six. She's gone."

"What the fuck do you mean she's gone?"

"Just that. Fisher beat you by twenty minutes. He went up to check on her, but the bedroom was empty. We've searched the house but there is no trace of her. I've got Fisher, Kai, Jude, and Baker out looking for her now. I've called in the rest of my security team and Wyatt's on his way too. We'll find her."

"Fuck. If she doesn't want to be found, you won't stand a chance. She's really good at hiding."

"Do I want to know how you know that?"

I glare at her, which she is immune to.

"Not the fucking time, V. I need to head to the woods. She won't come out for any of you, but she'll come out for me,"

"I hope so. It's getting dark and the temperatures are dropping."

"I hate to throw a wrench in the works, but you're in no fit state to go traipsing through the woods, especially on crutches," Danny points out.

"I don't have a choice. If anything happens to her..." My voice cracks as I turn back to Viddy.

"I promised her she'd be safe here. I promised her I would always come for her. I've broken one of those already, like fuck will I break the other one.

"Fuck. Fine, you stubborn bastard. But Danny will be your fucking shadow. I'll radio ahead and have Baker meet up with you too. Accept the help, Will. If you want to find her, you do whatever it takes. But you'll never find her if you fall, rip your stitches, and bleed out."

"I wasn't going to protest. I know I need help. I just want to go now."

"You'll give me five fucking minutes to pad that wound with some extra bandages and shove some pain killers down your throat. And you might want to put something warmer on than a pair of scrubs," she snaps at me like I'm a child, despite the fact I'm far older than she is.

"Viddy, I'm okay. Nothing is going to happen to me." I soothe her, though the urge to head straight to the woods is riding me hard. "I'm sorry I scared you, but I'm okay."

She growls before turning and stomping inside.

"She was worried. Last she heard, it was touch and go. You lost a lot of blood. Traipsing through the woods is the last thing you should be doing, and you know it. You're putting yourself at risk. And worse, you're doing it for someone you didn't see worthy of meeting all of us. We are your family and you treated her like a dirty secret by hiding her. Obviously, I can tell it's more than that, but you have to see it from V's point of view," Danny tells me as I navigate up the steps with my crutches.

I stop and look at him, refraining from ripping his face off but only just. "Six was never my dirty secret. And you're lucky I need help finding her or I'd kill you where you stand."

"I'm only telling you what others are saying." He shrugs.

Viddy steps back into view, clearly having heard what Danny just said if her arms crossed over her body and set jaw are an indicator.

"Did you ever stop to think that this wasn't about you? You may be the top dog, V, but the world doesn't revolve around you. Six not coming to meet you, especially with the shit going on with Cash, was for her benefit as well as his. So I'm sorry if you don't like it. I do not give one flying fuck if I hurt your feelings. Six is the only one that matters."

Danny snorts beside me, making me lift the crutch to smack him one.

"Don't," Viddy hisses.

I pause and look at her, seeing the hurt on her face.

"I wouldn't have hurt her or treated her poorly and fuck you for thinking that."

I shake my head incredulously. "That thought never even crossed my mind." I cock my head. "Sounds to me you're still feeling shitty over how you handled Layla, but this is not the same thing. Not once did I think I needed to protect Six from you."

"Then why hide her from me? Because you were ashamed? And you'd better fucking believe we'll be talking about the fact that you bought a fucking slave."

I hold up my hand before quickly moving to grab the crutch before it falls.

"Don't," I snap, my patience gone. "My woman is out there scared and alone. I don't have time for your pissing contest. I work with you V, but I don't work for you. You are not the fucking boss of me and I can walk away from this relationship at any time. Yeah, it was shitty of me to forget that I had put in a bid for a slave as part of the plan you all came up with when you wanted Dale caught. I don't remember a single one of you mentioning canceling the bid afterward."

"We were kind of preoccupied with Cash getting shot and Lily and Jenna getting taken," she complains.

"Exactly. I care about them too. I was distracted too. It's a shit excuse for all of us but it doesn't make it any less true. Why you think I should be held to a higher standard is beyond me."

Danny adds his two cents. "Maybe it's because we didn't keep a woman after realizing we'd fucked up."

I shake my head. "So, I should have tossed her back? Out of sight, out of mind. Is that what you're saying? Does Six's life matter less than Jenna's?"

"You're putting words in our mouths," Viddy argues.

"Sucks, huh? You have no clue what happened to her or what would have happened if I sent her back. She's not an unwanted parcel. She's a fucking human being. And honestly, if this is the stance you're taking, I'm glad she never met any of you. Get the fuck out of my house. I'll find her myself."

"You're an idiot. Don't let your pride get in the way—"

"It's not pride, V. I don't want people around Six I can't trust with her safety. And right now, I'm not sure you guys have her best interest at heart."

I bypass Viddy and walk into the house, ignoring the pain as I make my way through the kitchen and into the laundry room. Propping my crutches against the counter, I rummage through the dryer until I find a pair of sweats, a long-sleeved thermal T-shirt, and a hoodie.

I ignore Viddy when she steps into the room, focusing on keeping my balance as I get dressed, praying I don't puke all over the clean clothes when the pain in my leg flares.

"I would never do anything to hurt you or someone you cared about," V's voice chokes out.

"I know, V. But I'm reminded of something Layla once said. You protect your circle like a ferocious beast. And there is nothing wrong with that, but what about those not in your circle? Just because they are not yours doesn't make them expendable."

"I know that."

"Do you? Because from where I'm standing it seemed a lot like you think I should have sent Six back."

She shakes her head and sighs. "It's not quite what I meant, and you know it. I'm all about helping the underdog but sometimes that means handing them off to someone else. I can't save everyone."

"Yeah? How's your boy doing?" It's a low blow I know. Viddy pulled DJ off the streets when she saw him being forced to give a dirty cop a blowjob.

She growls and takes a step toward me. "That wasn't nice."

"He matters to you. I get it. But Six matters to me. Do you know how Six got her name? It's her number. She has never been called anything else because she was born in captivity and never knew what life was like beyond those walls, barring what she read in books."

She looks at me like I've struck her. "What?" she whispers as I step closer and wrap my hand around her arm.

"I've given women cars, jewels, hell, even given them apartments in my lifetime. And none of them came close to showing the happiness Six did at seeing windows." My voice comes out gruff as I swallow hard.

"Fucking windows, V. I have enough money to give her the world and all she wants is windows."

"Oh, shit." She face plants against my chest, wrapping her arms around me.

I hold her for a minute, letting the cracks in our friendship heal a little.

"I'm sorry. I should have told you what was going on," I admit. If the shoe had been on the other foot I'd have been pissed too.

"No, I should have known better. You're my Will. You're a good man and I let my temper cloud my judgment. I'm the one who's sorry. I was so mad it was like my past and present were smacking together, but those were my issues, not yours. It won't happen again. I…" She blows out a breath and looks up at me.

"It's not an excuse but my hormones are out of whack. I cried yesterday because I dropped my spoon," she deadpans as her words sink in.

My eyes widen. "You're pregnant?"

She nods and for once the formidable woman I've grown to love looks scared. "Yeah."

I grip her to me hard and press a kiss to her forehead. "Congratulations."

She pulls back and gives me a wobbly smile. "I'm terrified out of my mind, but I'll figure it out. For now though, let's finish getting you ready and go find your girl."

I give her a grateful squeeze and let her take over, knowing she needs to mother me. Viddy puts on a brave face but there is a part of her that's still that same young girl terrified of losing one more person she loves. Fears aside, I can't think of anyone who'll make a better mother than V.

"Okay, all done. This is as good as it gets. Please, for the love of god, take it easy. Danny and Baker can do the hard part."

"I know, V. Just, if she comes back, don't let her leave again."

"Go. I've got this. Liam and Jed will be here with me in a second, the rest of my team will be out searching with you. Keep your coms open. She might not respond to others but if they spot her at least they can give you the coordinates. Be smart and be safe."

I press a kiss to her cheek and follow Danny, who is lurking nearby outside.

"Baker and I can cover more ground than you. We'll help you to each area so you're in shouting distance, then the two of us will fan out. It's getting dark now. I don't want her out all night any more than you do. How do you know she'll even be in these woods?"

I shrug. "I don't, but it's where she feels most comfortable. She has only been off my land once since she got here. She'll stay somewhere close by, at least until she can get news about my condition."

Danny pulls his cell out and texts someone before shoving it away.

"I texted Liam and Jed to do another search of the house when they get here, just in case she was hiding before. They'll let us know if they find anything."

"Thanks."

He nods. "Let's do this."

CHAPTER THIRTY-NINE

SIX

The cold wracks my body as I crawl to the pile of my discarded clothes. They are still soaked and ice cold so putting them on won't help. Even so, I shrug the T-shirt over my head, covering my breasts at least. For someone who spent their whole life virtually naked, I feel too exposed being naked down here with a woman who peeled away my layers until she left a raw and bloody wound.

I look for something that might offer me some warmth but there isn't anything.

My eyes drop to M on the floor. Her top is soaked with blood and her pants are spattered with it, but they are still remarkably drier than mine. I hear Will's voice in my head, urging me to do whatever I need to survive. I squeeze my eyes shut before blowing out a breath.

I move before I can talk myself out of it. I pull off her boots, socks, and jeans, made difficult by her dead weight. Her chest still moves up and down despite the pool of blood surrounding her, but she won't last long without help. As much as I hate her, she has a lot of information I won't be able to get from anyone else.

I use my wet hoodie to tie around her chest. It's not much but it's all I've got. She groans as I struggle to get it around her slight frame and tie it as tightly as possible.

Once I realize that's as good as it's going to get, I tug her socks on before shoving my feet into her boots that are easily two sizes too big.

I sit next to the door and wrap my arms around myself, trying to imagine I'm sitting next to a roaring fire, but it does little to keep the chill at bay.

Something in the pocket of the pants gouges into my leg so I shove my hand inside and touch a piece of metal. Tugging it free from the tight denim, I stare in surprise to find an antique-looking key.

I look up at the door and see the keyhole before I scramble to my feet.

"That lying bitch," I snarl as I shove the key into the lock and turn it. The door opens with a resounding click. I yank it open and wince when the bright light hits my eyes.

I move to run but pause, looking back at M lying on the concrete floor.

I should leave her. I owe this woman less than nothing, but if I let her bleed out on the floor of the house I made my home, she'll forever taint the peace I've found here. It will make me just like her. We might share some DNA markers, but that's where the similarity ends.

"Fuck." For someone who spent forever biting their tongue, I seemed to have developed a fondness for curse words.

I slip the key back in my pocket and move over to M. Gripping her under her arms, I drag her toward the door. She's heavier than she looks and my body is weak, battling the effects of shock and exhaustion.

By the time I have her up the steps and through the door that leads to the utility room, I'm dripping with sweat and on the verge of passing out. I collapse on the floor beside M for a moment to catch my breath.

My eyes land on a pile of clothes in the corner of the room that I don't recognize. They look like something a doctor would wear, pale blue and clinical. They are completely out of place and for some reason, they make the hairs on my arm stand on end. How did they get here?

M moans, making me jump. I scramble to my feet, my hip catching the dryer door that's been left open.

Dry clothes! I yank off my wet T-shirt and bra and tug one of Will's T-shirts over my head. I rummage around for a sweatshirt but come up empty-handed so I slip on the jacket that hangs next to the back door.

I pause when I hear what sounds like laughter. I frown, sure I must be imagining it. But I hear it again as I move closer to the kitchen.

Voices talk too quietly for me to hear but there is definitely more than one person here. I move to open the door, hoping it's Fisher, or better yet, Will. I stop when a sense of foreboding washes over me.

M told me Will was dead. I have no idea if she is lying but even if Fisher made it to him on time, they would be at the hospital right now. If Will was awake, he'd be losing his mind worrying about me. What he wouldn't be doing is laughing with friends in his kitchen.

Shit. M must have brought people with her. I'd naively assumed that R was it. But why aren't they looking for her?

Or maybe they are and there are more of them out there. Someone killed James, after all. I swallow a wave of grief as I remember him laughing as he taught me how to bake cookies. James might be gone, but I'm clinging to the hope that Will made it and if he did, he'll find me.

The sound of a chair scraping in the kitchen has me swinging around to face the door while backing up. My fear of being detected makes me forget briefly that M is behind me. I stumble over her, falling on my ass as she cries out.

I scramble to my feet as footsteps race toward us. I yank open the backdoor just as a voice rings out.

"Hey!"

I turn on reflex and see a man drop to his knees beside M as a woman appears in the doorway opposite me. She takes in M with a look of horror before lifting her eyes to mine.

I stand frozen, taking in her fiery hair and pale face. She pulls a gun, aims it at me, and fires.

CHAPTER FORTY

WILL

*E*very step threatens to bring me to my knees. It's only sheer force of will and my absolute need to get to Six that's keeping me on my feet.

"Okay, that's enough," Baker snaps, grabbing my arm when I teeter.

"I'm fine." I grit my teeth, shaking him off.

"Yeah?" He pushes me and I stumble, landing on my ass with a curse.

"What the fuck, Baker?" Danny curses.

"He's being an idiot. Not only is the motherfucker going to get himself killed, but he's slowing us down."

Baker crouches in front of me. "Your leg is bleeding again. You've torn your stitches and the wound is far too close to your femoral artery to risk tearing it further. I know you want to find your girl. Man, I get it, but I can move faster on my own. Think with your head, not your heart. If we take much longer, it's gonna be dark and we'll stand no chance of finding her."

I look at his earnest face and drop my head. "She won't come for you."

"Tell me something to convince her I'm friend, not foe. Something that could only come from you."

I lift my head and think over his words. "Firefly," I choke out, feeling the noose tighten as the sun dips lower in the sky.

"Firefly?" He frowns.

"Yeah. She'll understand. Please, just find her."

"I won't come back without her." He claps me on the back before standing.

"Baker." Danny sighs.

"I know, I know. We work in teams. But Danny, sometimes the rules have to be broken, even by you. Can you get him back?"

"Please. I carried heavier packs in the desert," he mutters, making me shake my head.

"I can walk," I grumble.

"You could suck my dick too. Doesn't mean I'm gonna let you."

"Go. I'll call when I get him back and head back out," Danny tells Baker who nods before jogging off.

I look up at Danny, who looks resigned as he bends down and hauls me up. "This is going to hurt, isn't it?"

"Like a motherfucker," he agrees, dipping down to toss me over his shoulder. I'm granted a small reprieve when his cell rings.

He stands up, yanks out his cell, and barks out, "You found her?"

Whoever Danny is talking to says something that has Danny looking at me and swallowing hard.

"We're on our way."

He hangs up and I brace myself, his face not bringing me any kind of comfort.

"That was Viddy. They have Six. She's been shot. It's not looking good, Will, I'm sorry."

I roar with anguish. "Fuck."

Danny grabs my arms and shakes me. "Brace man. I'm sorry in advance." He dips and tosses me over his shoulder before turning and running.

How I don't barf down his back is a miracle. Not that I give a shit. All that matters is Six.

God, I promised her she'd be safe.

My stomach pitches as my leg bumps Danny's shoulder, but I swallow down the vomit as it rushes up my throat.

It feels like it takes years before we get to the house. We walk through the door to pandemonium.

Danny lowers me to the ground before stepping up beside Viddy and giving her the once over, but I can't tear my eyes from the scene on the floor.

V's man Jed leans down over the prone body, blood pooling on the kitchen floor around them both.

"Six," I whisper, dragging myself toward her, my hand wrapping around her ankle, trying to anchor her to me.

Jed turns at the sound of my voice, revealing her face and making my breath stall in my throat. Dazed bloodshot eyes meet mine a moment before clarity flashes within them.

"Who the fuck is this?"

I turn to Viddy, who steps closer with a frown marring her

face. "It's Six," she tells me softly but I'm already shaking my head.

"I don't know who that woman is, but it's not Six," I hiss as the woman wraps her hand around Jed's back and draws his weapon.

With the last of her strength, she aims the gun at me. Jed, realizing his error, grabs for it.

Everything after that plays out in slow motion, the gun swinging wide and pointing at Viddy when it fires. Danny throwing himself in front of her a second before Jed punches the woman in the face, knocking her out cold.

Everything speeds up at once, the carnage accompanied by Viddy's screams that cut into my soul even over the ringing in my ears.

I try to get to my feet but my leg buckles so I crawl toward her as she leans over Danny. When I'm next to her, I understand why the woman who is always as cool as a cucumber is falling apart.

Danny blinks rapidly, trying to catch his breath as blood oozes from a wound in his chest precariously close to his heart.

"Fuck." I press down over it to staunch the flow but the blood gushes up through my fingers and runs down my arms, saturating the floor beneath us. There seems to be more blood outside his body than inside. The bitch must have hit an artery.

A look of acceptance washes over his face and I know Viddy sees it when she starts sobbing. "No Danny, please don't leave me."

He lifts his hand and holds it against her cheek, love shining in his eyes. "It was worth it, V. Every single day. So worth it."

His hand drops to her belly, pressing against the small baby inside he just saved. He smiles as his eyes drift closed and his chest moves one more time before it stops moving altogether.

"No," she whispers as his hand drops to the floor. She leans over him, crying into his chest as I cup her head. She lifts her head to look at me, grief etched into every line of her face. "He can't be gone, Will. He just can't."

"I'm sorry, V."

She presses a kiss to his forehead before she sits back up, wiping her face of all emotion. I see her shutting down as she turns to face the woman on the floor. With a grace that belies her sorrow, she stands, pulls her gun, and shoots the woman in the face. Half her skull explodes, but that isn't enough for Viddy.

She fires again and again, emptying her clip until the gun clicks over and over.

Somehow, I get to my feet and stumble toward her, pressing my front to Viddy's back. As soon as she feels my heat, she drops the gun, turns, and crumples in my arms.

"Call Kai and Jude," I tell Jed, who discreetly wipes a tear from his eye before nodding.

I don't tell him to call Baker, the man who is out there looking for the woman I love. How can I tell him to stay out there until he finds her when his best friend lies dead on my living room floor?

CHAPTER FORTY-ONE

SIX

My arm burns but I know it could have been so much worse. Thankfully my feet had become unfrozen at the sight of the gun in the woman's hands. I ran just as she fired, the bullet winging my arm as I swung the door closed behind me.

I kept running until I hit the woods, my pace awkward because of the ill-fitting boots but I push through. Its only when I reach the tree line, I stop to catch my breath.

Not sure the best way to go, I decide to head to where I last spoke to Will. If he's there, I'll know I was too late. I'll walk right into that lake and give up because I can't do this anymore. I don't want to. I can't go back to the girl I was before Will turned me into a woman. I've felt too much to go back to being numb.

I traipse up the hill and head left, picturing the layout of the land in my mind. It's much darker now, which I hope gives me an advantage over anyone else M brought with her. Thanks to Will, I've learned to navigate these woods pretty well with limited visibility and someone hot on my heels.

It's quiet out, almost too quiet. An oppressive silence hangs in the air as the sisters of fate decide which strings to cut.

I lock down all thoughts of Will and head in the direction I left him. I can't afford to let the thought of him dying overwhelm me or I'll never make it. All I can do is put one foot in front of the other and pray.

I wish I'd been able to bring James's cell so I could call Fisher, but it was pointless if I couldn't open it without James's thumbprint.

At the crack of a twig, I pause and look around. I can't see or hear anyone so I keep going, carefully picking my way over fallen logs and scrambling up muddy slopes. The cold makes my bones ache, the icy wind chafes against my cheeks that already feel tender from snagging them in my haste to run through the woods earlier.

When I reach the place I left him and see nothing on the ground but blood, I drop to my knees as my breath rushes out of me. Fisher found him. I know he did. Now all I have to do is stay alive long enough for Will to find me.

I head back into the dense shrubbery, looking for somewhere to hide that will offer me an element of shelter as well as keep me hidden from anyone who comes looking for me. I'll move around when it gets darker. It sure as heck wouldn't do well to stay in one place for too long. But right now, I'm so exhausted I'm struggling to keep my eyes open.

If I don't rest now, I'll make a mistake, which could lead to me falling and injuring myself. That's the last thing I need right now.

I spot what I'm looking for by accident as I slip and grab a low branch for balance. There, tucked under the low bowing branches of the tree, is a huge hollow void in the wide base of the trunk. I dip and crawl until I reach it and squeeze inside the space big enough to sit in, and that's what I do. I pull my legs up to my chest and lay my head upon my knees, allowing myself to think back to the woman who fired on me. She isn't someone I recognize from the facility and neither was the guy working on M. Or at least if they are, I've never seen them. It's likely she hired them from somewhere else. But something about the woman doesn't sit right with me and I can't quite figure out what.

She looked horrified when she saw M on the ground, so maybe they are old friends or even lovers perhaps. But that still doesn't explain the vibe I felt.

Reading people is still a new concept to me and more often than not, I fail at it. Not because I'm stupid, but because I've never seen raw emotions on people before coming here. Anger and lust were pretty much the only things I was familiar with. But now? Jesus, I never knew people could be so expressive.

Maybe seeing someone so gorgeous and put together looking at me with such loathing is what's throwing me. Maybe she reminded me of M. They both had this—

I sit up straighter when I figure out what was bugging me. That woman wasn't a minion. She didn't cower or panic or look to M for guidance. That woman was in complete control and exuded confidence. If I had to point out the most powerful person in the room it would have been her.

But what does that mean? Did M lie about everything? Is

she working with this woman to take me back to the compound? As soon as the thought occurs to me, I shake it off. Once upon a time, perhaps. But when she locked me in the basement, she had no intention of letting me leave there alive.

The sound of a gun firing in the distance makes me jump as birds overhead flee in panic.

"Will," I whisper.

All sense of reason leaves me as I scramble to get free. I don't care about myself at this moment. All I care about is Will, but as I shift my weight, I'm aware of the sound of someone cursing nearby.

I freeze, my breath sawing in and out of me loudly. I cover my mouth with my hand and try to be as quiet as possible when I hear the sound of multiple footsteps running in my direction. I don't move a muscle, even though I'm not as covered as I'd like. There is too much bracken and broken branches on the ground for me to avoid making a noise. All I can do is hope their attention is on the sound of the gun firing, like mine was only moments ago.

For once someone must be listening to me because the sound of footsteps running past makes me tense so hard my muscles cramp. There are at least two of them. They don't make noise beyond their running. They don't hesitate or look around. They run in the direction of the house, ignoring everything else around them.

I wait for them to pass as another series of gunshots ring out into the night. I have to shove my fist into my mouth and bite down to stop myself from screaming.

Wanting to go back, but knowing I need to move farther away, I slowly inch my way out from my hiding spot. A glance around doesn't show anyone close by, but the encroaching dark hampers my visibility.

I take the risk, scramble to my feet, and run, only to find myself colliding with a man I've never seen before in my life. I bounce off his chest and lose my footing. Before I fall, the stranger wraps his arms around me. I struggle in his hold, but he doesn't let go.

"I'm not going to hurt you. Will sent me."

I fight harder, knowing he wouldn't send a stranger.

"Firefly!" he bellows as I kick him in the shin. I freeze.

He looks down at me, his face angry as he takes in mine. For some reason, I don't think the anger is because I kicked him but because of the fear he can see.

"Will told me to tell you firefly. He said you would know what I mean."

Tears run down my face at the innocuous word that would mean nothing to anybody else. "He's, okay?"

"He's okay. Cranky as hell because he's worried about you."

I pull back and wipe my tears from my face, still wary of this man who is twice the size of me.

"My name is Baker. Are you injured?"

"Just bumps and bruises."

He pulls his cell phone from his pocket, but I place my hand on his arm.

"I don't know you and I have zero reasons to trust you. But there is no way anyone except Will could have told you to say firefly to me."

He nods, but I'm not finished.

"There are other people here. Dangerous people. I don't think it's safe to go back. I think we should just go to the hospital where Will is —"

Baker frowns, holding his hand up to cut me off.

"It's safe. We have people looking for you. That's who else is out here."

I shake my head. "No, there are others. I heard gunshots and men ran past me. But more than that, someone shot at me at the house."

His eyes widen. "Will's at the house with Viddy." He places a call as a muscle flexes in his cheek. Nobody answers so he curses and hangs up.

"Look, I know you're scared. I get it, but I have to go help them if they are in trouble. I'm armed. I can keep you safe. I'm asking you to trust me blindly when I say I've got you."

I chew my lips, studying him. Truth is, he could have incapacitated me at any point, but he chose not to. If Will's in trouble, I want Baker to be able to help him.

"Okay. Let's go."

He holds out his hand and after a beat, I slip my smaller one into his. He tugs me but I stop him.

"No, this way. It's quicker. I know these woods better than you."

At least I assume so. I somehow don't see this man playing naked tag with Will.

"If you need me to carry you, you just let me know."

I offer him a small smile at his sweet offer, but the only arms I want around me belong to Will. With how freaked out I am, I can't guarantee being so close to Baker won't trigger me, which is something neither of us can afford right now.

CHAPTER FORTY-TWO

WILL

I watch Viddy stare into space. Jude and Kai, who rushed in moments earlier, watch her with worried eyes from either side of her.

"He's on his way to the funeral parlor now, Viddy. They are expecting him. The clean-up crew will be here any minute." Trevor, a professional cleaner who has done work for both Viddy and me before, tells us solemnly. "Does he have a family that needs to be notified?"

Viddy swallows before shaking her head. "We are the only family he has. Baker, for all intents and purposes, is his brother." She stops talking again as her head bows with grief.

Jude smooths a hand up her back and turns her body into his. She goes without a fight, practically collapsing against him. He looks at Kai and me over her shoulder, his anguish at not being able to take this pain from her easy to see.

"Thanks, Trevor." Kai rises to see the man out.

When he returns to the living room, his face is still grim when he faces me. "He told me he forgot to tell you that they've taken care of James and his place too. Fisher is on his way down there now to sort everything out. He said he'll call in the others to help search for Six."

I nod, my chest tight as the stark feeling of loss invades me once more.

"How did this happen?" Viddy mutters from beside me.

I turn to look at her as someone's cell rings.

Kai pulls his cell out and looks at the screen, then stares at me before answering. "Baker?"

Viddy tenses beside me, lifting her head to look at Kai.

"In the house."

He frowns before replying again. "It's safe, but how did you know? Never mind. You find her?"

Kai's eyes shoot to mine once more. "In the living…" his voice trails off as Baker appears at the door.

"Room," Kai finishes before hanging up.

"Did you find her?" I ask, gripping the edge of the sofa.

He steps aside to reveal Six, whose eyes lock on mine and widen seconds before she starts running for me. When her eyes land on Viddy, she stops so abruptly she almost trips.

"Firefly," I coax, easing myself up taking in the bloody scratches on her face and hands.

Viddy hisses from beside me, but I ignore her as I step toward Six.

She takes a step back looking around for an escape.

"What's wrong?"

"Who is she?" she whispers, her voice dripping with hurt and worse—betrayal—as she looks at Viddy.

"That's Viddy. Remember, I told you about her? Come on, you're hurt, let's get you cleaned up."

Instead of calming her, my words seem to make her more agitated. "I don't understand. I thought..." she backs up, looking ready to bolt.

"Baker," I warn him just as Six turns. Baker is right there, keeping her in place and giving me time to reach her.

"Why are you so scared? You know I would never hurt you." I reach for her, pulling her into my arms. She is stiff as a board for a moment before she melts into me, her face buried in my neck, tears soaking my skin as she grips me tightly.

"She's not scared of you. She's scared of me." Viddy's voice rings out, making Six tense again.

I turn to Viddy, keeping my arms around Six in case she decides to run.

"Why didn't you warn me?" Viddy whispers, the pain in her voice making me suck in a sharp breath.

I look down at Six in confusion. She looks at me with a frown.

"He could still be alive if I'd known."

My eyes fall on Baker, who is frowning now too. I see him scan the room before his gaze moves to Viddy. "Where's Danny?"

Viddy sniffs, a stray tear slipping down her otherwise blank face as she climbs to her feet and walks toward us.

"He took a bullet meant for me. He didn't make it," she tells him softly as a mask of fury and pain sweeps over Baker's face.

"Who shot him?" he snarls as I pull away from Six, ready to restrain Baker if needed.

Viddy turns her angry eyes to Six. "That's what I'd like to know."

Six shrinks into herself. I reach for her, but Viddy is quicker, reaching out for a handful of hair and yanking Six to her with a painful scream.

I move to stop her when Kai grabs me from behind and Jude reaches for Viddy.

"V, that's enough." He squeezes her hand until she lets go.

Six scrambles away. She looks at me and seeing me restrained snaps something in her. She runs toward me but instead of touching me, she moves to my back and starts whaling on Kai.

"You let him go," she yells, thumping him and kicking him enough that he has no choice but to loosen his hold, which throws me off balance and knocks me to the floor.

"Shit," I curse as pain stabs me in the leg.

Seeing me on the floor, Six stops attacking Kai and runs to me, dropping to her knees and moving in front of me in a protective stance.

Everyone stares at her in shock. I'd find the whole thing funny if it wasn't so heartbreakingly sad.

"I won't let you hurt him. You can do whatever you want to me. I won't cry. I won't scream, but you will not touch him."

God, I love this woman. This fiercely protective woman, who has been to hell and back, is facing down a roomful of strangers to keep me safe.

I smooth my hands up and down her arms, trying to soothe her. "I'm okay, Six. They won't hurt me."

"You're not okay and I don't trust them. Except for him." She points at Baker, who looks surprised for a minute. He steps around Viddy and walks toward us, crouching on the floor in front of Six.

"I won't hurt you. I promised, right? And friends keep their promises."

"You want to be my friend?" she whispers.

"Yeah, sweetheart I do. I have a feeling I'm going to need one." His head bows as he struggles to get his emotions under control.

I watch in awe and with a bit of jealousy as she reaches out and places a shaky hand on his head. At her soft touch, he lifts his head, his eyes red, his face looking ravaged.

Her hand slides to his jaw, leaving a smear on blood on his skin. "I've got you. Trust me," Six murmurs.

Baker swallows hard, his hand reaching up to cover hers. He nods before swallowing. "What happened to Danny?"

"I don't even know who Danny is," she answers him, which is true. Right or wrong, I've kept Six away from everyone. I wanted to wait until she was ready before I let them all barge in with their loud personalities and opinions, making Six retreat back into herself out of self-preservation.

"That woman shot him," Viddy chokes out but her anger is slipping now, giving way to grief once more.

"M?"

"Who is M?" Baker asks Six gently.

"She was one of my trainers. Is she dead?"

"Yeah, she's dead. I shot so many bullets into her face I nearly decapitated the bitch," Viddy snaps.

"Good." Six relaxes a touch at her answer. "Until today, the last time I saw her was when she told me I was being delivered to my owner. She was blissfully happy about what was to come for me. She hated me from the start, but I never knew why until she turned up in the basement."

"Wait, what? Back up. You were in the basement? My basement?" I grimace. I'd kept that room from her for a damn good reason. It's not a basement but a torture chamber.

"Why don't you start from the beginning?" Baker encourages her.

She blows out a breath and leans back into me. Despite the pain, I don't move her, needing her in my arms now more than ever.

CHAPTER FORTY-THREE

SIX

*W*ill holds me while I let Baker clean my hands and face before I start.

"We were on the boat one minute and the next we were in the water with bullets flying around us. I'm not sure when I realized that someone was trying to kill us. I was in shock, I think, but Will got us safely to shore."

"The first bullet fired was the one to hit me. I yanked her in and toppled the boat. I didn't know how many people were out there," Will tells them quietly.

Viddy and the man behind her move to the sofa, followed by the man who had Will restrained. They sit either side of her protectively, each one picking up her hand in one of their own, almost in a mirror image of each other.

"He couldn't walk and I couldn't carry him. I got him as far as I could, then found him somewhere to hide. I covered him as well as I could and ran for help."

I blink back tears as I tell them the next part. "I went to James's place. At first, I thought it was empty. But…" I shake my head. "Someone had stabbed him. I couldn't leave him like that."

"He was alive when you got there?" Will questions.

I turn back and look at him. "Yeah, barely. It was as if he was waiting."

"For me to save him?" Will curses.

"No. He knew he was dying. He was waiting for Claire. He spoke to her just before he slipped away. After that, I used his cell to call Fisher. He promised to rally the troops if I swore to hide. But I couldn't just leave you there to bleed out, Will.

"My head was a mess. I didn't think to bring any medical supplies or anything. I just had to get back to you and let you know Fisher was coming. I had to give you a reason to hang on."

His hand cups my cheek before he kisses me gently. "You were the reason I hung on Six, never doubt that."

I nod and offer him a small smile before carrying on. "I was soaked and freezing so I grabbed his jacket off the door and a knife from the block on the counter and headed back the way I came. But then a gunshot rang out and I forgot about all the reasons I was supposed to be stealthy. My only thought was getting to you. That's when I ran into trouble."

"What kind of trouble?" Baker asks, drawing my attention again.

"A man was in the woods. R. He was another trainer. He wrestled me to the ground and pinned me down. He was pissed

243

and apparently because I was already damaged goods, it meant he could have a little fun with me first."

Will growls so I reach around and snag his hand in mine. "I had the knife in my pocket and when the opportunity arose, I took it.

"I killed him. I panicked and was about to run. But then there was a gun pointed at my face before everything went black and I woke up however long later in the basement."

"Are you saying you were in the basement the whole time I was here?" Viddy questions.

I shrug. "I don't know how long I was in there or who was up here at the time. When did you get shot?" I look at Will.

He confirms what I already suspected. "Yesterday."

"When I saw you in the utility room, I had just gotten free," I tell Viddy softly.

"Wait, you saw, V?" Baker frowns.

I chew my lip. "Do you want me to skip the next bit or carry on?"

"Sorry, carry on. We'll come back to that," Will murmurs.

I nod before continuing. "I woke up alone with no idea where I was other than it was cold, dark, and windowless." I choke on the last word and feel Will lean in closer and wrap his arm around me.

"I'm not going to lie, I freaked out. I don't know why it was so bad. You'd think I'd be used to it, but it was awful. Like being given a beautiful butterfly to hold only for its wings to get ripped off."

"Panic attack." Will sighs.

"That's what I figured out eventually, but it was hard to calm down when I was down there. I was so cold and all I could think about was if Fisher made it to you in time. I'm not sure how long I was down there before the door opened and M appeared, scaring the crap out of me."

"And she was one of the trainers? You said that earlier, but I don't really know what that means. What were they training people to do?" Baker frowns.

"Follow orders without question. Be submissive. Suck dick."

His face goes an alarming shade of purple while Will's arms tighten around me.

"What?" Baker hisses.

I blink and tilt my head, confused. "I was a slave." I can say it now because the most powerful word in that sentence is was.

"But—" I reach out and touch the back of his hand.

"Don't try to understand. You'd have to be evil to even attempt to understand why they did the things they did. And in the end, none of it mattered. It was all a lie." I bow my head and close my eyes for a moment, trying to remember the woman I thought was my mother, but it's been so long and I was so young.

"What was a lie, firefly? I don't understand."

I don't answer Will but the room at large. "I was born in captivity. Until Will liberated me, I'd never known what freedom was beyond my dreams. My mom died when I was so little still. And although I loved her, she didn't show affection in any way. I understand why. It would have made me a weapon to be used to keep her in check, so I never held it against her. But now I know it was more than that. She didn't shower me with motherly love because she wasn't my mother. M was."

"That woman was your mother?" Viddy hisses.

"So she said. Her sister married a man who got her killed. M purposely got pregnant by the same man to use me as a weapon in his downfall. I'd been told I had been purchased when I was still in my mother's womb but that wasn't strictly true. It's just what M told everyone to protect my virtue. She wanted to trick my dad into taking it."

"That's fucked-up and I don't understand half of it." Baker scowls.

"Honestly, neither do I. She said something about me having brothers too and club whores. She told me she would get rid of my dad's current woman and kid and then…" I shiver while filling in the blanks.

"She didn't say anything, but I know her. She'd have had it recorded and used it as blackmail material at the very least."

"Club whore? So your dad is a biker. She give you a name?" Viddy sits forward now, her eyes dry even though they are still red.

"No. She did say that her sister had been undercover though, and something my dad did got her killed. I'm not sure she even had all the details herself. She did say someone else was helping her until they died. A Cohen? I don't know if that's his first name or last."

"Holy fuck," Kai curses. He looks at his brother who is identical to him, making me glad they both opted to wear different colored hoodies today.

"What?"

Both Kai and Jude look at me but it's Viddy that speaks. "Cohen caused a lot of trouble for two MCs so it wouldn't be that hard to figure out who your father might be," she tells me calmly, but there is a slight lilt to her words. I know instinctively she knows more than she's disclosing.

I don't answer, not sure I'm ready for that. Or if I'll ever be ready.

"She told you all that?" Will asks. I look over my shoulder at him and see him frown.

"She wasn't going to let me go. She said she had enough evidence to send to my dad, so she didn't need me anymore. She was going to kill me and probably take photos or videos of herself doing it on her cell."

"You figured that out or she told you?" Jude questions.

"A little of both. She told me I wouldn't be leaving alive. But when she made me strip, I knew she'd record it. There was no reason for it otherwise."

Will soothes his hand up and down my arms.

"She had the gun pointed at me and I just…lost it. I started taunting her. I wanted her to feel an ounce of the humiliation she heaped upon me over the years. I swept her legs out from under her and grabbed the gun as soon as she dropped it."

My face feels wet, so I reach up and swipe my cheeks, surprised to realize I'm crying.

"I tried to get out, but the door was locked. She said it locked from the outside and that we'd die down there. She reached for me and I shot her. Turns out I'm a terrible shot. I aimed for her chest but hit her shoulder. She just wouldn't stop coming for me, so I fired again and this time I hit her in the stomach. That's when she told me there were two bullets, one for each of us and I'd die down there alone. It's possible I lost my mind for a while again. Things are hazy and well…things never get hazy for me."

"We all forget things. Don't worry about it," Baker offers.

"Not Six. She has hyperthymesia, meaning she remembers everything she experiences," Will answers.

"What? Seriously. That must come in handy," Jude points out.

My face must take on a somber expression because he frowns.

"Maybe if you lived the all-American dream, but not for someone like me."

His face goes pale, and I see him thinking about all the possible things I've witnessed. Each one is something I'll never forget. I'm haunted every second of every day by bloody memories and terrified faces.

"On the plus side, now I've had a chance to look at you both properly, I'll always be able to tell you apart."

He smiles. "Challenge accepted."

"How did you get out of the basement?" Viddy interrupts.

I turn to look at her as she watches me with guarded eyes.

"My clothes were still wet from being in the water with Will. I had the jacket but my jeans…" I shake my head.

"Getting dressed in those again would have just resulted in me getting sick faster. M's T-shirt was soaked with blood, but her pants were not too bad. So I stripped them off her, along with her socks and boots, and put them on. That's when I found the key to the door in her pocket."

Will curses. "She must have taken it from James. He's the only person other than me with a key, but he wouldn't have given it to her willingly." Which is likely why he's dead.

I look at Viddy, knowing how important she is to Will. But I'm not sure there is anything I'm going to be able to do to bridge the gap between us now that her friend is dead.

"She wasn't dead. At first I was going to leave her, but I couldn't. Not because she could be my mother but because I had to believe I'm nothing like her. Plus, if I let her die, she couldn't answer for her crimes. I'm not the only person she trained. There are others out there waiting and praying for someone to find them."

I plead with my eyes for this woman to understand. She might have blood on her hands, more than all the men in this room put together, but she has a heart. I can tell by how fiercely she loves them and by how devastated she is over the loss of one of them. I'm not like her though. I already have a heavy cross to bear with my condition. I don't even need to close my eyes to see Ten swinging from the bars of his cage. A person can only carry so much before they bow and then break. I'm wise enough to know that the load I carry is already too heavy to be adding more to it.

Like killing my mother.

"I dragged her to the utility room and then I put on a clean top of Will's, knowing it would be warmer when I was back in the forest."

"You knew you were going to run. You didn't get spooked? What the heck? Why would you put yourself in danger like that?" Baker complains, making Viddy look at him in question.

"I didn't know if it was safe. James was killed in his home. I had been locked in the basement and nobody had noticed. I already knew there were at least two people because I'd hurt them both, but I had no way of knowing just how many people M brought with her."

I look at Viddy and hold her gaze. "And then you came. You looked at M as your friend worked on her, and you looked horrified before you lifted your gun and shot at me."

Will goes solid behind me and Baker's eyes widen.

"What?" Kai questions, looking at Viddy.

"I thought this M person was Six. Fuck, I'd had tea with her earlier in the day. I'd helped her to bed, encouraged her to take a shower, and all the while you were in the basement." She swipes a hand over her face, looking exhausted all of a sudden.

"If you had told me," she whispers, but I shake my head.

"You wouldn't have believed me. You had tea with her. She turned off her hatred and turned on her tears to reel you in. You'd have shot me before letting me explain. It's only because I saw in your eyes that you were going to pull the trigger that I moved before you fired. You clipped my arm but I'm fine, its a tiny graze." I rush to reassure Will. "But if I hadn't turned, you'd have hit my chest. I'd have died before Will even realized I was in danger. And if that had happened, you'd have broken what the two of you have."

CHAPTER FORTY-FOUR

WILL

She's not wrong. It's taking everything I have not to destroy the house and kick everyone out except Six.

"I loved him," Viddy tells Six softly. Even though I'm so fucking angry, my heart hurts for the pain emanating from her.

"He was my friend and I loved him, but he's dead and I can't fix dead. I can fix almost anything but not that."

"I know. I wished more than once that I could fix that too. But we can't. We are responsible for our actions, but we're not God. We can't possibly know the ripples those actions will have until they play out. I'm sorry about your friend, Viddy, truly I am. He sounds like he was a good man who died protecting someone he loved. I didn't know him but it seems to me like he died doing what he loves. Nobody chooses to die. But if we could, how do you think he would want to go out? A car accident? Cancer? Or saving someone who meant the world to him?"

Tears stream down Viddy's cheeks now, as Six's words penetrate her shields.

"I hate that he's gone, V," Baker says softly. "But this is who Danny is—was. He was never going to go silently into the night. That man was destined to go out in a blaze of glory. Don't be angry at that."

"I'm—" Viddy's cell rings, cutting off what she was going to say. She wipes her tears before answering. Her voice is so steady and clear, you'd never know two minutes ago she was falling apart.

I lean down and breathe Six in, holding her tighter to me. My leg is throbbing like a bitch from sitting on the floor too long, but I don't want to let her go just yet.

"I'm on my way," Viddy replies before standing and smoothing down the front of her dress. "Jenna's in labor."

"Go. I think Six and I need some time alone to regroup."

Jenna's pregnancy has been problematic from the start, something to do with scarring caused by years of abuse. But the baby is a fighter just like its mom. Though it's making an appearance earlier than expected, I have no doubt mom and baby will be okay. Even so, the last thing Wyatt will want is a waiting room full of people to deal with.

"Will, I—" Viddy starts but I shake my head.

"Not now, Viddy. Go be with Wyatt. He needs you. Everything else we can figure out later."

She sighs but nods. Jude stands and wraps his arm around her shoulder and tugs her toward the door, tipping his head at me on the way out.

Kai steps around me and moves to follow but stops and

turns at the last minute. "She reacts before she thinks. I get that more than anyone. It's the same instinct that's kept her alive all these years. I know you're pissed. If it were me, I'd be the same, but this is who she is, Will. You can't love her for all her strengths and abandon her when she shows a moment of weakness. She just lost Danny, don't let her lose you too."

"I almost lost Six today because of her. Stand there and tell me if Six had fired at Viddy you wouldn't have been calling for blood."

"Oh, I'd have snapped her neck. Because like V, I react first before thinking. But you're not me, Will. You're better than that."

His eyes drift to Six, a small frown marring his face. "She fucked up," he tells Six softly. "A few years ago, she stepped in front of my brother and took two bullets that were meant for him. I nearly lost her there and then. Nothing much scares me anymore but losing her." He shakes his head and swallows. "I'd follow. In life and death, I'd follow her anywhere, but it doesn't mean I'm oblivious to her faults. If you give her another chance, I can promise you won't regret it. When V loves, she loves with her whole heart. And you could be a part of that, not just for Will, but for you too. She can give you a family."

"Kai," I warn. I get where he's coming from but this stinks of mental manipulation.

"It's okay, Will. I understand what he's trying to say. I've never had a family, but I understand what one is on a fundamental level. I've read about them and since coming here, I've seen movies, and..." Her voice trails off before she turns her head and looks up at me with sad eyes.

"I witnessed it between Will, Fisher, and James." She turns

back to Kai and nods. "I get it. Family messes up but if you love them, you forgive them."

"Well, yeah." He winks. "Within reason, of course. If your father is Zodiac, you don't mend bridges, you burn them."

Six freezes in my arms.

"Six?"

She doesn't answer but her breathing picks up.

"Six?" I shake her, but her breathing is way too fast and she's not hearing a word I say.

"She's having a panic attack. Pull her back flush to your front and get her to breathe with you," Baker orders.

Ignoring my pain, I do just that, vaguely aware of Kai talking to someone.

"I'll meet you there Jude. Stay with V."

"Take deep breaths, Six. Listen to Will's heartbeat behind you. Can you hear it?"

After a moment, she nods.

"Good girl, now match your breathing to his."

I take a deep breath and blow it out slowly, repeating the process until she finally mimics me.

"That's it. You've got it. Nice and slow," Baker praises as Six relaxes further.

We sit there for a while longer, Baker and me helping Six calm as Kai stands sentry over us.

"I'm sorry," she whispers, what feels like hours later.

"Nothing to be sorry about, darlin'," Kai answers in a gentle voice as he squats next to us. "Something I said set you off. You up for telling me what so I don't trigger it again? I might be a bastard, Six, but I don't like seeing you like that knowing I caused it."

"It wasn't your fault. I just never expected to hear that name again."

"Fuck!" Kai runs his fingers through his hair.

"Jesus, was there anything that man wasn't involved in?" Baker hisses.

"You know he's dead right?" Kai ignores Baker and keeps his focus on Six.

"Really?"

"Really. Did he hurt you?" he asks her.

I tense but Six shakes her head. "He scared me. And given the type of people I was surrounded by, that's saying a lot. He threatened me and I was wise enough to know he wouldn't care about the hands-off rule placed on me. He told me as much. He wasn't scared of my owner and now I know it's M, I understand why. Women were beneath him. There is no way he would recognize her as a power he should be wary of."

"That's exactly the reason Viddy was able to bring him down. He thought as king he was safe in his castle, but he was too misogynistic to realize the power a queen can wield." Kai stands and offers Six his hand.

"Let's get you both off the floor. Will must be due some pain meds."

She turns to look at me before worry fills her eyes.

"I'm fine, I promise. But Kai's right, I'm due some pain pills and I want Baker to check where the bullet grazed you, so let's move to the sofa, alright?"

She nods and after a beat slips her hand inside Kai's. He helps her up. Before I can figure out how the fuck I'm going to get off the floor, Baker is there, pulling me up, slipping his shoulder under mine. I wince but manage to bite back a moan as I make it to the sofa and gather Six close to me once more.

"I'm glad he's dead. Is that wrong to say about someone's father?" Six asks.

"Not when it concerns Zodiac. Why he would need to go to a place like that is beyond me. He had enough victims to keep him busy as it was." Kai grunts.

"I can only guess that out here people, even criminals, often have lines they won't cross. And forcing children to have sex with them is one of them. Where I was held though, nobody asked questions or frowned upon his activities." She looks sad as she gets lost in the past.

"More than that though, I heard some of the trainers talking once. And the gist I got was that he traded with them. He wanted easy access to younger girls, and he was willing to supply an endless number of women as a trade-off to do it. It was a win-win for the trainers. They didn't have to give the child up, only rent her out and they got paid handsomely for it. The only time they got mad was when the damage was so extensive that the child didn't make it." She swallows.

Kai looks like he wants to kill Zodiac all over again but Six, sensing how close to the edge he is, reaches up and grabs his wrist.

"Maybe there is a record in his things at the place I was held at. I can't direct you there as the only time I left was when I was blindfolded and delivered to Will, but if you find something and can pull up photos, I'll be able to tell you if I recognize it. There were also a lot of people in and out over the years, so if you have photos of people you want me to look at, I could tell you if they were involved or not. It's not much but it might be enough to bring Zodiac's castle of stone to rubble."

He looks down at her, something moving over his face I'm not familiar with. It has me tightening my hold on Six. When his face softens, I realize it's affection, something he usually shows for nobody except Viddy.

"You'd do that, even knowing it might trigger another panic attack?"

"I'd do anything to get every man, woman, and child out of there."

CHAPTER FORTY-FIVE

SIX

I didn't realize how much I needed to do this until the words are out of my mouth. Before, I had no way of finding them. If Will had an army ready to help me, I had no location to give him. Kai has given me hope that perhaps Zodiac left a clue behind we could trace back to them.

"I'll look into it. Honestly, Zodiac considered himself untouchable and for the longest time, he was. But what that means, is he kept records, records any sane man knew would incriminate them. But not him. Zodiac had always been able to get himself out of everything. A lot of it seemed inconsequential, so I placed it aside. But now...well, now I have a place to look. You take some time to mourn James and spend time with Will. I'll stop by with what I find. Okay, Six?"

"Okay, Kai."

"Now I'm gonna go and catch up with the others. I'll let you know when the baby is born," he tells Will.

"You coming?" he asks Baker as he stands and pats my shoulder.

"I'll be right behind you. I just want to quickly check this wound."

"Alright, I'll meet you outside."

When he leaves, Baker bends down in front of me and asks me where I was hit so I slip the jacket off and show him my arm. He cleans it up before agreeing it's just a scratch then takes my hand in one of his. I feel Will tense at me touching another man, but he doesn't say anything. There is a connection developing between us. There is nothing sexual about it. He reminds me of Ten.

"I lost my best friend today." He takes a second to compose himself before blowing out a breath. "But I like to think I made a new one too. It's as if Danny boy knew I'd need you as much as you'd need me."

He looks at Will. "I had a sister once, but I lost her a long time ago. Six reminds me a little of her. I know you need time for the dust to settle, but if you need me, call. You have my number, even if it's just so I can sit with her while you deal with shit you have going on."

"Thank you. I might just take you up on that. Six is new to the whole making friends thing but she's pretty fucking good at it. Seems everyone who meets her loves her."

"Not everyone," I whisper.

Viddy sure as heck doesn't and I worry her dislike might filter down through the rest of their group. I don't want Will to have to pick a side.

"Trust me, Viddy doesn't dislike you. Everything was messed-up, but you'd know if she hated you."

"How?" From where I'm standing, I'm not sure I can tell. She is so hard for me to read and I struggle with understanding people at the best of times.

"Because you'd be dead," Baker answers softly.

I surprise us all as I giggle unexpectedly. "When you put it that way, it does seem pretty clear cut."

He smiles before standing. "Take care, Six. And Will, call me when you need me."

"Thanks for finding her and bringing her back to me. I know you love V, but I know what it's like to live in a house that does nothing but remind you of what you've lost. If you need a break, there is a room here with your name on it."

Baker grips Will's shoulder, his face full of gratitude as he nods and follows Kai out the door.

"Can you pass me those, firefly?" He points to the bottle of water and pain meds Baker grabbed earlier.

I hand them to him and let my eyes rove over his face as he takes them. His skin is pale, his eyes have shadows under them. Brackets around his mouth show me he's in far more pain than he's letting on.

"Do you want me to help you to bed?"

"No. I'm fine right here. Lay with me for a minute?"

I kick off my shoes and help Will lie back, pulling his shoes off as gently as I can so I don't jar his leg.

I lie down next to Will and tug the blanket from the back of the couch over us before laying my head against this chest. He runs his fingers through my hair, soothing me to the point I know, despite the horror of the last few days, I'm about to fall asleep.

"I thought I'd lost you," I admit. Saying it out loud, even though I'm wrapped up in his arms, hurts me.

"Never. Not when I have you to come home to. I love you, Six. I'd survive a hundred bullets if it meant waking up to you just one more time."

"I love you too," I whisper, tears dripping over my cheeks at how freeing it is to speak the words that have held me captive for so long.

"I know you do. I never needed you to say it to know it's true. I feel it when you touch me. See it when you look at me. I know it as surely as I know the sun will rise and fall. You were the one with reservations, but not once did I ever doubt your love for me."

I turn my head and look up at his face, which is blurry through my tears. "I prayed for you. I was ten years old, and I prayed that one day a prince would come along and rescue me. He would love me. He would think I was the most precious person in the world. He wouldn't hurt me or lie to me or scare me. He would be brave and strong. But more than that, he would teach me how to be brave and strong too. You did that. You make me stronger because I don't see the worn-down little girl in the mirror anymore. I see myself through your eyes. I see the girl who got knocked down a hundred and one times but I always got up. I never gave up, never gave in," I whisper, thinking briefly of Ten.

"I held on because I knew one day you would come."

"Always, Firefly. I will always find you."

"Why do you call me that?"

"Because where you saw darkness, I saw luminance. You were lost. You spent so long trying to find the light that you didn't see it was inside you all along. You are the light, Firefly."

He presses a kiss to my forehead, his voice gruff with emotion before tucking my head under his jaw and holding me tightly as we both drift off to sleep.

I sleep deeply. I had prepared for nightmares, but it seems sleeping wrapped in Will's arms kept the monsters at bay.

When I do wake up, it's because I'm melting. I shove the blanket away and crack my eyes open. It's just starting to get light out, which casts the room in a gloomy gray.

I pull away from Will gently, needing to strip my clothes off. When I do, I realize it's not me that's hot, it's Will. I place my hand over his forehead, which is pale while his cheeks are flushed, and gasp at the heat radiating from him.

"Will?" I nudge him gently, not sure what to do. I've never had to look after someone who is sick before. Surprisingly, considering the environment I was raised in, I rarely get sick myself.

"Will, wake up for me." I tap him lightly on the face, making him groan, but he doesn't answer me and he doesn't open his eyes.

I feel myself panicking so I fight it back and try to think. I'm out of my depth and don't want to mess this up.

I spy Will's cell on the table and carefully climb over him to retrieve it. I tap in the PIN he made me memorize and scroll through his contacts until I find the one I want.

I hit the call button and pray he answers. He does, with a groan.

"Will?"

"It's Six. Something's wrong with Will and I don't know what to do," I tell him, fighting back my tears.

"Okay, Six. Calm down." I hear the sound of rustling as he moves. "Tell me what's wrong with him."

"I don't know. He's really hot and I can't wake him up."

"Shit. Did he change his dressing before you guys went to bed?"

"No, we fell asleep on the sofa. Should I do it now?"

"No, don't worry about that. I'm coming over. Is Fisher there?"

"I haven't seen him."

"Okay, don't worry. I'll call him. Right now, I want you to soak a cloth and place it on his head. See if you can cool him down a little. I'll be there as soon as I can."

"Thank you, Baker. I didn't know who else to call."

"You did the right thing. I'm on my way, Six. Promise."

He hangs up and for a moment I stand there as I absorb yet another blow. I've never been one to ask for much. I've never begged or pleaded for more. I moved through life under the gossamer threads of my dreams, resolute in the knowledge that there was more for me out there. I just had to hold on. And I did. I held on through everything even when it would have been easier to lie down and close my eyes. I fought through every trial life threw at me. I passed every test. But everyone has a limit and I've reached mine. The tangible hold I have on my sanity is fraying at the seams as I struggle to keep holding on. My fingers fist as they grasp those gossamer threads, but in the end, it doesn't matter. If Will falls now, so will I. I'll lie down beside him, close my eyes, and we'll take our final journey together. Some people might see that as cowardice, but not me. I was born to be his and the only way I'll let him leave this earth is if he takes me with him.

CHAPTER FORTY-SIX

WILL

I wake up with the mother of all headaches. I groan and crack my eyes open, blinking rapidly when the light blinds me. My mouth is drier than the desert. If I didn't know better, I'd have thought I'd been on a drinking bender.

Once I've adjusted to the light, I take in the room and realize I'm not where I fell asleep.

I focus on the antiseptic smell and the dreary gray paint and figure out pretty quickly I'm in the hospital. I swear these rooms are so depressing that it's a miracle anyone can find the will to live. Perhaps that's part of their master plan—make us hate the place so much we fight harder to get well and leave.

I turn when I feel someone move beside me and find Viddy asleep in the chair next to the bed with her head resting near my leg. I reach out and touch her, making her jump.

She looks around wildly before her eyes land on me and she relaxes slightly.

"What happened? Where's Six?"

Viddy scrubs a hand over her face. I study her and realize how exhausted she looks.

"Six finally passed out. She's been running on fumes so I took advantage and ordered Baker and Fisher to take her home and make sure she ate and slept for at least four hours before she could come back."

She shakes her head and whispers, "You scared the shit out of me."

I reach out my hand, tug her closer, and wrap my arm around her. She grips me tightly and we stay like that for a few minutes before she pulls back and sits back down.

"There was a reason the doctors didn't want you to leave so soon after getting shot. But did you listen? No. Stupid stubborn man. You got an infection in the wound. God knows what was in the lake. Six called Baker and by the time he got to you, he knew it was bad. He got you to the hospital and hasn't left her side since. And she hasn't left yours until today. I'd call her and tell her you're awake, but she really does need to sleep, Will. I doubt she's slept more than a handful of hours in the last three weeks while she watched over you like a Valkyrie."

"Three weeks? Shit, V!" I groan. Six must be frantic.

I ease myself up and feel sweat bead my forehead.

"Take it easy, Will." Viddy moves to help rearrange the pillows behind me.

"I need to get home. Six must be worried sick."

"She is. But if you think she'll be happy to see you stroll back in your front door, you're crazier than I thought. She needs you to get better, Will. And if that means spending a few more days here, then so be it."

"Viddy—"

"No!" she snaps, cutting me off. "You nearly died again. She can't handle losing you, Will. I can't handle losing you either. Please, for the love of god, stay put."

When I open my mouth to argue, she pulls her damn gun and points it at me.

"I'm not above shooting you in the other leg if it means you stay in bed."

"Fine. It seems counterproductive to me, but whatever. Tell me what I've missed."

She eyes me for a minute, likely gaging whether I'm going to leap from the bed. She needn't worry. I doubt very much that my legs would support me even if I wanted them to.

She tucks her gun away and sits back down with all the grace of a queen. "Well, let's see. Fisher took over the temporary running of your company. Jude has been on hand to help if needed, but Fisher seems to be holding his own. Oh, Wyatt and Jenna's baby girl came kicking and screaming into the world twenty minutes before you were brought in. She was small and needed a little help in the neonatal unit, but she's due to go home today."

I smile at that, knowing Wyatt and Jenna must be over the moon that everything worked out in the end.

"What did they name her?"

"Esme Megan Turner."

"Damn, I bet Megan is over the moon with that. You're not jealous they didn't add Vida to the mix?" I tease, the tension between us falling away.

"Fuck no, I hate my name. Besides, Megan saved her. It's

because of her that Jenna even met Wyatt in the first place. Speaking of…"

"What?"

"I told Megan what M told Six, wondering if any of it sounded familiar."

"And?"

"Melly, or Melinda, was Megan's mom. She was some type of law enforcement agent who died undercover because her handler was a dick. There is a lot more to it but—"

"You know who Six's dad is, don't you?"

"Megan has two half-brothers. They were both born while Melly was working undercover. Both their parents were agents. Orion and Diesel, otherwise known as the current President and Vice President of the Kings of Carnage MC.

"I'd still recommend she do a DNA test rather than take the word of a psychopath, but if this is all true, then I believe that King is Six's father."

And suddenly all the shit about undercover agents makes sense.

"Ah, fuck. If he is, then the shit is going to hit the fan."

I try to imagine what I'd feel like, learning I had a daughter after all these years, plus discovering she'd been held captive her whole life.

"I know. It's why I've sworn Megan to secrecy. Six is going to need you by her side to deal with this. She is still fearful around people and now she is going to find herself with the title lost princess of Carnage. Brace, Will. I can't even begin to fathom what the fallout of this will be."

"The key players are dead. M, Cohen, J, even Zodiac. Who's left?"

"That, Will, is the million-dollar question."

She turns at the sound of the door opening. Surprise jolts me when I see Cash walk in. I hadn't seen him much since Layla's funeral. He needed space and time to grieve and we understood that. Then with everything that was going on with Six, he slipped my mind. Jesus, I'm a shitty friend.

"Cash, it's good to see you." And it is. And it has to be said he looks a fuck of a lot better than he did the last time I saw him. Aside from the angry scowl that is.

"Are you fucking kidding me?" he roars.

"Cash—" Viddy starts but he cuts her off with a glare.

"You nearly died twice and nobody thinks to, I don't know, give me a call?" Disdain drips from his words.

"You had enough on your plate," Viddy tells him softly.

"That was not your call to make, and you know it. You don't get to decide what I can and can't handle, V."

Her shoulders slump. "I'm sorry. You're right. If it helps, I was coming over later to talk to you," she whispers, her arms wrapped around herself.

He takes her in before his anger melts away. He steps forward and yanks her into his arms. "I'm sorry about Danny, V. He was a good man."

"The best," she agrees as she buries her head against his chest.

He looks at me over the top of her head. "How are you now?"

"I'm okay. Tired and I'd murder for a greasy burger right now."

Cash's lips twitch. "I'll see what I can do."

"How are you doing?" I question.

Viddy pulls back and looks up at Cash, waiting for his answer.

He looks down at her, a wide smile spreading across his lips. "I'm good, Will. Really fucking good."

"Where's Lily today?"

"She's at home...with my wife."

Viddy and I are silent as the news sinks in before we both burst out with a million questions.

He waves his hand to shut us up.

"It's a long story that I don't think either of you knows about in its entirety. To understand the choices that were made, I'll need to start at the beginning."

"Well, I'm apparently hospital-bound for the next few days. I have nothing but time, so tell me what's been going on."

He pulls up the seat beside Viddy's and tells us his version of the story of him and Layla and all the twisty turns they navigated.

By the time he gets to the end, we are both stunned into silence.

"She's alive?" Viddy shakes her head incredulously.

"Alive and well. And more importantly, she's safe."

CHAPTER FORTY-SEVEN

WILL

*T*he weather fits the mood. Two funerals in two days and the skies weep along with the rest of us. James had been the first to be laid to rest, in the plot beside his beloved wife. I'd hated saying goodbye, but I took comfort in the fact that he was now reunited with the only woman he had ever loved.

I'm thankful I even made it. Viddy held off as long as she could, hoping I'd wake up.

Fisher stood on my left, head bowed, and Six stood on my right with her arm around my back and her face pressed against my shoulder.

We said our goodbyes before heading home. Kai and Jude lit the fire pits while Baker grilled food and Jenna and Viddy made sure we all ate something.

Layla stunned us with her arrival and her drastic change in appearance. She seemed to struggle with what to say or do, which ironically ended up drawing Six in. Neither of them is great with crowds and found comfort in each other that had the potential to grow into something great.

While Layla snuggled under Cash's arm and chattered quietly with Six, who leaned against me, I knew Six would find friendship with Layla far easier than she would with V. Six and V had put their differences aside while I was sick. Although there is peace between them now, I doubt they will ever be as close as V is with Jenna and Megan. It's sad, but sometimes the damage is too extensive, the wound too deep. Time can help mend it, but we would have to see how it played out.

Danny's funeral is a much larger affair. The church is filled with the family Viddy built and welcomed Danny into, but the graveside service gave other people the chance to say their goodbyes.

Standing with Six's hand in mine, I can't tear my eyes from Viddy. She stands up front between both her men, her face pale, her expression blank as she hides her pain from the world. Pain they would see as weakness.

I turn at the sound of motorcycles drawing close to see the Chaos Demons MC pulling up. They line the perimeter of the cemetery in a show of solidarity. The lead rider, Viper, climbs off his bike and extends his hand to Megan sitting behind him. Once she is steady on her feet, he watches her walk through the crowd to the front, nudging Kai aside so she can wrap her arms around Viddy.

Viddy dips her head and leans against Megan's shoulder, a single tear escaping as Megan whispers something only Viddy can hear.

"Who is that?" Six asks quietly from beside me.

"Megan. Viddy's sister, even though they don't share blood."

"Some of the strongest families have not a drop of blood shared between them. It doesn't make them any less brothers or sisters than Kai and Jude. Just look around at all the people here. Sure, some came to say goodbye to a good man, but others, they came for Viddy."

She's right. Chaos has no ties to Danny. Most probably never met him. But V loved Danny and Megan loves V. It really is as simple as that.

More bikes approach, an endless amount until I realize it's not just the mother chapter of Chaos but the sister chapter too. I see Scope with Mercy behind him and Wizz beside them. Then Blade rides in with his Raven Souls colors flying and Carnage bringing up the rear.

Six is right. Danny was loved, but these brothers and sisters came for V.

I tense when I see King hanging back. He doesn't leave his bike. He nods to something Sunshine says from where she sits behind Conan, but his eyes never stray from the scene in front of him. A man like King can't afford to let his guard down. He has too many enemies who would do anything to hurt him. Six is a testament to that.

He sees me looking and nods. He takes in Six, his head tilting for a second before he turns and takes in the people closer to him, arguing.

I relax a little and shake my head. I'm being paranoid. There is no way he can tell who Six is just by looking at her. Unlike Diesel and Orion, who have the same dark hair and light blue eyes he has, Six looks nothing like him. At least from what I can see at a distance.

Six looks up at me and nods in the direction of Baker, who stands up front with Viddy and her men but off to one side, detached and in his own world.

I press a kiss to her temple and release her hand. "Go. I'll be right here."

She offers me a sad smile and walks to the front, slipping under Baker's arm much as Megan did with V moments before. He folds her into his embrace and I have to swallow when I see his shoulders shake, finally giving in and allowing himself to grieve.

It's hard to lose a good man at any time, but Danny had become so much more than just a member of V's security team. Friend, brother, and hero. I can't help but think as I gaze around at all these people that Danny would have been happy with the turnout.

CHAPTER FORTY-EIGHT

SIX

$\mathcal{I}$ sit on the edge of the sofa as Kai spreads photos and papers across the floor. Neither of us speaks, both of us knowing this could turn out to be nothing or be a game-changer.

"Jude is gonna be here in about thirty minutes with pizza. He said he has a contact who might have a few extra things to add so he's gonna swing by for those first."

I look at him and nod before looking out the window where Viddy and Will sit.

Kai follows my line of sight. "They've been through too much to throw their friendship away, but he would have. For you, he'd give Viddy up in a heartbeat."

I open my mouth to protest, but he stops me. "It's as it

should be, Six. When you love someone so wholeheartedly, little else matters."

"I don't know about that, Kai. I understand losing yourself in a person, but there was a moment when Will was sick when I was more than lost. I couldn't see the point in holding on when he was slipping away. If you take away my reason for living, I might as well lie down and die too. But then I realized something."

"What's that?"

"How utterly selfish I was being. Will pulled me out of hell and gave me this whole new world. He gave me love and happiness. He gave me safety and a home. He gave it all to me freely, wanting nothing in return. By giving up, I'd be throwing it back in his face. He didn't save me for him. He saved me for me. The only way to honor it is to do just that—live. It would hurt to have to do it without him. It would hurt so bad that just the thought of it feels like a knife plunging through my heart, but I'd do it anyway. He gave me a life. How can I do anything but live it?"

He stares at me, which is hardly surprising given that it's unlike me to waffle, but I've had a lot of time to think about it. While Will lay there in that hospital bed so close and yet a million miles away, I ignored the toxic whispers that threatened to pull me under. That insidious voice that spent a lifetime murmuring its poison into my ear.

Instead, I took that fear and wrapped it up as a shiny promise.

I wouldn't give up. Somehow, I'd find my way to happiness once more. I knew how to recognize it now. Knew what it felt like, what it tasted like. It had changed me, filled me, and reshaped me from a scared girl into, well, a scared woman.

One that now had the tools and the will to fight back and to recognize my worth.

"At first glance, it's hard to see how you two could work. The differences are staggering. But after watching you together, somehow it just makes sense. Like it had to be him for you and you for him. Perhaps that's why I never really saw him with a woman the whole time I've known him. He was waiting for you."

I smile widely at him. "You know, people told me you were a little rough around the edges but you're nothing but a teddy bear really. Don't worry, I'll keep it a secret so I don't blow your street cred."

He looks at me for a beat before throwing his head back and laughing loudly. It draws the attention of Will and Viddy, who looks at Kai with a sparkle in her eye before she looks at me with a soft smile on her face.

Why do I get the feeling he doesn't let go like that very often?

I smile back just as softly. Maybe we'll never be as close as she is with the others, but it's hard to dislike someone when they care so deeply about the man I love. Even if that person is a little psychotic and a whole lot scary.

I pull my eyes away and focus on the photos spread out before me. I don't know why I was expecting mugshots. Clearly, I'd become somewhat addicted to the crime channel since being introduced to it.

These photos hit harder than any mugshot could have. They are candid pictures taken of various people and in different places. People who laughed and smiled with each other. They were friends, family even. Knowing that predators were lurking within the group makes me feel sick. It's so easy to see evil as a black entity that looms over everything, smiting people with its cruelty. It's something we convince ourselves we'll be able to detect and avoid. Smart people know the signs, right? Trouble is, evil is smart too. They were taught the same signs and like any true predator, they adapt.

Lurking in the shadows is a thing of the past. Hiding in plain sight is often the simplest way to avoid being caught. Nobody suspects their brother-in-law or neighbor or school-teacher of having a black soul. Because you're smart enough to spot a killer, right?

I see a picture of a young-looking Layla standing beside an older man. They both smile at the camera as they pose. Both of those smiles are masks. His to hide his lack of emotion, hers to hide her wealth of it. But the eyes don't lie. His dark ones are cold and empty whereas Layla's look haunted. It makes me want to reach into the photo and wrap my arms around her. I'd whisper in her ear that everything would be okay, to hold on a little longer.

"She looks so young. There was a moment when I met her. I stood by and let her get hurt. Then, to live with myself, I forgot her. But looking at the younger version of her now, I have to wonder how I managed it," Kai says from beside me.

"Self-preservation. Humans are capable of both amazing and horrendous things in their bid to survive. It doesn't make it right, but it doesn't necessarily make it wrong either."

"Maybe one day that will be true."

"The facts don't change, only the way in which you inter-pret the information. I have witnessed many atrocities. There have been moments where I've tried to help, moments I've run, and moments I've stood by and done nothing. I'm not infallible. I'm good and bad. Both and neither. Life is all about balance.

You take lives. Each one leaves a taint on your soul but if you hadn't, perhaps your life would have taken you in a different direction. Perhaps if you never pulled the trigger all the times you did then the butterfly effect that led you here would have changed its course. You are who you are now, a loving partner, brother and in some people's eyes, a hero because pulling that trigger shaped you.

"People have died at your hands, Kai, but people have lived because of those hands too."

"How the fuck do you have so wide a view of the world when you grew up in a cage?"

"Being forced into a cage didn't make me small, it just made me bend. Being forced to mindlessly comply didn't steal my dreams. People only have power over you if you give it to them. I didn't really understand that until Ten. But there are always choices. All you can do at the time is pick the one you can live with."

"Maybe. I still feel like I could have done more to help Layla back then."

"She told me, you know, about that night. She forgives you because she too made a choice. You both chose to live. Any other move you made would have resulted in your deaths. They were awful choices, but they meant you both lived to fight another day."

He says nothing, but I can see my words are getting to him.

"I don't recognize her husband. If he did come to the facility, I never saw him." I look over the photos some more, taking my time to study each of them, pointing out any faces I think look familiar.

"Her." I point at a young blonde woman with her hand on

the chest of a handsome man in a dark suit wearing an even darker scowl.

"You recognize her? I have to admit I'm surprised. I thought if anyone it would be the man beside her."

"Why? Who is he?"

"Dimitri Aslanov."

I shake my head. The name is not ringing any bells.

"No, I don't recognize the name or his face and that's not the kind of face I'd forget."

He smirks at me, making me blush.

"That's not what I meant. He…how do I put it? He exudes power, even in a photograph."

And he does. Even with the scowl firmly in place, there is something alluring about him.

"Anyway, it's not her I recognize, it's the crest. You see that pin on her bag?"

He leans down and picks up the photo and scans it.

"I've seen that before, more than once in fact. If memory serves, and let's be honest, it does, I've seen that same crest eleven times. That doesn't mean there weren't more, that's just the only time I spotted it."

"Where did you see it?"

"On the jackets on some of the new slaves that got brought in."

"Oh fuck," he hisses.

"What? What does it mean?"

"That crest is an emblem. It belongs to Willow Creek Academy—a privately funded school for troubled rich kids whose parents have more money than god and fewer morals than a hooker blowing a priest."

I grimace at his gross analogy, then freeze when his words penetrate.

"They are recruiting from the school? How is that even possible? Surely someone is missing them. One child should raise eyebrows, but eleven?"

Viddy's voice sounds out. "That's something I'd like the answer to as well. And luckily, I know just the person."

I lift my head and see Viddy and Will looking at the photo. I never heard them come back in.

"Who?" Will asks before I see a lightbulb go off over his head.

Will might have figured it out, but thankfully Viddy explains it to the rest of us. "Dulce. She's undercover. Or was. The person she was looking into was swept up in the investigation Layla triggered, but this school isn't far from there. Dulce was playing girlfriend to the dickhead's son so I'm thinking she could work this to her advantage and switch schools to finish out the last half of the year."

"Who is Dulce?"

Viddy looks at me and grins.

CHAPTER FORTY-NINE

WILL

"*I* can't believe they are taking these girls from their school and nothing is being said about it. How is that possible, Will?"

I stroke her hair as she lies on my chest.

"I don't know. Hopefully Dulce will be able to figure something out."

She sighs but doesn't say anything else. I understand where she's coming from though. Even after everything I've seen and done, nothing turns my stomach more than knowing children are being preyed on for the sexual gratification of an aging flaccid-dicked banker with a god complex, who can't get it up for anyone unless they are smaller and weaker than he is.

"I need to talk to you about something else."

She lifts her head to look at me, the sheet slipping down to reveal her bare back.

I trail my fingers over her skin, which pebbles with goosebumps.

"What is it?" she asks quietly, making me wonder if there was something in my voice that made her guard go up.

"I didn't know all those bikers were going to show up yesterday. I figured Megan and one of her men would come, but I had no clue that many people would turn up."

"Okay?" She frowns, not getting what I'm putting down.

"One of the men in the crowd is the man I suspect of being your father. If he is, then two of the other men are your brothers."

She gasps, looking at me, unsure.

"Do you know him?"

"Not well, but I know of him. Everyone does. He is somewhat of an enigma. I'm not sure who the real man is. I doubt many are, barring his old lady. I will say he's a good man. One who has made some fucked-up decisions, most in the name of protecting people, but not everyone was happy with his reasoning. There is some animosity between King and his boys, but it's based on their history, not yours. Don't let their opinions of the man get in the way of you forming your own."

She frowns. "Do you not remember who you're talking to? I seem to remember you telling me how pigheaded, stubborn, and rebellious I am. If they dislike him, I'd probably like him just on the principle of the matter."

I chuckle, knowing she's right. It's pretty amazing to see how far she's come. Once scared of her own shadow, she's now determined to stand strong even when she's afraid.

"What if he doesn't like me or wants nothing to do with

me? I mean, if my own mother didn't want me, why would he? He already has his two perfect boys. What more could he want?"

"His beautifully imperfect daughter." I tug her higher. Her bare breasts press against my chest as I kiss her, softly at first before deepening it.

I pull away but only so I can murmur against her lips. "He'll love you. How can he not?" I nip her lip and soothe the sting with my tongue.

I'm hard as a rock and two seconds away from picking her up and yanking her down on my cock when she pulls away.

"Can...can I..." she bites her lips, hesitating.

"What is it? You can say anything to me, firefly. You know that.

"I don't think I can do the running through the woods thing while you chase me anymore. Not after everything," she admits. I pause before reaching up and tucking a strand of hair behind her ear.

"Do I love hunting you down and fucking you while you're helpless? You know I do. But it's not a deal-breaker. If you only want vanilla sex from now until the day I die, then it will still be the best sex I've had in my life."

"I like the feeling I get when you chase me. Sure, there is fear involved but it only heightens everything. When you catch me, you consume me, taking everything you want. But you give more than you take. I trust you not to hurt me, but I like it when I have no control. It makes no sense given the way I grew up. But with you, instead of wanting to rage at the cage, I want to grip the bars while you fuck me."

I groan, my dick throbbing at the literal image that paints.

"Can we do something else that will trigger the same kind of responses, just not…"

I place my finger over her lips. "We can do anything you want. There are so many things I want to show you, teach you. And if you find you don't like something, then we don't do it again. It's as simple as that."

I move her so she's straddling me. "While my leg still hurts, you're going to have to do all the work." It's bullshit of course. It would take more than a bullet to stop me from flipping her over and thrusting my cock inside her.

"Are you wet for me, firefly?"

She nods.

"Show me."

She slides a hand between her legs and dips a finger inside her pussy, her knuckles brushing against my dick. Slipping her finger free, she holds it up for me to see.

Gripping her hand, I bring it to my mouth and suck her finger clean, reveling in her sharp inhale.

"Hmm…delicious. You are wet but I think you could be wetter. Climb up and straddle my face, firefly. I want to taste the nectar from the source."

Her eyes widen as her breathing picks up. I grip her hips and lift her until she takes over and climbs up my body, settling her pretty little pussy over my mouth.

"Such a good girl. Now time for a reward."

I don't tease her. I yank her down hard against me until she is all I can taste and smell. I feast on her as if she is the last thing I'll ever eat. And if I get my way, she will be.

CHAPTER FIFTY

SIX

I grip Will's hand tightly. I know he said he wouldn't leave my side, but I have to be sure.

I've faced down and attacked a crazy mom and a sex trafficking ring, not to mention a whole host of shit that would make most people crumble. So why the heck is meeting the man who could be my father the one thing to send me into a downward spiral of self-doubt and worry?

"Everything is going to be fine, firefly. I promise," Will murmurs before pressing a kiss to my temple.

The two bikes stop at the end of the driveway. I watch as both men climb off and hang their helmets on the handlebars before walking toward us.

I glance at the man with startling green eyes, but my focus is all for the man beside him. He's tall and muscular, his body fit and belying his age that is only given away by the silver threaded through his once dark hair.

As he draws closer, I feel my palms begin to sweat, especially when he seems to be studying me as much as I am him.

He's a handsome man. I can see why ladies might like him, but I have to wonder what it is about him that inspires such insane behavior. Will didn't hold back the info he had on King. Truth be told, what he gave me wasn't much more than what is already public knowledge. But one look at the man and I can see straight through the non-threatening slightly hunched vibe he is trying to give off. After the men I've been exposed to, he doesn't stand a chance of hiding his true colors. Normal everyday people I struggle with, but people with a dark side and a hidden agenda, I can read like a freaking book. Regular nice people, not so much. They were as foreign to me as windows and snow before I came here.

"King. Blade. Thanks for coming. Let's take this inside, shall we?" Will offers.

Both Blade and King look from Will to me, neither of them making a move to enter.

"Who is this?" Blade asks Will, making me roll my eyes.

"You could just ask me," I point out. I'm not going to let them speak over me or pretend I'm not here. I've had enough of that to last a lifetime.

"Indeed," Blade concedes.

I scowl at him, which I turn onto Will when he chuckles.

"This is Six."

"Six. That's an unusual name," King replies, his voice deep and soothing. I get a brief flash of what it could have been like as a little girl listening to him reading me stories about kings, princesses, and dragons, causing a sharp pain in my chest over all that might have been stolen from us because of someone else's misguided quest for vengeance.

"I'm an unusual woman," I answer when I realize I was staring at him.

He cocks his head before looking at Will once more. "This gonna be something Six here can hear?"

"This is about Six and it's about you too. Come on, let's sit down. It's not an easy story to tell."

Will turns and tugs me down the hallway, leaving the others no choice but to follow. He leads us to the living room and indicates for them to sit, while taking a chair himself and pulling me onto his lap.

"Okay, Will. You have us here and well, patience never was my strong suit. So what's this all about?" King asks, leaning forward with his arms resting on his legs in a deceptively casual pose. I cock my head, fascinated by him, not just because he could be my father but because he seems so at odds with himself. It's like he is so much more than the persona he shares. If anyone can relate to that it's me.

"I'm not even sure where to start," Will admits, his hand squeezing my thigh lightly. "What I know about you could be written on a postage stamp. Oh, I've heard rumors from everything declaring you a terrorist to the next person in line for the presidency." He smirks before shaking his head. "Facts, however, are harder to come by. All I ask is that you keep your cool around Six while we try to figure it out."

One short sharp nod is all he gets from King while Blade does nothing but watch me with interest.

"Orion and Diesel's mom was called Melinda, right?"

King tenses, his body strung tight as he waits for what comes next. I can see we caught him off guard. In all the likely scenarios he prepared for, the mention of his ex-wife likely wasn't one of them.

"Did you ever meet Melinda's sister?"

He frowns and shakes his head.

"Melly never had a sister."

I look at Will, anxiety humming just under my skin.

"Are you sure?" Will asks, holding up his hand before King can reply. "We know Melinda and you were deep undercover. What I'm asking is if Melinda had a family she distanced herself from, to keep them safe perhaps?"

An expression passes over King's face that's gone before I can get a read on it. He stands abruptly. "We're done here. Melly is none of your fucking business."

Will lifts me gently before getting to his feet. He doesn't grimace even though I know his leg is still causing him pain, but I see his hands tense at his sides.

He moves forward and places me at his back protectively. "I asked you to keep your shit together, King. I'm not the bad guy here. I'm trying to be diplomatic, but if you want to throw your attitude around, please have at it."

"What I want is to go home to my woman."

I peek around Will's back and see Blade watching me with a frown. I can see the cogs spinning in his head as he tries to put the pieces together.

"Did Melinda have a sister?" Will repeats, a touch of anger threaded through his voice. I slide my hands up his back in a soothing gesture. He's so worried about me getting hurt. What he doesn't realize is, with him beside me, I'm untouchable.

"I don't know what you're talking about."

"Look —" Will snaps but I step beside him and slip my hand into his.

"He's protecting his boys. He's protecting the memory of their mother," I tell him quietly.

King's eyes flash to mine in surprise, but it's Blade that speaks. "Are you claiming to be Melly's sister? Because I hate to break it to you sweetheart, it's impossible."

"Why?" I frown. I mean I'm not, but how can they be sure?

"Because Melly's parents were dead before she even joined the bureau. It's one of the reasons why she was recruited. If you were her sister, you'd be a fuck of a lot older. I don't know what game you're playing but —

"I'm not Melly's sister," I tell him, cutting him off.

"But it turns out she could be my aunt."

That shuts them both up for a minute. They relax a touch but that soon changes when the next words leave my mouth. "And there's a very real chance that King is my father."

The bomb drops and I brace myself for the fallout.

Will pulls me tightly to him, ready to protect me if needed. But truth is, I owe this man nothing. If he wants nothing to do with me, it will leave a mark, but it won't be noticeable on a heart already littered with scars. I've survived worse and lived to tell the tale. I'm not going to beg for scraps from anyone.

King doesn't say a word as he storms out.

I swallow as Blade levels an angry glower on me.

"Don't," Will warns him but Blade ignores him.

Blade looks me up and down and clearly finds me lacking. He sneers and steps forward.

Will moves to step in front of me but I halt his movements with a hand on his arm.

"Smarter women than you have tried to bring King down. Each and every one of them failed. You're no different than the rest of the greedy bitches with dollar signs in their eyes, you're just working a different angle."

Will reaches for his gun but again I stop him, turning my back on Blade completely. I don't like him, but I don't believe Will would let me anywhere near a man who would shoot me in the back.

I look up at Will's angry face and smile, reaching up to cup his cheek.

"Don't. It's not worth it. They're not worth it. I have everything I'll ever need standing right in front of me. You showed me what I'm worth, Will, and it's more than what they're offering." I shrug. "Seems I might have made a lucky escape," I tease as he tugs me around the neck and yanks me forward. I faceplant against this chest and let his scent soothe the sting of Blade's disdain. I meant what I said. I don't need them in my life.

"I asked you here today as a favor. I asked you here even though Six had reservations because I thought King needed to know, and you just shit all over it. Get the fuck out, Blade. Go back to King, tell him to keep his head buried in the sand. Believe me when I say it's his loss."

I turn to face him and see his anger has fled, leaving only curiosity.

"Look—"

"No. It's time for you to go, Blade. Whatever you do though, warn King to be wary of any suspicious emails. Some things you can't unsee."

He looks like he's going to say something else but thinks better of it. He heads out to follow King. When the door closes, I feel my shoulders slump, half in relief and half in disappointment.

"I'm sorry, Six."

"Nothing to be sorry about. You didn't do anything wrong. If he changes his mind, he knows where I am, but I'm not chasing him."

"Good girl."

CHAPTER FIFTY-ONE

WILL

"What are you guys doing here?" I ask as I step back and let Viddy and Wyatt through.

"We come bearing gifts. Okay, mine's a pretty shitty gift. It's more photos and building specs Kai found sifting through the files. The trouble is, there is so much shit that it takes time. He's in a unique position that he's been on the inside so he can see things the rest of us don't but it's a slow process. Wyatt, on the other hand, has a welcome to the neighborhood gift Jenna had Luna put together."

I look at his empty hands and raise a questioning eyebrow.

"It's in the car. I wanted to make sure you were home first. That thing weighs a fuck-ton. Christ knows what she put in there."

I laugh and usher them inside. "We were just going to have lunch if you want some."

"I'm good," Viddy answers at the same time Wyatt replies, "I could eat," making Viddy roll her eyes comically.

"Where's Jenna and Esme?"

"Megan and her men have come for an impromptu visit, so I've been kicked out," he grumbles.

"I thought you got on with the Chaos boys."

"He did until they started stealing his daughter from him. Now he just gets pissy and growls."

"Hey, if they want to hold a baby, they can go hold their own," he complains.

"See?" Viddy laughs as we enter the kitchen, where Six is making sandwiches.

"Oh, hey. Do you want me to get out of your way?"

Viddy waves her off as she sits at one of the stools next to the counter. "You're fine. We aren't here for Will anyway. We came to see you. I can't remember if you've met before, but just in case—Six, this is Wyatt, one of my best friends. Wyatt, this is Six."

"Nice to meet you officially. Sorry it's taken so long but life has been a little hectic lately."

Six laughs. "I understand that. It's been quiet here for a few days so I'm waiting for the SWAT team to storm the house or for a swarm of deadly locusts to lay plague on the world."

Viddy snickers before placing the file she's carrying on the counter.

"These are from Kai. He and Jude are working on something today, but he wanted me to get these to you ASAP."

"No worries. I'll look over them while I eat. Do you guys want one?"

"I'm fine, thank you, but Wyatt has hollow legs so he'll take whatever you're offering," Viddy jokes.

"I've got it, Six. You sit and look over the photos." I know it's been playing on her mind a lot lately, wondering what's happened to the others, especially now M and R are dead.

She sits beside Viddy and takes a bite of her sandwich as I make one for myself and Wyatt.

"What's that all about?" Wyatt asks me as Viddy and Six talk quietly, pointing to the images.

"They are trying to locate the facility Six and the other slaves were being held in."

"Slaves? What?"

I look at him and realize just how much he's missed. "Shit, pull up a pew, this might take a while," I warn him as I start at the beginning and tell him everything, from the second I met Six to the confrontation with King a few days ago.

"Jesus, fuck. I feel like I've been living in a bubble. If I'd have known—"

I cut him off with a shake of my head. "We didn't want you caught up in this, not with Jenna needing you. She and Esme rightly needed to be your priority. If we'd have brought you in and your mind was with Jenna, you'd have ended up killed. And that's not something any of us were willing to risk."

"This is it!" Six exclaims, drawing our attention.

"What? You found it?" I walk over to her and stare down at the photo in her hand.

It's a room that brings a new meaning to neutral. Everything inside it is cream. Cream walls, cream rugs, and a long cream sofa with a dark wood end table beside it—the only item in the room that's not cream. On top of it seems to be a selection of tools but I can't quite make out what they are in this shot.

The picture itself is pretty unremarkable. Nothing inside it captures my attention. In fact, it's the kind of image I'd scan my eyes over before moving on to the next. Perhaps that's exactly the point.

"How can you tell?" Viddys asks.

"I spent so many wasted hours and days kneeling on that rug I'd know it anywhere. This is the main playroom, usually favored by X. He said the warm ambiance kept him calm, then focused his training around that theme. He projected the need to sit still and be quiet, even when he was deliberately attempting to distract us just so he could dole out punishments like candy."

"Plus, she has a memory that won't let her forget. If Six says this is the place, then it's the place."

"Do you know where this photo was taken? I can tell you it's the correct place, but I still don't know where it is."

"I'm not sure, but Kai might know. Let's see if there are any others that came from the same place." Viddy says, sifting through the pile. In the end, there are three shots. The original one, one of a room that looks more like a dormitory and I'm assuming is the place trafficked women were kept, and the last one—a photo of a small shack with the desert as a backdrop.

"Son of a bitch. You were in the desert. Makes sense, it's quiet and secluded. Nature works against your ability to escape. By the same reasoning though, a building like that would stand out. It must be hiding in plain sight as something else or there would be a lot of questions raised."

"Military base perhaps? If so, I'm guessing Nevada."

"That was my guess too."

"Wait. You mentioned Cohen before. He was a part of it?" I remember her mentioning his name but as he's dead I didn't dwell on it much.

"M mentioned him, but I don't know the name to be able to apply it to a face. If he were a trainer, we would only ever use an initial. I don't recall a trainer called C in any of the compounds I was held at over the years."

"That would make it too easy," Wyatt grumbles, scrolling through his cell phone.

Turning it, I see a news article pulled up on his screen about the man's untimely death. Beside it is a photo.

Six studies it, her head cocking to the side as her brow furrows.

"He's familiar but I've never seen him before in my life. He just reminds me of someone else."

We all look at her waiting for her to continue.

"Who?"

"He looks like X. He was the nicest of all the instructors. They have the same coloring and bone structure. Their eyes are the same color too, but X is older. His hair is mostly gray, but it's threaded with blond that I assume is his natural color."

"Oh, fuck," Viddy hisses as Wyatt taps the screen once more, this time bringing up a second image.

He spins it around to show Six.

She nods before looking up at our grim faces. "That's X. What's going on? Why do you all look like that?"

"Because that is Xavier F Michaels. Cohen's uncle and the former vice president."

CHAPTER FIFTY-TWO

SIX

I stare at Wyatt, trying to process his words.

"Vice president as in Vice President of the United States of America?" My voice squeaks.

I know who the president is because I'd watched enough television to catch his name, but I had no clue who the vice president is or was.

"We never stood a chance, did we?" I murmur, the sickening realization making me sway.

Will reaches out and steadies me before tugging me to him and holding me tightly. "He isn't in power anymore. He stepped down after Cohen's misdeeds came to light, casting a shadow over the man and what he stood for. Or at least that's what we thought. Now it's clear to see that he left to stop people from digging any further into his personal life. What I don't understand is how? The whys don't matter. People do fucked-up things all the time that make no sense to anyone but themselves. But the hows are different. How did a man that high profile manage not just to visit a facility holding trafficked slaves but do it without detection? You said this place was littered with guards. How did one not sell him out? They could have asked for any amount of money and they'd have still had the media bending over for them wanting an exclusive," Wyatt points out.

"He never entered the building where we were kept. We only saw him when we went for training. It was always the same guards on the door so maybe only a select few knew he was there," I muse. It seems unlikely that someone so high profile could keep his anonymity, but I guess everyone there had secrets to keep.

"It's possible. Or maybe everyone just knew if he went down, he would take them all down too." Viddy sighs. "See, this is why I hate politics. The ratio of dirty politicians to genuine ones who want to make a difference is largely skewed in the wrong direction."

"Perhaps with all the media coverage lately, thanks to Layla naming all those names, the public is demanding more answers and wanting people to be held accountable. Too many times bigwigs with more money than morals have run good people, innocent people, into the ground. It's at the point where enough is enough," Will adds.

"The irony isn't lost on me that as these so-called law-abiding citizens fall from grace, I become more popular." Viddy sighs, making Wyatt and Will grin.

"You're a modern-day Robin hood. Before, people whispered about you. They heard the rumors. You dealt out punishment where you saw fit. But you protected the innocent and that's something people so desperately want to see now that their faith in the system has been obliterated," Wyatt replies before finishing off his sandwich.

She rolls her eyes. "I'm aware, but it's annoying and it's trickling down. Do you know the police commissioner offered Jude his job back?"

I look at Viddy in confusion.

"Jude was an undercover detective. He gave it up for Viddy," Will fills me in quietly.

"Oh. Yeah, that will never work." I shake my head, making Viddy laugh.

"That's exactly what Jude said, and damn was he pissed. Whatever I feel about it all matters little, but Jude believed in what he was doing. He might have made some questionable choices, but he genuinely believed he was saving lives by taking down Zodiac. And he was. He just never stood a chance against all this."

She moves her hand over her petite frame, making me chuckle.

"I'm guessing he told them to take a running jump?" Will smirks.

"Oh yeah, but with far more F-bombs."

I let my eyes drift back to the photos as they talk among themselves for a minute. It seems so bizarre looking at a snippet of the world in which I was held captive through a lens.

"We need to call in King."

Wyatt's voice has my head snapping up. He watches me, a soft look of regret on his face.

"I'm sorry, Six. I understand from what Will said that he's not your favorite person right now, but he might be the only person who can shine a light on this. He knew at least two of the players personally, possibly more. He could be the key."

My shoulders sag. I didn't want to bother King again. I didn't want him to feel like I was forcing the issue or trying to build something with him when there is no foundation. He might well be my sperm donor but that doesn't make him my father.

None of that matters though, does it? Not when I'm on the outside looking in. I swore I'd do what I could to find the others and I meant it. If that means I have to deal with King's disdain, then so be it.

I think about the cryptic speech M gave me about my dad messing things up again and wonder if it's all connected somehow.

"Whatever you guys think will help. I can handle anything thrown at me if it means there's a chance I could help the others."

Viddy bites her lip and looks away. I recognize the look for what it is. Avoidance. Not because she doesn't want to help but because she doesn't think the others would have survived this long.

"I have to try, Viddy. If not me, then who? Someone needs to stand up for them."

She looks at me with what I think is respect. It's not something I'm used to seeing so I'm not one-hundred-percent sure, but when she nods and reaches for my hand to give it a brief squeeze, I figure I'm right.

"We'll find out what or if King knows anything. But he doesn't get to take potshots at your expense. I don't care who he is. You're Will's and that makes you mine too. If he upsets you, I'll geld him," Viddy growls.

"That's the nicest thing you've ever said to me."

Wyatt laughs. "Girls are so fucking weird. Speaking of. I have a gift for you, courtesy of my woman and her friend. A friend, I should point out, who is with Orion, your could-be brother."

I shrug. "He doesn't know about me, so I doubt anything is poisoned."

Viddy snorts as Wyatt shakes his head with a grin. Will wraps his arm around me and chuckles.

"Orion wouldn't hurt you unless you tried to hurt his family or his club. He's a good man for a motorcycle president. The only reason I brought it up is that King might be burying his head in the sand, but if Orion and Diesel find out they have a sister, they'll want to know you. Trust me, this isn't the first time a sister came out of the woodwork," Wyatt says sardonically, making me feel like I've missed something.

"Wait, I have a sister?"

Viddy shakes her head. "Megan, Orion, and Diesel share a mom, not a dad. But I guess that makes you sort of cousins, I think. Jesus. My brain hurts just trying to figure it all out."

"Yes, I can see how this must be taxing for you," I deadpan, surprising us both with my sarcasm. Viddy recovers first. A grin spreads across her face as she winks at me.

"Sassy. I know grown men who aren't brave enough to speak to me like that," she says softly. Although there is a warning in her voice, I can tell she's not really angry.

"Way I see it, you've already shot at me once. Things can only get better, right? I mean, you love Will. I love Will. So we have that in common. You're..." I search for the right word. "Intimidating to the point I wonder if men's balls shrivel up like raisins when you walk past. But I know Will wouldn't let me anywhere near you if he thought you'd hurt me. The fact I'm here and not tied naked to his bed suggests you're not planning to kill me anytime soon. So I think maybe if you want, we could try the friends thing. I'm not sure I'll be good at it. I've never really had friends before but you're Will's, which means you're mine." I turn her words back on her.

She looks at me, her face giving nothing away before she nods. "Okay, firefly. Friends." She winks.

I know it cost her. When she sees me, she sees Danny dead on the floor. But if she can move past it for Will, I can move past the fact she shot at me too.

Something tells me though, in years to come when we're gray and old, these stories will be passed down to the next generation of crazy.

"I'll call King." She waits for me to object but I don't. I know it needs to be done.

"Do it. Hopefully he'll figure out an angle we overlooked."

CHAPTER FIFTY-THREE

SIX

I watch the calm water and try to emulate it, but it seems to be a fruitless endeavor. I've told myself all the reasons I shouldn't care, but it's impossible to completely snuff out the tiny flame. It's not that I want or need King's approval like so many other jaded kids. For me, it's more about feeling a void where my father should have been. My mother was evil. There are no two ways about it. She might not have started that way, but it doesn't change that the woman she became was likely someone her sister would have hated. I guess after finding out how awful my mom was, it would have been nice to have a relationship with King, if only to know that there was someone out there connected to me. It's hard not to feel small and untethered sometimes. Say what you like about being raised in a cage, but even a bird sings. There is comfort to be found in the familiar. Home is a place in your heart, not where you lay your head. Being out here in the big wide world while people pick apart my childhood with pitying looks and sympathetic coos makes me feel uncomfortable. And if I'm honest, a little lost.

The only thing keeping me grounded is Will, which brings up another issue I've been trying to ignore. Am I using the man as a crutch? I don't doubt my feelings for him, at least not now. But am I relying solely on him to make me happy? When I thought he was going to die I contemplated taking my own life so I didn't have to live without him. I know that's not a normal response. It can't be, or there would be no lost souls wandering the earth writing songs about heartache and grief. In the end I fought the urge. But would I always find the strength to push forward, or would it wear me down over time? I might not have a complete understanding of what Will does, but I understand enough to tell it's not the safest job in the world. There will be times I pace the floor, praying he makes it home in one piece. And there may come a time when the knock at the door in the early hours of the morning signals that he won't.

Can I live without him?

"What's got you thinking so hard over there?"

I jump at the sound of Will's voice. I hadn't even heard him approach.

"Sorry, I was in a world of my own."

He sighs and sits next to me on the chair beside mine, his warm hand sliding over my thigh.

"Talk to me, Six. No secrets between us, remember?"

Now it's my turn to sigh. I lean my head against his shoulder so I don't have to look at him, worried I might see answers in his eyes I won't like. The truth is a fickle bitch like that, not giving a shit about the blow she lands.

"I'm worried I'm too reliant on you. I don't want to bleed you dry but I'm scared of losing you. I don't think I can cope without you."

"I call bullshit," he answers with zero hesitation.

I lift my head and look at him, surprised by his answer.

"How can you say that? There was a moment when you nearly didn't make it that I wanted to give up."

He cups my cheek, his thumb skating over my bottom lip.

"You didn't though, did you? For three weeks I laid in that bed on the brink of death and yet you kept on fighting for both of us. That's all you can do, Six. It's all any of us can do. If I die, you just have to keep on fighting for both of us. I'm not saying it won't be hard. I'm not saying it won't hurt because it will, but the payoff is worth the risk. I'd rather spend one minute with you and die tomorrow than live another fifty years without you by my side. If you died, I would honor your memory. I'd keep fighting, even if only so I could sit out here at the end of the day and feel the specter of you beside me. We are all destined to die, Six. One day will be our last and when it's over, I want to take a million memories of you with me. Don't let your fear of losing me or losing yourself stop you from living."

He presses his lips to mine and kisses me gently. I grip his shirt and anchor myself to him, letting his words wrap around me like a cloak. I open my mouth when he demands entrance and melt into him when he takes control. He leaves me dazed and confused for a moment when he rips his lips from mine.

"Stand up."

I jolt at the tone of his voice. It's thick and heavy with lust.

I stand up and step in front of him, the blanket that was covering my lap slipping to the floor.

"Turn around."

I do as he asks and face the water once more, my breathing picking up and leaving little white clouds in the cold winter air. Without the heated blanket over me, I feel the cold nip at me, but it does nothing to cool the fire burning low in my belly.

His hands smooth up over my thighs to my hips before he hooks his fingers into the waistband of my leggings and yanks them down, taking my underwear with them. I gasp in shock as the cold air hits me, but Will seems impervious to it.

"Bend over. Keep your legs straight."

I hesitate for a moment before bending at the waist and exposing myself to him. His groan of appreciation causes a rush of heat between my legs. I know he can see how wet I am and damn it if that doesn't just make me wetter.

"Such a pretty pussy," he murmurs almost to himself.

I wait for his fingers but gasp when his hot wet tongue lashes at me instead. I grip my shins, needing something to hold onto as Will begins to assault me in the most delicious way.

Just when I think I can't take anymore he slips a finger inside me.

"Will," I groan. Now that he's moved his mouth, the cold air hits my pussy, making me shiver. But it only adds to the pleasure.

"What do you want, firefly? My fingers?" He thrusts a second finger inside me and scissors them.

"My mouth?" He must move because I feel his hot breath against me.

"Oh, do you want something else?"

"I want you to fuck me." No point beating around the bush. If he doesn't fuck me in the next five seconds, I'm going to take matters into my own hands.

"You only have to ask." He tuts, letting me hear the smile in his voice.

I feel him moving around and hear the clink of his belt opening before the noise of his zipper makes my pulse quicken.

"Come sit on my lap facing the water," he orders me.

I stand up, pausing for just a moment as the blood that previously rushed to my head rushes back the other way. Hands on my hips guide me onto his lap, but before I can get comfortable, they slip under my ass and lift me.

"Put me inside you, firefly," he growls in my ear.

I reach between my legs and take hold of his cock. With my leggings still around my thighs, it's not the easiest thing to do but I maneuver enough to place his cock at my entrance. As soon as he feels my wet heat, he surges up while yanking my hips down, ripping a scream from my lungs.

He holds steady for a moment, giving me time to adjust as he reaches down, snags the blanket from the floor, and wraps it around us.

"Now we're both in our favorite place. You near the water and me inside your pussy." He bites my ear as he guides my hips up and down in a steady rhythm.

I grip the arms of the chair and use my arms to help lift me. He feels so deep in this position. There is a tiny bite of pain when he bottoms out inside me, but it doesn't put me off. I like the sharp edge it brings to the sweet pleasure.

I lean my head back and close my eyes, letting the sensations wash over me. Hot and cold, sweet and sharp. There is a duality to our lovemaking reminiscent of the differences between us.

We shouldn't work. On paper, this relationship was doomed to fail before we even started, yet we fit together as if we were made for each other.

"You unman me, Six. Christ, the things I want to do to you."

"Hmm," I moan. "Like what?"

"I want to paint you with my cum. I want to trace your lips with it, watch it drip from your tits, and rub it all over your clit while I force it inside you with my fingers."

"Yes," I agree, but I have a feeling this man could have me agreeing to anything. I rock faster, needing more.

"This is what it feels like to live, firefly. And one day I'm going to fill your belly with my babies. Pretty little girls with red hair just like their mama."

His words kick-start a storm inside me. I'd never thought much about having children of my own. There was no point looking toward the future when it was unlikely I'd survive very long.

"You want that?"

"I want everything with you," I whisper as his grip tightens and he moves me faster until my body is wound tighter than a coiled spring.

"Pinch your clit, Six. I want us to come together."

I reach between us and stroke my clit before pinching it hard and releasing it. The pulse of pain sends me hurtling over the edge. I tighten around Will and bite my lip hard enough to draw blood as I come.

"Yes. Fuck yes," he hisses as I feel his cock throb inside me as he comes too.

"There is nowhere on earth I'd rather be than right here inside you," he whispers against my ear as I lean back into him.

He pulls the blanket up high, tucking it firmly around us both while we catch our breath. I don't climb off him and he doesn't ask me to move. We sit, connected in the most primal of ways, joining my favorite place with his.

I never want to move. Moments like this are the closest I've come to heaven. But when Will's cell rings, it shatters the magic we created, letting real life spill into our bubble.

With a sigh, he lifts up, making me gasp and moan when I feel his softening cock start to harden once more.

I thought older men needed longer to recover?

The cell keeps ringing so I glance over my shoulder and find him frowning at me.

"I'll show you just how quickly I can recover, firefly, once I take this."

Crap. I didn't realize I said that out loud.

I look at him sheepishly as he answers his cell. I don't pay attention to what he's saying because the sneaky man slides his hand between my legs and starts playing with my already sensitive clit.

"Yeah, that's fine. See you then." He hangs up before urging me to stand up.

Once I do, he follows and stands behind me. "Viddy and King are on their way."

I reach down to pull my leggings back up when he spins me and bends me over the chair.

"What are you doing?" I gasp, gripping the arms of the chair so I don't fall over.

"Showing you what my recovery rate is like," he teases before his now hard cock thrusts inside me once more.

"But they'll be here—" My words get choked off as he thrusts into me harder and faster, his grip on my hips likely to leave bruises later.

"Then we better hurry up."

He's trying to kill me but as he bottoms out inside me, I realize I can't think of a better way to go.

CHAPTER FIFTY-FOUR

WILL

S he fidgets nervously beside me, her hand holding mine so tight her knuckles are turning white.

It makes me want to punch King in the face.

He sits opposite us, his eyes so laser-focused on Six that if he were anyone else, I'd have slit his throat. He sighs, turning his head away from Six to look at me.

"Tell me what you want from me."

"I don't want anything from you, King. Honestly, I'd rather you not be here at all. You acting like a dick is hurting Six and that makes me want to hurt you."

He looks back at Six before crossing his arms and leaning back against the chair. Viddy steps up behind us, letting King know where her loyalties lie. King's lip twitches but he wisely doesn't say anything. Viddy would have no problem shooting him just to wipe the smile off his face.

"Okay, I'm listening. Tell me your story," King tells Six, who tenses further.

"It's not a story. It's my life. I don't know you but everyone I've spoken to seems to think you're the only person who might be able to help. If it were just about me, I'd walk away and you'd never see me again. But it's not about me or you. It's about so much more than that."

She shakes her head, her face taking on that hazy look she gets when she's thinking about her past.

"There have been a lot of us over the years. More Twos and Fives and Eights than anyone could comprehend but there has only been one Six in eighteen years and that's me. We might find some of the others but most of the originals are long gone. For a lot of them, I will be the only one who'll remember them."

"Them?" he asks, his eyes going sharp.

"The other captives."

His eyes widen a fraction before he can school his features. "Trafficking?"

Six nods, still squeezing my hand. I brush my thumb over her knuckles, letting her know I'm not going anywhere.

"It wasn't the same for me though. I was always different. I never understood that until I was older. The guards treated me differently, which meant the other captives did too."

"Why? What makes you different?"

"I was born in captivity for a start, not stolen or sold into it like the others. All my life I was told that I'd been sold before I was even born. I was to remain pure but to receive the same training placed upon all captives. Until I turned eighteen, which is when my owner would collect me. M used to love telling me all the horror stories about what I could expect."

A psychological head game from a woman who orchestrated it all. Her mother was a sick fuck and if she wasn't dead, I'd wring her neck with my bare hands.

King looks from Six to me, his face clouding with anger as he makes his assumptions about how Six came into my life.

"Don't," Six says softly, drawing all our attention once more. "Don't look at him like that. He saved me in more ways than you can ever imagine. He never once made me feel weak or small, even when I was fragile enough that a single blow would shatter me. He helped me to heal so you, of all people, don't get to sit there and judge him."

Viddy steps forward and places her hand on Six's shoulder, lending her support, but Six doesn't need it. She's stronger than she realizes and in her defense of me, she's like a warrior walking through fire.

King leans forward, his elbows resting on his thighs. "How did you end up here?"

Six doesn't relax. Perhaps if King had apologized to her, she would have, but he's far too stubborn for that. Looking at the two of them now, it's not hard to see where Six herself gets that streak from.

"There were two of us being delivered to separate buyers. Two died in transit so I swapped places with her. With hoods on and the same dress, we passed as each other without too close of an inspection. All I had to do was switch the numbered hoods."

She swallows hard, likely remembering her friend.

"Let me get you some water," Viddy offers, squeezing her shoulder before heading toward the kitchen.

"So where do you come into this?" King asks me.

"When we were trying to track down Dale, we had a backup plan in place. He was supposed to meet with a recruiter. The only way to get access to the man was to order a slave. The problem is, we never banked on Cash getting shot or Lily and Jenna getting kidnapped. As shitty as it sounds, we just forgot until I got an encrypted email telling me my order was ready to be collected."

"And you thought, why the fuck not? I've already paid for her."

"That's your last chance. Say one more thing against him and I'll get Viddy to shoot you. I think she'd even enjoy it," Six snaps, jumping to her feet.

"Easy, killer. King's just being an asshole for the sake of it. It's who he is."

"I've had enough of dealing with assholes for a lifetime." She sighs as Viddy walks in with water and hands her the glass.

"Say the word and I have a bullet with his name on," she whispers loud enough for us to hear, making Six chuckle and King mutter under his breath.

"I couldn't just throw her back. At least here I could help her and find her somewhere safe to move on to, but then Two turned out to be Six and…"

Six jumps in with a soft smile. "I refused to let him go."

"I couldn't have let you walk away if my life depended on it."

She blushes that pretty pink that spreads over her chest, which in turn makes me think of her tits, which is not good. Sitting in front of King with a hard-on for his daughter, yeah that will get me shot even if he hasn't claimed her yet.

"What you said before about me being your father? It's not possible."

She looks at him and I see the brief moment of sadness cross her face, not for her but for him. Everything he believed is about to come tumbling down like a house of cards. He might be formidable, part myth, part legend, but he is still just a man. He still bleeds and feels pain like the rest of us.

"We were attacked. Will was shot and I was locked in." She looks at me quickly before answering. "The basement." I almost smirk at her trying to protect me but she needn't have bothered. King probably has a far more sinister setup than I for extracting information from people.

"That's when M told me who I really am. Who she really was."

CHAPTER FIFTY-FIVE

SIX

"She told me about having an older sister she loved. They were close, even more so when their parents died, making it just the two of them. I'm not sure what happened after that, but her sister was recruited and sent deep undercover."

"She thinks Melly was her sister?"

I nod. "She found out where she was sent and what happened to her and, for whatever reason, held you account-able. I have no idea if she was always twisted or if losing her sister broke something inside her, but everything after that became about revenge."

"Even if it were true that she was Melly's sister, and I'm not saying that it was because I couldn't see Melly just cutting her out like that, but how would she have found out where she was?"

I look at King, trying to read him, but the man is like a vault. Is he so sure that Melly wouldn't leave her sister behind? Because I'm not. I'm not saying she was a bad person, just that sometimes we make decisions that are best for ourselves, not for others around us. That's not necessarily a bad thing, but it's not to say it can't hurt others.

Viddy had filled me in about what Megan had learned from her mother. I don't doubt that she loved her kids and did what she could to protect them. But I'm still aware, as someone looking in from the outside, that it was her decisions that led her to put her kids in a volatile situation to begin with.

I'm not judging her. My heart breaks for all that she endured. But I'm not convinced she is the innocent angel they paint her as either. Death has a funny way of swaying people's perceptions. Flawed people in life suddenly become sainted in death. People who died alone find their names whispered on the tongues of people who only called themselves friends after they were gone. Again, I can't judge. I'm an outsider, but sometimes it takes someone looking in from a different angle to see what others have missed.

"The man who recruited Melinda told her where to find you and his version of what happened."

"Cohen?" he growls his name with so much hate it makes me shiver.

"Yeah. He helped her put together this plan and while that was taking shape, she was one of the lead trainers for their side business."

He rubs his hand over his face and sighs. "Tell me the rest."

"She came to Carnage and posed as a…" My voice trails off as I try to think of a term that isn't disrespectful. I've heard them called club whores, but I hate the term. They might be sleeping with all the men, but the men who are sleeping with all the girls don't get called whores. The double standard makes me grind my teeth.

"Bunny. Mercy asked them once what they prefer to be called and most went with bunny." Viddy laughs, picking up where my thoughts have gone.

Weird, but okay.

"Alright, bunny it is, but I'm not sure that's right either. Bunnies are at the club full time, right? M just went to party for one night."

"Ah, we get plenty of those too. They are just party girls looking for a wild night with a biker before going back to their safe and predictable lives." King shrugs.

I shrug too, not caring about MC politics.

"She came, intending to seek you out and sleep with you. She did, after slipping you something to make you agreeable. I'm not sure what exactly, as she didn't tell me. Her plan was to get pregnant, and she did. With me. I don't know if she would have kept coming around if she didn't get pregnant straight away or if she would have tried a different approach. A lot of her plan really did seem to rely on luck. But what she lacked in smarts she made up for in patience."

"You believe her? You said she was a psycho, so why would you take a word she said seriously?"

"Because she fucked up and I got away. This changed her entire plan. She decided to kill me and send you pictures." I keep that part vague, including what her original plan was. Some things he doesn't need to know. "She thought my death would hurt you. But given how you feel about me, I'm not sure her plan would have worked."

"You want a DNA test?" he asks me slowly.

Do I? I'm not sure anymore. Seems to me it might be better to leave this can of worms firmly shut but…"Yes."

"Fine. I'll arrange for one to be done tomorrow."

"No need. I already took the liberty of getting one done. Oh, don't look at me like that. It's not exactly hard to get a hair sample from either of you. I was just saving you both time." Viddy huffs when both King and I glare at her.

She pulls a sealed envelope from her bag and hands it to me.

"I don't know the result. That's between you and King, but this will at least give you an answer one way or another. What you do with the knowledge is up to you."

I want to be mad at her, but I know she didn't do it out of spite. If I want any kind of closure, I need to know.

"Tell me the rest first," King says softly, reaching out to take the envelope from me.

I don't let go straight away, worried he might rip it to shreds before I can read it. But trust has to start somewhere. With a reluctant sigh, I release it.

He places it on the table in front of us, staring at it as if it's a swarm of bees. I'm not sure how I'm supposed to feel right now. He looks so horrified that I could be his. Despite making my peace with not having him in my life, it hurts.

I start talking, needing him to refocus. "There was a hands-off order in place. I was to be trained just like the others but no penetration."

It works. He looks at me with sadness in his eyes. He's a

smart man. He knows that no penetration doesn't mean I was spared anything else.

"At the time, I was told it was because my owner wanted that honor. But M enlightened me on a few things. She was technically my owner. I was supposed to be delivered to wherever the heck she planned to keep me while she implemented the next part of her plan."

"God, I don't even want to ask what it was, do I?" He shakes his head and I watch him brace himself.

Fuck. Moments ago I'd convinced myself to keep my mouth shut. But then it would always be a secret between us.

"She was going to get rid of your woman and send me in to comfort you, likely with a pocketful of drugs that worked so well the first time around. She wanted you to fuck your virgin daughter. Knowing her, she'd have had it recorded too, for blackmail purposes. She wanted to hurt you. I was just the tool to do it with."

He looks like he's going to be sick, so I add the last part quickly, like ripping off a Band-Aid. "I cut my hand not long after I got here. Will took me to the hospital to get it stitched. While I was there, the doctor took some blood and asked me about any medications I was on.

"I hadn't thought about it until she asked, but for about three months before I left the compound, M started me on a bunch of vitamins. I didn't know why but I knew better than to argue. I memorized the names and that was that, until the doctor asked.

"Turns out what I thought had been vitamins were actually fertility drugs. I freaked out but the doctor insisted my contraception was still working as long as it was still inside me.

Thankfully it is. My guess, M planned to have it removed before sending me to you."

"Jesus fuck!" King looks green. I don't know what to say to him so I turn to Will, who looks at me with a frown. I hadn't told him about the drugs.

"I was afraid you'd send me back."

He shakes his head and sighs, tugging me closer until he can wrap his arms around me. "What am I going to do with you?"

"I'm sorry. A lot happened in such a short period of time."

"I get it, Six. But I hope by now you can tell me anything."

"I know," I mumble into his chest.

"Six?" I lift my head and turn at the sound of King's voice.

He picks up the envelope and waves it at me. "We should open it now."

I shake my head. "There is more you need to know without that clouding your mind. It isn't the reason we called you back." I turn around and lean against Will.

"We've been trying to find the location where I was being held so we could try and free the others, but I only know what the building itself looks like, not its location. They can't get out of their cells alone. The guards have access, but they have to answer to someone. So who is feeding them?"

"M and R are dead, which leaves X. I didn't know who he was before. How could I?"

"Slow down, Six. You've lost me. Who is X?"

"Cohen's fucking uncle," Will hisses before I can answer.

"You have got to be shitting me." King jumps to his feet and begins pacing. His anger is a palpable thing, making me shrink back further into Will.

"We found photos among Zodiac's shit and Six was able to

pick out three images she recognized. We think we've narrowed it down to Nevada for one reason or another. You're the only person who has any inkling of who these people are and how they think," Will tells him.

King turns back to me with that damn blank expression on his face that I can't read. "Show me."

CHAPTER FIFTY-SIX

WILL

I can feel her shaking beside me, but fuck me I'm so proud of how she's holding herself together.

Viddy hands her the three photos from the stack. Six looks down at them and swallows. I wish there was something more I could do, but I know as well as she does that the longer it takes for us to find these people, the less of a chance there is of finding them at all.

Her hand shakes as she hands the photos to King. To his credit, he checks out her face before taking them, his expression softening when he sees her worry. He tugs them from Six's grasp and turns them around to look at. He studies each one, taking his time as he goes over each detail.

"I'm sorry but nothing here looks familiar."

Six's shoulders fall in defeat.

"What else do you have?"

She squeezes my hand at his question. "I...I have the other stuff laid out over there in the study. I've gone over everything a thousand times but nothing else is familiar to me," she tells him, indicating the small office area she has dedicated to all the stuff Kai gave her to look at.

King walks into the room and studies the table and all the paraphernalia littering it before his eyes drift to the wall. Six and Kai have made so many copious notes and lists, I've started to lose track of things. I'm sure they have a system, but whatever the hell it may be is lost on me.

"Do you have any coffee?" King asks over his shoulder.

"I'll make some," Viddy offers, leaving us alone. I stand in the doorway and watch as Six moves closer to King and points out the things they found.

She keeps a small distance between them. When King talks animatedly using his hands, she steps back, almost leaving a barrier around her. I don't know if King notices it, but after the second time she does it, he tucks his hands in the back pocket of his jeans.

"This list of names. What are they?" he questions when something catches his attention.

"Some are names we found in the information Layla collected from her ex-husband. Some are trails we followed before hitting a dead end. Why, what do you see?"

"That one there. Marigold Systems. It is, or was, a government-funded project back in the day. It was one of the first of its kind that pioneered projects sourcing renewable fuels. It's been years since I've heard the name. It's a fossil compared to the huge companies out there now. What about the names underneath? I don't recognize any of them...wait. What's this one at the bottom? There is something familiar about this one."

I step forward as he taps the name on the bottom of the list.

"Untainted Saints? Is that another MC?" I question. If it is, it will help narrow the field.

"No, if it is, it's not an established one. No, that's not where I know it from. The government sold the building used by Marigold Systems to the Untainted Saints twenty-five years ago but that's as far as we got. There are nine hundred properties in and around Nevada that could fit what we are looking for, and that's only if we keep our search narrowed in that area. The Untainted Saints building is just one of them. We never had a starting point to look at before so after a basic search, we've slowly been doing more in-depth ones.

"If it was a government property, there won't be much on it online, not if they don't want there to be."

He chews his lip before pulling out his cell and dialing a number. Viddy walks in with drinks for everyone, placing a tray on the edge of the desk.

"Bates? King. Listen, does the name Untainted Saints mean anything to you? They own a building down your neck of the woods."

He's quiet for a minute as Viddy studies the wall.

"Fuck off, Bates. People's lives might be at risk. Are you really so fucking selfish that you won't even listen?"

He's quiet for a few minutes before cursing.

"Yeah? And what if it's a possible threat. It's on your fucking doorstep, Bates. What about Reign and Willow's safety?"

I turn away and shake my head. King must have a screw

loose to mention the words threat, Reign, and Willow all in the same sentence.

"I still think it sounds like an MC," I mumble to Six, who stands quietly beside me.

Viddy chuckles. "Sounds like a church for judgmental assholes."

"What did you say?" King interrupts, looking at Viddy with wide eyes.

"I said, it sounds like a church of—"

"Fuck me." He growls before putting the cell back to his ear. "Bates? Where's Saint? No, put him on the phone now or I'll come down there and—"

He shuts up at whatever Bates shouts.

"I don't give a fuck. This is important, Bates." King's voice loses its hostility for a minute.

"What's going on?" Six whispers to me, but I'm as lost as she is.

"Bates, Priest, and Saint are the Carnage mother chapter presidents. If anyone but King spoke to them like that, they'd peel them alive and set fire to them. But King is King." Viddy smirks. What she's amused about is lost on me. The last thing we need right now is to get caught up in a club war.

"Saint? Yeah, it's King. I have a question. Does the name Untainted Saints mean anything to you?"

He's quiet as he listens to whatever Saint says before he lifts his head and looks at Six.

"I'll call you back, Saint, but if this is what I think it is, you'll need to gear up."

He hangs up, slipping his cell back into his pocket.

"The original chapter of Carnage was presided over by two presidents, Flex and Coil. Fraternal twins who were undercover agents using the club to infiltrate the criminal element that was running rampant in Vegas at the time."

"Wait…this sounds familiar. Are you talking about the guy that ended up being a serial killer?"

"That was Flex, AKA Garrett. I won't go into all the million reasons this whole thing was fucked from the start, it's of no consequence right now. Saint is Garrett's son. When Garret took Reign, Saint's woman, he took her to a church that he was virtually raised in. I say church loosely because they were really a fucked-up cult hiding behind a cross and a bullshit made-to-fit version of the Bible."

"Okay, but what does that have to do with…Oh, are you talking about the Uncertain Saints?" Six asks excitedly.

"The church was called All Saints chapel. It's gone now, burned to the ground after everything that happened to Reign, but this story goes back before then. The All Saints were a small group that set up the church after breaking away from their origins. It was big news when it happened, especially since people were still reeling from the Manson murders."

"Oh, shit," Viddy curses, likely figuring out where this story is going.

"What? What am I missing?"

"The church deacon ordered a culling and like sheep being led to a slaughter, each and every member, bar the select handful who had supposedly been touched by God died in a mass murder-suicide."

"Oh god, that's horrible. All those people."

"That's not all. Garret was in cahoots with Cohen, and he was also the heir to the family throne."

"The deacon was Garret's great Grandfather. The property would have passed to him."

"So, this is it?"

"I don't know for sure, but I don't believe in coincidences."

"Does this mean Saint is now the rightful owner?" Viddy asks.

"Him and Ava, his half-sister, yeah. And if nothing else, it gives us a damn good reason to go check the property out."

Six turns into me and bursts into tears.

"Shh, I got you." I slide my hand into her hair and hold her tight as she cries.

King watches us with a look of sadness on his face as his eyes drop to Six. "I think it's time we look at the results, Six," he tells her softly.

She sniffs and turns her head to face him. "Why now? We could wait."

He shakes his head. "At the moment, you're just a girl. You mean nothing to any of the MCs. They won't risk themselves or their women for you."

Six flinches, but King steps closer, his hand reaching out to her. He holds it in the air and waits for her to decide her next move.

After a beat, she pulls from me and slips her hand into his.

"And if the test shows you're my dad?" Her voice cracks and I have to fight the urge to yank her back into my arms.

"Then you'll be an MC princess and we'll rain down fire for you."

CHAPTER FIFTY-SEVEN

SIX

I watch the world whiz by outside my window, seeing more of it now in a colorful blur than I ever have before.

"You doing okay?"

I turn to face Will and nod. He looks at me briefly before turning back to the road, his hand sliding over my thigh.

"What if they don't like me?" I whisper, feeling pathetic saying the words out loud. It was bad enough dealing with King's emotions, but now, thanks to one tiny slip of paper stating that King is categorically my dad, I have to prepare myself to meet two brothers too.

I'm not sure why it's worse. Maybe it's because it's the one thing I wanted more than anything else when I was a kid. I wanted an older brother to protect me, to make me feel safe, to show me how to fight. Now I have exactly what I always dreamed about but they already have lives. What if I don't fit into their world? I don't know how to be normal. They're gonna think I'm weird. Oh god, I can't do this.

I don't realize the car has pulled over until I'm being yanked out of my seatbelt and onto Will's lap. He surprises the shit out of me by shoving my T-shirt and bra up my chest, exposing my breasts. He quickly sucks a nipple into his mouth before I can protest.

"What are you doing?" I gasp, looking around wildly, but I can't see anyone else.

"If I have to explain it to you, I'm clearly not doing a very good job."

"Will, someone will see."

"So let them. Let them see that I'm the luckiest fucking man on earth because I've been blessed with an angel who has a body built for sin."

"Will," I groan as he switches to the other breast.

"Relax, they were all ahead of us. They'll think we stopped for gas or something. They more than likely won't come check on us."

"More than likely?"

"Well, they might worry, I suppose," he admits as he slides his hands up my thighs, dragging the denim of my short skirt with him.

"Lift."

I do without conscious thought, finding my skirt now around my waist. "If they come back—"

"They'll get an eyeful, that's for sure," he agrees, sliding my panties aside before flicking his fingertips over my clit.

"Oh god, Will. I don't want my father to see us fucking." I

protest even as I start grinding against his hand. He makes me so damn weak when he touches me like that.

"Better hurry up then, firefly, because we're not moving until I feel your sweet pussy ripple around my cock, milking me dry."

His words cause my stomach to clench. He slips a finger inside me, finding me wet. His smug grin makes me want to growl and kiss him, so I do both, letting go with wild abandon. I get lost in the feel of his mouth on mine that it takes me a second to realize his fingers are gone and the blunt head of his cock is now pressing inside me.

Any worry I had about being caught dissipates in a cloud of pure need. I center my hips, which allows him to drive himself inside me. I whimper at the sensation, feeling overwhelmed, and yet I want more.

His teeth bite into my shoulder as he grips my hips and guides my movements. "That's it, firefly, fuck me," he growls as I throw my head back and groan.

He presses against something inside me in this position that has me seeing stars with each thrust. Nothing else matters in this moment, not the steering wheel digging into my back, not the worry about the journey ahead, all that matters right now is me and him.

"I swear I've never seen anything sexier than watching you bounce up and down on my cock."

My movements pick up, urged on by his dirty words as he slips a hand between us and strums my clit.

"So tight, so hot, Jesus. From the minute I open my eyes in the morning until the second I close them at night, I imagine myself right here inside you. Watching my cock disappear as you stretch to accommodate me makes me feel like a fucking teenager battling the urge to come too soon."

His fingers move faster, making my movements falter, but I don't stop. I need to come almost as much as I need to feel him erupt inside me.

His head dips again, biting his way up the column of my throat. He lifts his free hand to toy with my nipple as the other flicks my clit.

It's more than my body can handle. I hurtle over the edge of pleasure into a dark abyss as my body undulates with sensation. He comes right after me, spilling himself inside me as he whispers my name reverently in my ear.

I collapse against him as his hands move around to my back. He traces my spine with the tips of his fingers as we catch our breath.

"Feel better?"

A giggle escapes me before I can stop it. "Did you just fuck the worry out of me?"

"I don't know, did it work?"

I think about it for a second. Although I'll admit I'm still terrified of how it's all going to play out, I don't feel like I'm going to have a panic attack anytime soon.

"Yeah, I think it did. You and your wonder cock saved me."

Now it's his turn to chuckle.

I lift off him and feel our combined juices drip from between my legs. "I never really thought about how messy sex could be until I started leaving more slick trails than a snail. Please tell me you have some napkins or something."

He slides his cock free before pressing his fingers inside me. "I don't know, Six. I like the idea of my cum streaking your thighs, especially as we're going to be surrounded by a bunch of hedonistic bikers."

"You're such a caveman."

"Perhaps, but I just don't give a fuck. You're mine, firefly, and I'll kill anyone who fucks with that. I couldn't care less if it starts a war. I'd fight to my last breath for you."

"I'm both flattered and horrified, but you don't need to worry. Nobody is going to be looking at me like that. They know I'm yours. It's about family, that's all."

"And I hope for your sake they welcome you with open arms. But if they don't, it's their loss. You don't need them, Six. You already have a family in me. You have Baker and Fisher, hell, you have Kai and Jude and Viddy and Wyatt. You are not alone anymore. If you welcome them into your life, I want you to do it because you want to, not because you feel alone."

I lean forward and press my lips to his forehead, feeling tears well up inside. His ability to go from dirty talk to sweet nothings renders a girl like me defenseless.

"I have a feeling they'll love you, firefly. But remember, I loved you first and I'll love you last."

And just like that, I know everything is going to be okay. I might take a few knocks today, but I'll get back up. I always do. Only this time, I won't be alone.

CHAPTER FIFTY-EIGHT

WILL

A much calmer Six hums beside me with nervous anticipation as we pull up outside the gates of Carnage. The original plan was to head straight to the Vegas chapter, but King insisted we stop here first so Six could meet the rest of her family. If things go well, I can only assume we'll make the last part of the journey with a leather-clad entourage.

I park the car near King's bike and look at Six.

"Are you ready for this, firefly?"

"I think so. As long as I don't throw up on anyone, I should be fine, right?"

I grin at her. "It's a biker clubhouse, sweetheart. I'd imagine it's seen its fair share of vomit over the years."

"Oh gross." She cringes as I unclip my seatbelt and lean over her.

"You want to leave at any time, and we're gone. I don't care about anyone here but you."

She looks into my eyes before lifting her hand and cupping my cheek. "Sometimes you make me wonder if I'm still locked up somewhere dreaming of you because there is no way you can be real," she whispers as I turn my head and press a kiss against her palm.

"I'm only half the man I am because of you. I'm a big believer you get what you deserve. Someone up there decided I deserved you and I'll be damned if I ever give them a reason to take you from me. If that means proving to you every day that I'm worthy of you, then so be it. It's no hardship, not when I start my day with the taste of your mouth on my lips and end it with the taste of your pussy on my tongue." I wink before climbing out of the car.

A crowd is building but I ignore them as I move around to Six's door and open it for her. I lean inside and unclasp her belt before helping her out. She grips my hand tightly as I nudge her aside so I can close and lock the car. I'm not worried about anyone stealing it, but I wouldn't put it past one of these assholes to hide it so I can't leave with Six. Of course, if they think that would stop me, they are in for a rude awakening. Aside from the fact I have my chopper on standby, I'd carry her home on my back if I needed to.

"Jesus, back the fuck up. Nosy bastards," King grumbles as he comes over to stand in front of Six. He bends his tall frame as Six ducks her head. He slips a finger under her chin and tips her head back.

"Head high, little girl. You have no reason to hide from us. The boys will love you, but no matter what, I want to be a part of your life if you let me. I'm sorry I made it so hard—"

Six steps into him and lays her head against his chest, tugging me along with her as she refuses to let me go.

"You know I love you, firefly, but hugging King is not really something I ever imagined doing."

Laughter erupts from her, making her whole body shake. King looks up at me as he wraps his arms tightly around her, a look of respect tinged with wariness in his eyes.

I meet his gaze head-on. I don't back down. The sooner he realizes this, the better. When it comes to Six, I will never back down, never walk away, never give her up. He'd better get used to my pretty face because he's going to be seeing it over Christmas dinner for years to come.

"Guys, seriously. Let them through." A woman's voice rings out, making me look over to the clubhouse steps where a tiny blonde in a long floral dress stands with a hand on her hip. She looks completely out of place, like she stepped off the set of a whimsical flower child movie where the heroine finds out she's part fairy or something.

I know this must be the infamous Luna I've heard so much about. She is shorter than Six, with wild blonde curls, big blue eyes that at first glance look innocent, but a second look shows a shrewd and calculating woman behind them.

The sea of leather parts at Luna's words.

King leads us over as Viddy's SUV pulls up. I'm not sure how the hell we beat them here but when Jude steps out with a wicked smile on his face, I figure they pulled over somewhere too.

Hiding my grin, I nod to V when she steps out behind him, adjusting her dress.

"Hey, I'm Luna. It's nice to meet you, Six. Sorry it's under such shitty circumstances, but that seems to be the theme around here. Now, I don't like to brag or anything but I'm pretty awesome. So when King called and dropped a big old bomb on us a few hours ago, in that way that only King can do, I processed it despite wearing a thong today instead of my big girl panties."

"Christ, Luna." King curses but he leans forward and kisses her cheek, his love for this woman obvious in the soft smile he offers her.

"Hush, old man, you know what these boys are like. Big strapping bikers are terrible for spitting out their pacifiers when things don't go their way, so they are inside pouting." She fixes her eyes on Six. "Their pissy mood is on them, not you. You do not take shit from them, okay? If they say anything to piss you off, you come find me and I'll shoot them myself."

"I...okay. Thank you, that's um, really kind of you," Six replies softly. I have to hide my grin.

"Jesus Christ. Can we keep her?" Luna asks King.

Before he can answer I jump in. "Six is mine."

"Figures," she mumbles as she rakes her eyes over me from top to bottom.

"So, this is the famous Will Harris? You have excellent taste, Six." Luna winks as a big biker steps up behind her and grabs her hips.

"Woman," he growls.

"Why yes, I am, Demon, thank you for noticing. It was the boobs that gave it away, right?"

He dips his head and covers her mouth with his, not giving a single fuck about us watching on. It's quick but savage, a marking of one's territory, biker style.

Luna sighs when he pulls back and turns glazed eyes back

to us. "Will, Six, this is Gage, one-third of the cause of all my headaches, but the man has a cock the size of a—" The rest of her words get muffled as Gage tosses her over his shoulder and slaps her ass.

Six and I look at each other before turning to King, whose lips twitch.

"Welcome to Carnage."

CHAPTER FIFTY-NINE

SIX

This place is a sensory overload. I grip Will, knowing he'll keep me grounded, but I feel very much like Alice in Wonderland. This place is...insane. It's big and loud and full of people who either eye me curiously or glare at me.

Maybe things would have been different if King had always been part of my life but it's impossible to imagine being raised in this environment. I don't know why that makes me feel sad. No, that's a lie. I feel inadequate. Watching Luna made it glaringly clear where my failings are. She oozes confidence and though she is tiny, her strength is clear for all to see. I wonder if that's something you're born with or something that can be taught.

I never had a woman around to nurture me and show me the basic concepts that go along with being all a woman can be and I've never cared. In my world, women were pawns in a game I was forced to play. But now I'm not so sure.

I look up at Will as he surveys the room and wonder if he'll miss the sexy confident women he is used to. I don't doubt that he'll be faithful to me. Will is many things, but he's not a liar. My concern is that my novelty will wear off long before I've figured out who I am.

"You're doing it again," Will whispers from beside me.

"What?"

"You're letting your thoughts run riot. Stop, take a deep breath, and listen to your heart instead. You've spent too many years being manipulated to think clearly right now. It will come but it takes time. Your heart though, they never touched that. Trust it to lead you."

"Wise and sexy. I'm a lucky girl." I smile up at him.

"It's me who's the lucky one, Six. Never doubt that."

A chair scrapes, catching my attention before I can say anything else. I turn toward the noise and find myself ensnared in the gaze of a man who can only be one of King's sons. His eyes move over me as he takes me in before moving to Will.

"So, this is her?" He speaks, his arms crossed over his chest.

"Don't be a dick, Orion," King warns him.

"Sorry, Daddy, you don't get to tell us what to do anymore." A man I hadn't noticed grunts from the opposite side of the table. So, this is the other brother. When he stands up and moves next to Orion, he faces me and I suck in a sharp breath at how similar they all are. I can't see myself in any of them, which only adds to the feeling of being an outsider.

"Six, the big bastard in the middle is Orion, the President

of the Kings of Carnage. And the asshole beside him is the vice president, Diesel. Diesel, Orion, this is Six, your sister."

My heartbeat seems ridiculously loud in the now silent room. I notice that most of the bikers have cleared out, leaving only a few to witness my humiliation. As the silence echoes on, I study the two men I'd prayed for and know I have to make a decision. I can turn and walk away, cut my losses and go back to the way things were, or I can take a step or two in their direction and meet them halfway. I'm not going to pretend I'm not terrified. But I've been terrified before and I never let it control me. Why start now?

I let go of Will's hand, take a deep fortifying breath, and take a step forward. When nothing else happens, I take another step and another until I'm standing beside the table next to them. I've come as far as I can. The rest is up to them.

Nobody speaks, nobody moves. Hell, I don't know if anyone is even breathing anymore. The longer they take to decide, the faster the cracks begin to spread across my already damaged heart.

I'm two seconds from turning back when Orion moves around the table and steps up in front of me. He's so close I can smell him, an oddly comforting mix of beer and motor oil. I lift my head to look into his dazzling blue eyes and almost flinch at the pain reflected back at me.

I swallow hard. My mouth suddenly feels like it's filled with sawdust.

"Hi," I whisper.

He's quiet for a beat before he tags me around the back of the neck and tugs me to his chest. Tears fill my eyes when he wraps his arms around me tightly. I can feel him shaking as his grip tightens but I don't feel afraid. Despite my best efforts, my tears slip free as I grip the front of his leather vest.

I feel Will crowd closer, but he doesn't step in. He lets me know he's there if I need him.

"I'm sorry," I whisper as I pull back.

"It's not the first time I've had a pretty girl cry all over me."

I laugh when I hear someone cursing him out.

"Alright let me in." Diesel shoves Orion aside, nearly knocking me over in the process.

Before I lose my balance, I find myself tugged into Diesel's arms. This results in more tears, damn it. I'm not sure why I'm crying. This is exactly what I hoped for. After a few minutes, Diesel pulls back before looking down at me and swiping my tears with his thumbs.

"You'd better head back to your man. He looks like he wants to rip my arms off."

"He's very protective of me."

Diesel grins widely.

"As he should be, darlin'." He steps back a second or two before I feel Will at my back. His hands move to my hips when he turns me and studies my face.

"You okay?"

I nod. "Yeah, it's just a lot, you know? I'd convinced myself that they would hate me. That way it wouldn't hurt so much when they turned me away. I wasn't prepared for this."

He kisses my forehead before turning me back around. Everyone has gathered around the table now. Orion and Diesel watch Will and me as they sit. On the left of Orion is a handsome blond man who looks like the superhero in a movie Will and I watched last week. Next to him is the man who carried Luna off earlier.

I look behind me and see Viddy and Jude watching everything play out as they stand just behind King, who catches me looking and winks.

"So, you called, said we had a sister and that she needs our help. Aside from my fist in your face, what do you want?" Diesel asks King, full of hostility.

I frown and without conscious thought pull free from Will to step in front of King. A look of amusement sparks in Orion's eyes whereas Diesel grins widely.

"You don't need to protect dear old Dad from us. Trust me, if we wanted him dead, he would be six feet under by now."

I'm not sure what to make of Diesel. He's openly hostile to his dad and yet, I'm not sure he would actually hurt him. It feels more like a messed-up family dynamic than outright hatred.

"I don't like you being mean to him."

His grin grows wider. "He's a big boy. He can handle it."

"Just because he can handle it doesn't mean he should."

"Looks like you've got yourself a champion, old man." Diesel nods at King.

The man in question slings an arm around my shoulder, making me jump. It's the first time he's initiated contact with me since finding out the paternity results. It was like he didn't know how to be with me and honestly, it was the same for me. It's awkward as fuck finding out the stranger in front of you shares the same blood. It was a rare moment King seemed stunned, and I have a feeling that's not something he experiences much.

"So, what do you need?" Orion asks.

"I'm waiting for the others to get here so we only have to go over it once. We don't have a lot of time to waste," King replies.

"The others?" Diesel frowns.

"Conan and Blade are coming with a few men. Inigo is staying back with Sunshine and Alex who both have a stomach bug."

"You didn't think you should, I don't know, let the president know another club was coming?" Orion says sarcastically.

"You're right. I'm sorry. My mind was elsewhere."

"If you were still president you'd have —"

King holds his hand up and cuts Diesel off. "I said I'm sorry, D. Leave it alone. You don't know all the details yet. When you do, you'll understand why I was distracted."

"This something that needs the room cleared?" the man who carried Luna asks.

Orion addresses me. "Sorry, Six, this is Gage and Halo. These are my club brothers and the other two men who belong to Luna with me. I believe you met my old lady when you arrived?"

"You're all with Luna?"

He nods, crossing his arms over his chest, looking at me as if he's waiting for me to say something, but I don't know what. I'm just trying to keep track of everyone.

"Nice to meet you all. This is Will. He's mine. That's Viddy and Jude. They are mine too, although not in the same way I assume you all are."

"We know Viddy and Jude." Orion smirks. "Although I can't usually tell which Reid brother it is until he speaks."

"Really? Huh."

"Wait, you can tell them apart?" Diesel looks from me to Jude.

"Sure. Jude looks like he wants to handcuff most people

and toss them in the trunk of his car. He's not a big fan of people."

"That's pretty accurate," Jude remarks wryly, stepping closer with a laughing Viddy.

"What about Kai?" she asks.

"He looks like he owns handcuffs too, but mostly the bedroom kind. He doesn't like people either, but he wouldn't toss anyone in the trunk. He'd toss them off a cliff."

"And if that doesn't sum up the Reid brothers, I don't know what does." Will sighs.

I shrug as the doors open, revealing two older men—one with a cocky smirk that has likely been the cause of falling panties over the years. The other is the tallest man I've seen in real life, and he has a scowl etched into his face that has me gulping.

"Six, this is Blade and Conan. Guys, this is my daughter, Six." He looks at me then and frowns.

"It's just occurred to me that I don't even know your last fucking name."

I flush with embarrassment. "I don't have one. I've always just been Six."

"Not something to worry about, firefly. The only last name you need is mine," Will growls, making me gasp.

Wait, did he just propose?

CHAPTER SIXTY

WILL

J can feel the animosity beating against my skin like wings. They might have only just found Six, but men like these are born with a protective instinct a mile long and I'm sure they've already figured out she can do far better than me. Bad news for them—I'm a selfish fuck and I'm more than happy to take out Carnage if they attempt to come between me and mine.

"I'm not asking, firefly, because that implies you have a choice."

I hear a growl, but I ignore it in favor of listening to Six's laugh. "I'm not sure it works that way. What if I want you to get down on one knee? I'm only going to do it once, right?"

"Damn fucking straight. If you want me down on one knee, just smile at me. It brings me to my knees every single time.

346

"Oh, dear god I think I swooned. Either that or the cheese was bad at lunch." I hear Luna mumble as she enters the room.

"Later." I wink at Six before turning back to the others.

"What Six has to say isn't easy, so let her finish before you bombard her with questions. If you upset her, we'll leave. I don't give a fuck who you are."

"Oh, it's not the cheese. I definitely swooned." Luna sighs, making me chuckle. I turn to look at her and see her standing with a little girl on her hip with the same riot of blond curls.

"Sorry, I can't stay. This little one is going for a sleepover with Aunt Ava."

I nod but feel Six tense beside me. I look down and find her eyes fixed on the little girl with a look of awe on her face.

Luna must see the look of longing because she steps toward her. "Hey, Six, meet Ruby, your niece. Ruby, do you want to say hello to Auntie Six?"

The little girl lifts her head and smiles at Six. "Hi."

Six smiles back at her. Her eyes are glassy with tears, her voice soft when she speaks. "Hi. Wow, you're so beautiful. I bet you're smart too, huh?"

"Uh-huh."

Ruby turns her head to look at me and smiles once more. I'd be lying if I said I was immune to her cuteness.

"Hi," she whispers. "Are you a prince? Daddy H says I'm a princess."

"I'm not a prince, I'm afraid." I smile at her.

She sighs. "Balls."

Luna turns and glares at the men behind her while I struggle to swallow my laughter.

"What have I told you guys? I swear to god if she comes out with anything worse, I will burn your bikes, you fuckers."

"Yeah, fuckers." Ruby laughs and claps, making Luna freeze. But not me. The laughter I'd been holding back erupts in an instant, along with everyone else's.

"Now, Luna, what have I told you about your language in front of our impressionable daughter?" Halo asks with a straight face.

"I have to go. It was nice to meet you, Six. Don't be a stranger, you hear? Will." She nods before turning and leaving, ignoring her men completely, her head held high.

"Oh, she is so getting spanked for that later," Gage growls, but he doesn't follow after her.

"Alright, alright, sit down and let's get this shit sorted," Orion orders.

The chaos calms as everyone finds a seat. Will takes a chair closest to us and tugs me into his lap.

"Okay, Six, where did we get to?"

"That I have no last name. I've always just been Six." I go on to tell them my story, editing out the parts they don't need to know and glossing over the areas I think might hurt them. By the time I'm done, I feel inexplicably tired.

"What does, or did, this M look like? I'm wondering if anyone else here might remember her, or could have slept with her for that matter. I know you did a paternity test. I'm not disputing that. I'm just wondering if she interacted with anyone else."

"I have the footage we pulled from security cameras." I slip my cell from my pocket and fiddle with the keys until I'm able to pull up the image I'm after. "What's your number and I'll send it to you."

Orion rattles off his cell phone number, which I type in before forwarding the image. I'd shown King the image before we left but he has no recollection of the woman, which isn't surprising given that she drugged him.

"Can't say she's familiar to me. You guys?" Orion holds the phone out for the others but everyone shakes their heads.

"I'll see if any of the others recognize her. Maybe one of the club girls from back then. We don't get anyone coming here alone. They always have to have someone vouch for them, so someone has to remember her." Gage stands and heads off, leaving us to carry on.

"I don't even know what to say to you, Six. How did you not lose your mind?" Orion asks.

"What makes you think I didn't?" She laughs but it's forced this time. I'm not sure the others have picked up on it as I have.

"Trust me, I know crazy. So, what's the rest? Don't get me wrong, I'm glad to meet you and I'd love to get to know you better, but you came here for another reason altogether."

"I need help getting the others out," she whispers, her voice cracking.

"We think we've figured out where Six was being held and believe it or not, it all ties back to Garrett." King sighs.

"Ah, fucking hell. He's like Jason motherfucking Voorhees or something," Diesel curses.

"Who is he?" Six questions.

Everyone looks at her for a beat, making her skin turn pink.

"Nobody you need to worry about, Six." I wink before looking back at everyone.

"We're heading down to your mother chapter now. Because with Garret being dead, the property is technically Saint's."

"Makes sense. So why do I get the feeling there is more?" Halo, who had been quiet up to this point, asks.

"Because one of the trainers is the former vice president. Seems Cohen followed in his uncle's footsteps and with the media coverage, Xavier retreated to lick his wounds."

"How does a piece of shit like that end up in power? Jesus," Diesel spits out.

"Money. It's what the rich crave more of and what the poor take to look the other way and keep their mouths shut."

"He's a different kind of predator than the rest. The others were mean and cruel or just indifferent. We were nothing to them but property to be rented out. But with X, he loved us in his odd, twisted way. Not like equals, though, like pets. He was never outwardly cruel, even if he hurt you, which wasn't often. It was done with a soft smile and an apology on his lips. He was a big believer in aftercare, which was something the others never bothered with. It made the other captives favor him. They let their guard down more, believing his words when he told them false promises. He was a smooth-talking manipulator and because of it, he was perhaps the worst of them all."

"In what way?" Orion asks, his jaw tight with anger.

"The others prepared us for the horrendous lives we were going to end up living. They trained the emotion out of us with cruel words and brutal touches, but not X. His weapon of choice was hope. He infected everyone with it. He made them believe there was a chance of escape, or of maybe going to a kind owner. But it was all an illusion. I saw the ones that came back for reconditioning. It was just another day in the office for all the trainers. But not for X. Have you ever seen a kid spend an hour building a tower out of bricks only to knock it down with a smile of glee on their face before starting again? That was X. He liked to build them up just so they had further to fall."

Absolute silence after she finishes as everyone digests her words.

"But not you though, Six. You didn't fall for his lies, did you?"

"No, but then that's what happens when you forget nothing. I saw things he thought I didn't, and they plagued me. When I first noticed the odd contradiction between what his words said and what his face showed, I was still too small to understand. Whatever I hadn't been able to put into words, though, didn't matter because my psyche had already figured it out. I mentally withdrew behind my shields when I was in one of his sessions, just like I did with the rest of them. He was never my hero, no matter how hard he tried to mold himself to appear that way. How could he be when he held the keys to my cage?"

CHAPTER SIXTY-ONE

SIX

J was beyond exhausted. We had finally made it to the mother chapter of Carnage at around one o'clock in the morning. I was dead on my feet, which was a blessing in an odd sort of way because it dampened the shock at finding the clubhouse in the middle of a party. A patching over party I was told, though I have no idea what that means.

I'd been introduced to a few people but after a few minutes, names and faces began to blur. Will carried me upstairs to the room they offered to let us borrow for the night. Part of me wanted to protest. We were so close now, we should go rescue them before something else could happen. But that was my heart talking and not my brain. We needed a more solid plan than to angrily storm the keep with pitchforks.

I didn't think I'd be able to sleep, but the stress must have gotten to me more than I realized. I slept like the dead, only waking when Will trails his lips up my throat, his hand cupping my breasts, his thumb tweaking my nipple.

"Mmm…" I murmur, arching into him.

"It's time to get up," he whispers against my ear.

I open my eyes slowly, taking in Will's stubble-covered jaw before my eyes meet his heat-filled ones.

"I know today is gonna be hard for you. I really think you should stay here."

"You know I can't. I'm the only one who knows the layout of the place. None of the schematics Kai was able to find match what I have in my head. They've changed everything too much."

He growls, slipping his hand between my legs, finding me wet like always when he's near me. Spreading me wide, he fists his cock. Not bothering with foreplay, he thrusts himself inside me.

Grabbing my hands, he pins them above my head as he fucks me hard and fast, almost like he's punishing me for not agreeing to stay here even though he knows I'm right.

"You stay by my side. You hear me. Nothing can happen to you, Six."

I wrap my hands around his biceps and lock my legs around his hips. "Nothing will happen to me. I have you and a whole motorcycle club to keep me safe."

Dipping his head, he nibbles my ear, tugging the lobe between his teeth.

"Promise me, firefly."

"I promise I'll be safe, Will. You can't get rid of me that easily."

With a growl, he bites down on my neck where it meets my

shoulder. The sharp burst of pain is enough to make me see stars. He buries his head in my hair as he comes, whispering my name softly like a prayer.

"I love you," I tell him when I can find my voice. "I will always do everything in my power to come home to you."

"I'm going to hold you to that, firefly."

I might only have feelings for Will but I'm still a woman with 20/20 vision, so even I can appreciate the collective hotness in the room. It doesn't make me any less nervous, though. Large groups of men, and crowds in general, make me nervous. I'm not sure that will ever change.

I grip Will's hand so hard my fingers ache, but he doesn't complain. Viddy and Jude close in behind me, offering me their support, which I'm grateful for. I still feel myself trembling under the gaze of the club presidents Priest, Bates, and Saint.

"So, what you're saying is you have no clue what we could potentially walk into," Priest says, crossing his arms over his chest.

"Pretty much," King replies flippantly from beside me. Saint's eyes move over me in a curious way, making me feel like a bug under a microscope.

"There are parts of this story you haven't shared, King. I won't put my brothers at risk with only half-truths," Bates snaps.

"I've told you everything you need to know. The rest is not mine to tell."

That's when Bates and Priest look at me too. I have to fight the urge to slide down the chair and hide under the table. Shit. It's not that I'm ashamed. I know nothing that happened was my fault. But when people know my story, they look at me differently. Sometimes I just want to be Six, or better still, fire-fly. Not the poor little girl born in a cage.

I speak up. "He's trying to protect me." My voice shakes, but I straighten my shoulders, refusing to let them intimidate me.

"And what exactly is he trying to protect you from? No offense, sweetheart but you aren't Carnage."

"Actually, she is." Orion steps forward with a growl, Diesel flanking him. Up until now, they had stood silently at the back of the room, letting King take point.

"Six is our sister. She is Carnage."

Bates and Priest look at each other, but Saint never looks away from me. It's like he can see beneath my skin to the secrets I keep locked inside me.

"Orion and Diesel are my brothers. But I have other broth-ers, other sisters who aren't related to me by blood who need me now more than ever."

The silence in the room is deafening but I don't cower like I want to. This is too important.

"King said this building that is now technically mine is being used to house sex slaves," Saint states.

I flinch at his tone, but I don't look away.

I nod. "That's right."

"And you know this because…"

"Saint," King barks.

"It's okay," I tell King softly, reaching out blindly for his hand with my free one.

"I know this because I lived there. I was one of them. No, *I*

355

am one of them. The difference between them and me is Will."
I look up at Will and let him see all my love for him shining in
my eyes before turning back to Saint.

"I get it. You don't know me, don't trust me. You think I'm
a plant or, hell, I don't know what's going on in that head of
yours. And honestly, I don't care. You don't matter to me, but
my brothers are Carnage. They told me what you stood for. I'd
hate for you to make them liars. If you stand by and do nothing, then you're no better than the people who stole us or the
trainers who break us."

I swipe a stray tear before moving my eyes to Priest and
Bates.

"It's never just the bully but the circle around them
cheering them on. I thought Carnage would be better than
that."

Priest's fist hits the table. I feel Will reach for his gun and
feel the room begin to descend into chaos.

"Stop, just stop. I'm sorry we came to you for help." I
stand, Will and King standing with me.

"It's not your problem, right?" My voice cracks again,
which pisses me off, but I press on. "They have nobody to fight
for them. Everyone thinks they're dead. They're scared and
alone. They could be any one of you, any one of your women,
sisters, or daughters. You might think it's not your problem,
but we are all fucking human. They are all someone's daughters, all someone's sons," I whisper, my tears now running
freely.

"Fuck me, she really is Carnage," Bates curses.

"Okay, motherfuckers, we need a plan."

CHAPTER SIXTY-TWO

WILL

*H*aving Six here goes against every single instinct I have.

"She'll be okay," Viddy reassures me, sensing where my thoughts have gone.

"Yeah? Then why do I feel like there is a storm brewing and we're all about to get caught up in it?"

Viddy doesn't dispute it. Despite her words, she feels it too.

"She was right, you know, what she said before. I understand you not wanting to risk her, but if we do nothing to help, we really are as bad as them."

"I know this, V. Ask me if I care. Because I'm telling you right now, I'd sacrifice everyone in that building to keep Six safe. Now what kind of man does that make me?"

"It makes you the best kind. A hero would sacrifice one in

357

favor of many. But we aren't the good guys, Will. We never were. We'd burn the world to ash for our loved ones."

"If that's true, then why are we even here to begin with?"

"Because of her." She nods her head to Six, who is talking to Jude as he helps her slide her jacket over a bulletproof vest. "Because of Jenna and Layla and every other person who had something stolen from them that they refused to give freely."

I tuck a strand of hair behind Viddy's ear and see a shadow of pain cross her face, gone as quickly as it arrived.

"Because of you."

"It's not the same."

"It fucking is. Someone stole something from you too, Viddy, and everyone else turned a blind eye to it all."

"I survived. It made me stronger."

"No, fuck that. You were already strong. You took something that should have broken you and you let it fuel you. You became a warrior queen with an army who would die for you. You had something taken from you, V, but because of you and Six and Jenna and Layla, we can give something back. We can free them. We can get them the help they need to have a life beyond this prison. The sum of your collective experiences makes you all more than qualified to help them."

"And if we can't help them? Not everyone wants to be saved, Will. Some seek the peace only death can bring."

"Then we give them the freedom to make that choice. You said it yourself. We aren't the good guys. We live with our own set of morals and rules. I don't know about you, but I'm not about to take one more choice away from them."

She sighs and steps forward, closing the distance between us and resting her head against my chest. "I wish I could save them all, Will. But I know in my heart I can't. I just don't know how to be okay with that."

I tip her head back and look into her eyes and see the wary look as if the weight of the world is upon her shoulders.

"We get justice for them where we can, but when that fails, we get vengeance. It might not be enough, but it's something. Something more than any of the rest of you were given. You…" My words drift off when I see a familiar face heading our way.

"Well, I'll be damned. What the fuck are you doing out here?"

Viddy turns to see who I'm talking to and she takes a running jump at Cash.

He laughs at her excited greeting. It might seem overzealous, but for a long time we thought we'd lost the man.

"Lily, Layla, and Stuart are staying with Wyatt and Jenna for a few days. You didn't think I'd let you do this without me, did you? You've always had my back. It's time to return the favor."

"It's good to have you back, man." I reach out and shake his hand when Viddy dislodges herself from his arms.

"I'm sorry," he apologizes, but I hold my hand up to cut him off.

"I get it. The thought of losing Six?" I shake my head, feeling sick at just the idea of it.

"We get it, trust me," Jude says, stepping up behind Viddy and wrapping his arm around her shoulders. I know he's thinking about how close he came to losing her when a couple of bullets meant for him tore through her chest and stomach.

Six burrows herself into my side so I pull her close, ignoring the way her bulletproof shirt digs into my ribs.

"Hey, Cash. Thank you for coming. You sure you're okay leaving Layla? I don't want her to worry—" Cash steps forward and cuts off Six's words.

Dipping his head so he can see into her eyes he speaks softly. "Layla wants me here too. It's important to you, therefore it's important to us too. You matter to more than just Will. You matter to all of us."

She blushes and ducks, but he cups her jaw and forces her to look back up.

"Look around you, Six. Will's my boy but I came for you just like every single person here has."

"Really?" she whispers, shocked. A few tears slip down her face that Cash wipes away.

"Really."

She takes a deep breath, lets go of my hand, and steps into Cash's arms.

His eyes flash to mine in shock. I just nod and stay beside my woman where I belong.

Everyone around us is quiet. Those closest to us know how hard it is for Six to give her trust, especially to men. Yet Kai, Jude, and Cash have somehow weaseled their way into it, three of the biggest assholes on the planet. That's not including the friendship she has with Fisher and Baker or the bonds forming between her father and brothers. It was a nightmare getting Fisher and Baker to agree to stay back, but someone needs to run the place in my absence. It's the same reason Kai had to stay behind. I swallow down the memories of James and Six laughing in my kitchen, the moments bittersweet. There is no chance I would have been able to convince him to stay back. He adored Six.

"Right. Viddy, time for you to head back to the car. I'll call as soon as the coast is clear."

"I hate that I'm not coming," she complains but Jude shakes his head, his hand sliding over her still flat stomach.

"You're carrying precious cargo now, Red. I'll lock you in the trunk if I have to."

I half expect her to argue. Thankfully she doesn't, knowing he's right.

"Okay, motherfuckers, it's go time. Everyone knows what they are supposed to be doing, yeah? Good. Don't get dead," Bates yells out, making me shake my head. The guy is nuts. I'm just glad he's on our side.

CHAPTER SIXTY-THREE

SIX

I squeeze Will's hand before letting go so he can draw his weapon. I know he hates me being here, let alone being one of the first to enter. But with nobody— including Wizz and G, friends of Carnage from another MC who are supposedly the best hackers—able to break into the closed-circuit surveillance, we were left with no choice.

"Keep ahold of my belt loops. Don't let go for anything and if I tell you to drop, you fucking drop to the floor," Will orders.

"I know. I've got it," I reassure him, slipping my fingers through his belt loop.

I don't bother trying to make him feel better about me being here, because I know it will fall on deaf ears. The only thing I can do is keep my promise to make it out in one piece.

The man forgets that I'm the only person wearing a

freaking bulletproof vest. To say I wasn't happy about that is an understatement. The MC only has a handful of vests and they purchased them with the women in mind, so they fit small and tight. I've never had a chance to think about sexism. It sure as heck was wasted on me living in a cage. But knowing I'm the only one out of these people protected makes me want to scream at the unjustness of it all.

When we get out of here, I'm going to have to talk to Will about supplying the MCs with these vests. I know he makes them along with a shit ton of weapons, so maybe it can be our way of saying thank you.

We all hold still, waiting for the signal. King is a few feet from me with Diesel and Orion flanking his side. Cash nudges me back when he sees me trying to peer around him, making me huff.

A small bang and a puff of smoke before a beeping noise and Cash taps my shoulder three times, telling me to go. Will yanks the door open and we head inside.

I send up a silent prayer for all the others fanning around the property. I open my eyes and a wave of fear washes over me at the sight of the familiar surroundings. I push it back and point to the left. Will nods and heads that way, with me following and Cash covering my back.

I look behind me and see King and my brothers went the other way as planned.

Please God, keep them safe.

Directing Will through the series of tunnels and corridors, we keep quiet, even though we don't encounter another soul.

The more time that passes without seeing a single guard, the more the panic creeps in.

As we make the final turn toward where the cells are, Will

freezes. I crash into the back of him. Cash steadies me but we don't speak until Will relaxes.

As we step inside, I realize what the issue is. All the cells are empty. We're too late.

"This is where they kept you?" Cash hisses from behind me.

I lift my arm and point to the cell on the right at the far end. "That one was mine."

Will growls just as the lights cut out.

"Fuck," Cash curses, but the lack of lighting brings me relief. It means there is still someone here and if the lights are off, they have something to hide.

"The training rooms," I whisper to Will.

"Jesus, which way?"

Instead of directing him verbally, I grip both his hips and nudge him. Taking the hint, he walks until I urge him to turn. I feel Cash's hand on my hip as I lead him too, back to the room I hoped I'd never set foot in again.

Our eyes adjust to the light when we make it to the courtyard.

"That building there is where the main training area is. There are other rooms, those would be used for...one-on-one training if the person required something more vigorous." I try to keep inflection out of my tone but it's hard when I can still hear the screams from the people who ended up there.

"This door will take us into a narrow corridor, which will lead to the main room and four smaller ones. The other six are only accessible through the main room."

"Sounds like that room might have been the original sanc-tuary of the church."

"It's big enough," I confirm. I always wondered why they

never used it as something else but learned to be grateful that it wasn't being used to house more slaves.

"There are no windows, no glass panels in the doors. You won't be able to see inside. I'll have to go first because I'm the only one wearing one of these." I press my hand to the vest lurking under the zip-up jacket Jude gave me.

"Like fuck. You stay behind me, Six, or I'll take you back right now," Will snaps.

"Will—"

"No, Six. I'm serious. Cash and I know what we're doing. It's not the first time we've been shot at but if you get hit then I'll burn this motherfucking place to the ground. And then all of this would have been for nothing. Do you understand me, firefly?"

I close my eyes in defeat and nod. Not because I necessarily agree, but because for one fleeting moment, I saw more than anger in Will's eyes. I saw fear.

This time, I'm not just pushed behind Will but behind Cash too. Everything in me rebels at the idea of these men being in danger, but we don't have the time to argue about it now.

Will places his hand on the door and nods to Cash, who pushes me against the wall and covers my body with his. Will shoves the door open and ducks behind the wall. When nothing jumps out at us, he gives us the all-clear.

Stepping into the corridor means stepping back into the dark. The absence of sound makes this place even eerier. Each of these rooms is soundproof for a reason, and it's not because of the slaves screaming. It's to offer privacy for the trainer to dabble in whatever they wish without being judged by their peers. I doubt I'd have realized that if I hadn't been here as long as I had.

"Which one is the main room?" Will whispers.

"Last door on the left."

It's dark, but not the absolute blackness from before. The door to the building remains open, spilling a small amount of light inside. It's more than enough to guide the way. That's not what is unnerving, but the utter silence. Since I escaped, my life has been filled with color and noise and now it feels like all life has been drained from this place. It's as if the vast emptiness just opened its mouth and swallowed everyone whole.

I'm so lost in my own world, I almost miss Will's nod—the same signal to Cash as before.

Cash moves me, his body covering mine once more before Will pushes the door open. There is a click and the sound of a breath being sucked in, but Will doesn't move to hide this time. His eyes are frozen on something in front of him.

A voice calls out, "Ah, guests, please enter. It's rude to loiter in the doorway." A voice I recognize as X's.

My eyes find Will's over Cash's arm, his face carefully blank as he looks at me but speaks to Cash. "Get her the fuck out of here now."

CHAPTER SIXTY-FOUR

SIX

"No." I shove at Cash, but he doesn't budge.

"Come now, Six. I would hate to make a mess of your friend here. I should tell you though, I'm a very good shot so at least you won't accidentally get hurt," X calls to me loudly.

"Cash, go," Will hisses but I know how this will play out. Will means nothing to X. He will kill him in a heartbeat, but he won't kill me, not unless he absolutely has to.

"I'm sorry," I whisper to Cash before I lift my knee and slam it into his balls as hard as I can.

He reacts instinctively, bending to cup himself as he tries to remember how to breathe. I take the moment to push him away and dive in front of Will.

Will grips my hips and growls as he tenses to move me, but I stumble forward, leaving him no choice but to follow me.

As my eyes sweep the candlelit room, I see what stopped Will earlier.

X stands before us on a dais of sorts, in that fucking throne he likes so much. In his lap is a naked girl who can't be any more than eight or nine years old.

Her long dark hair is a mass of tangles and there is bruising around her wrists indicating she's been restrained recently. I can't see any other visible injuries, but that doesn't mean she isn't hurt.

"Oh, Six, how I've missed you." X smiles. The thing is, he's not lying. He's not very good at hiding his tells, which was why I was so surprised to find out who he really was.

"Hello, X. Or would you prefer I call you Xavier now?"

He looks sad for a moment and a little lost, making him look almost boyish in his reaction. But when he sees Will, or more importantly Will's hands on my hips, his expression changes. Like a spoiled toddler, he never did like other people playing with his toys.

"I see you brought me someone else to play with."

I shake my head. "No, he's mine."

"And who do you belong to, Six?" he purrs, stroking his hand over the little girl's hair. She doesn't move an inch but the haunted look in her eyes is one I'm all too familiar with.

I let my eyes scan the room once more, this time taking in the shadows in the corners. I tense, my hands squeezing into fists.

"Why?" I whisper.

He doesn't pretend he doesn't know what I'm talking about. He looks behind him, his hand still stroking the little girl's hair. I use his distraction to step closer, Will moving with me.

X turns back to me, looking sad once more.

"They weren't you," he answers. I move my gaze once more to the shadows and the bodies I can just make out, lying discarded on the floor like yesterday's trash.

I let my tears fall. I cry for each of the people I was too late to save and for the little girl who likely witnessed it all.

"I'm here now. Why don't you let her go?" I nod to the girl.

He pauses his stroking, tipping her head back by her hair, making her whimper.

"But you won't stay, will you?" he says, his eyes on mine.

I hear movement behind us. I don't look, keeping my focus on X even when I sense more people enter the room.

I hear King's voice. "Let her go, Xavier. It's over."

"Ah, King. Last I heard, you were dead."

"Turns out death is overrated. Why don't you let the girl go and we can talk?"

"I let her go and you'll shoot me, which would be really bad, King."

"You know how this is going to play out," King replies softly, but my focus is on X's words. Not so much what he said but how he said it.

That, teamed with the lack of guards and the lights cutting out...he knew we were coming.

"Wait—" I shout, sensing King move closer. "You knew we were coming. One little girl, as protection against an army? That's not grand enough for you."

X beams a smile at me like it's proud of me. He lifts the girl from his lap but keeps hold of her as he stands. I gasp and hear everyone around me curse when the vest he's wearing comes into view.

"A bomb?" I choke out incredulously.

"It's like King said. I know how this is going to play out. It's why I have all my toys behind me and my little kitten by my side."

I swallow the bile but filter through his words, my eyes going to the doors at his back.

"The others are back there?"

I thought the bodies on the floor meant he'd killed them all.

"Of course. I couldn't leave them here alone. Who would take care of them? This way we can be together forever."

"You'll kill us all," I whisper.

"If there was another way, Six." He shakes his head solemnly. "But no. It has to be this way."

"This asshole has lost his fucking mind," Cash hisses, making me jump.

I turn to see him over my right shoulder.

He looks at me, a scowl on his face. If he was pissed about me kneeing him, he's going to hate me for this.

"Lily needs you," I whisper.

Pain crosses his face. So much pain and guilt and I know I can't let him die. I can't let any of them die. Not Will or Orion or King or Jude. All these people matter, and right now, they matter more than me.

"I'm the only one who can stop him," I mouth. Cash frowns at Will, who has moved to see what we're talking about.

"Grab Will. Now," I murmur. When Cash's eyes go wide, I elbow Will in the stomach. When Will releases me, I run forward.

I ignore the roar of anguish behind me and stare at X, who

is now almost in touching distance. He pulls a gun from behind the girl, making me throw my hands up in surrender. But he doesn't aim it at me. He aims it at Will.

"No, stop. I chose you, X. Me and you. You let everyone else go and I'll stay with you to the end."

X's eyes flick to mine and although he tries to hide it, hope blossoms on his face.

"You'll die."

"But we'd be together. That's what you want, right?"

"No, Six. Fuck no." Will's anguished voice shouts out over the sounds of his struggling, but I shut him out. I can't let him die. I refuse to.

X's anger lashes at him, making him aim his gun and press his finger over the trigger.

"If you hurt him, the deal is off. If you hurt him, I walk away and you'll die alone."

"You think I'll let you leave?" he laughs.

"I think you'll go to hell, but not me. I'm a good girl, remember? I can be your good girl again, X." I reach up with shaky hands and unbutton the fly on my jeans, lowering the zipper and pulling them down as I kick off my sneakers.

The confused voices and angry shouts make me hesitate as I pull the denim free from my feet before I hook my fingers in my underwear and slide them down my legs.

X's eyes fix on my naked pussy as he licks his lips. Moving the gun, he presses it against the girl's temple, making her cry silent tears. He fumbles behind her and hands her something.

I can't make out what it is, but when she takes it from him, he presses his thumb down over hers before winking at her.

"Hold it tightly now, kitten, or we all go boom and we haven't reached the finale yet."

Fuck me. He's given the girl the detonator. She's too young to understand what's happening but one look in her horror-filled eyes and I know she understands all too well.

X nudges her so she covers his front once more, the gun still firmly against her head as I take a step closer.

"To take her place, you'll have to take the detonator."

I can't make a grab for her and knock her to the ground, keeping her out of harm's way.

"I can do that, X."

"Take off the rest. You know the rules," he orders, slipping back into training mode.

The room around me is deadly silent, each of the men fighting between wanting to grab me and waiting for the perfect moment to strike.

I draw down the zipper on my jacket, revealing the bullet-proof vest. His eyes narrow at that, but he doesn't say anything. Unlike Will.

"Don't you do it, Six. Don't you fucking dare," he snarls.

I silently beg for forgiveness while I unstrap the vest. I don't pull it off though. I maneuver my arms through the tank top beneath it and shimmy the tank down over my hips, leaving me in my sports bra and the vest.

"What happened to you, X?" I ask him softly as I lift the vest over my head, holding it in front of me as I slip the small flick knife from my bra.

In case I never get the chance again, I turn and face Will. He's not alone, the room is filled with people, but I focus only on him.

"I'm sorry. I love you," I choke out, throwing the bullet-proof jacket at him.

I turn when he shouts for me, his tortured expression engraved on my brain.

"You lied. You're not mine. Not yet anyway," X snaps before lifting his gun, aiming it at Will, and firing.

Fighting against every instinct I have, instead of turning back, I lunge forward, my eyes on the little girl.

"Don't let go," I tell her before flicking open the blade and reaching for X.

Mindful of the explosive vest, I cup his jaw in a soft caress, my tears falling freely because I can't hear Will, or anything, anymore. My ears are ringing from the noise of the gunshot.

"Even in death, I will only ever be his," I vow as X looks down at me triumphantly. I lift the blade and jam it up with all my might into the soft part under his jaw.

His eyes go wide and he reaches for me, but I'm already pulling away, wrapping my arms tightly around the girl and taking her to the floor with me.

"Don't let go. Don't let go. Don't let go," I chant to her over and over, knowing I'm putting the weight of the world on her shoulders.

I cover her body with mine, ignoring the chaos around us as a stampede of feet heads our way.

When I feel hands on me, instinct takes over. I fight them, my mind splintering apart, refusing to let me look up and see that Will's gone.

But those fucking hands are persistent. I curse when I'm pulled away from the girl, who screams. But then Bates is there holding her with Jude beside her, taking the device carefully from her tiny hand.

I sob and turn to my captor. King looks at me in shock

before I wrap my arms around him and break apart into tiny pieces.

"Tell me," I whisper. Even though it's chaos in here, he hears me.

"You saved him, sweetheart. The bullet hit the jacket you tossed him. Bates had to knock him out to stop him from grabbing you. You scared ten years off my fucking life, girl. It goes without saying, you're grounded."

I snort out a laugh but quickly dissolve into tears again.

I feel hands on my back and look up to see Orion shirtless behind me, his T-shirt in his hands. He slips it over my head and helps me pull my arms through before pulling me in for a hug.

"You have bigger balls than my old lady and that's saying something."

"Is X dead?"

"Snapped the fucker's neck myself."

Instead of being horrified, I squeeze him tighter. That's until I'm yanked out of his arms and into Diesel's, who holds me a fraction too tightly.

"You're crazy. I want to kiss you and kill you. Fuck, I need a drink. Here, she's all yours."

I'm turned into Cash's arms, who looks as if he wants to kill me too.

"I'm sorry."

"I swear to god if you were my woman, I'd put you over my knee."

"I couldn't lose the only family I've ever had, and I couldn't let Lily and Layla lose you, not now."

"You stupid, stupid, brave girl." He presses a kiss to my

forehead before wrapping his arm around my shoulders just as my name is bellowed across the room.

I take off running in that direction, shoving people out of the way before I collide with a familiar chest. He grips my arms and shakes me.

"You fucking promised me, Six," he snarls.

A sob breaks loose. "You rescued me over and over. It was my turn to rescue you. Please don't be mad. It had to be me, Will. It was always going to be this way."

He growls, yanking me against his chest. He holds me so tightly it hurts but I don't complain. I soak it in, knowing how close I came to almost losing it all, and send up a silent thanks to whoever was looking over us.

CHAPTER SIXTY-FIVE

WILL

I watch her as she washes her hands and dries them, knowing I'm taking things to the extreme, but I can't stop. Letting her out of my sight right now is not an option. If that means I follow her to the fucking bathroom, then so be it.

I'm grateful I can hold her and fuck her and love her, but Jesus Christ I'm pissed. I'm so angry that she put herself in harm's way, even knowing that if she hadn't, none of us would have walked away.

I'm the one that's supposed to protect her and yet I'll never get the sight of her plunging that knife into his jaw out of my head. As she stood chest to chest with a bomb.

"Okay I'm done," she tells me softly, stepping closer to me

and pressing her hands against my chest. "I'm sorry, Will. I know you're mad at me and I deserve it but—"

I cut her off, slamming my mouth over hers. The thing is, I know she's sorry. I know she did what she thought she had to do, but I can't unsee her standing naked in front of him, completely vulnerable as she traded her life for mine.

I press her against the wall and grip both her hands in one of mine and pin them above her head. Ripping my mouth from hers, I shove my leg between hers and rub my thigh against her pussy. My lips hover over hers, taking her little gasps and swallowing them down.

"Do you know what it would have done to me to lose you?" My voice is so rough I barely recognize it myself.

"I couldn't let you die." She cries out when I shove her shirt up to her waist and slide my hands underneath it, cupping the bare skin of her ass. I pull her leg up and hook it over my hip before snagging the thin strip of her G-string and ripping it from her body. She yelps from the sharp sting of the material ripping, but that soon turns into a moan when I dip a finger inside her.

"You couldn't let me die, yet you'd condemn me to the same fate?"

I'm being unfair. I know it, she knows it, but I can't help it. I want to destroy everything around me. But with the enemy dead, I have nowhere to direct my anger but inward.

The trouble is, there is just too much to contain so it bubbles over and spills out, seeking someone else to attack.

"I'm sorry. God, I'm so fucking sorry, but I'd do it again. You taught me how to love, Will. How to recognize it in others. And showed me all the reasons why I deserved to have it. This is what that love looks like. It's not this pure white entity I used to think it was. It's so much more than that. Love is both light and dark, pure and dirty, rebellious and obsessive, and all fucking consuming. Asking me to leave you to your fate is akin to asking me to cut out my own heart with a rusty spoon. You built me into this woman who stands before you. You made me strong, but that strength is a double-edged sword. You can't make me strong, then expect me to crumble when you need me most." She pleads for me to understand.

With an agonized roar I slip my finger free of her, pull back my fist and smash it into the wall beside her head. She doesn't flinch, knowing I'd never lay a finger on her in anger. I press my forehead to hers, gritting my teeth as I try to corral this swirling viper inside me.

"I liked you better when you capitulated to me."

"Liar," she whispers before ghosting her lips over mine. "But I am sorry I scared you. Maybe you'd feel better if you punished me."

I pause, knowing the word punishment used to act as a trigger. The heat in her eyes now is telling me something else altogether. Her idea holds merit.

"So be it, firefly," I whisper before stepping back and spinning her around until she faces the mirror.

I push her over the counter, her hand grabbing the sink for support as I rip open my fly and pull my hard cock free. I slap her ass hard, making her gasp before rubbing my weeping dick over her reddening skin.

She centers her hips, but I slap her other cheek this time, telling her without words I want her to stay still. I nudge my cockhead against her pussy and pause long enough to wrap my fist in her hair and yank her head back.

"Do not come," I order before surging inside her.

She screams at the intrusion, but I don't give her time to adjust. I fuck her hard and fast, each stroke more brutal than the last. Right now I'm more animal than man, fucking her with a savagery that will leave bruises. But I don't stop. I couldn't even if she begged me to.

Maybe that makes me a monster. But the need to mark her, claim her, and remind her that she belongs to me overrules every other ounce of logic.

"You are mine, Six. Mine. And if you ever try anything like that again, I'll tie you to my bed and keep you there. Don't think for a second I'm joking because I'm not."

"Will!" she screams. "Please let me come."

"No, don't you fucking dare. When you sit down later, your pussy hot and aching and dripping with my cum, I want you to remember why you're being punished."

I thrust and hold myself fully inside her as I start to come. I pull myself free and finish by coating her pussy and ass.

Dipping a finger in my cum, I trail it up to her ass and press lightly against the tight rosebud. She tenses but she doesn't stop me.

"When we get home later, I'm taking you here." I press just the tip inside her. "Then you can show me just how sorry you are."

I pull back and look at her in the mirror, her flushed cheeks and glossy eyes will show everyone outside this room just what we've been up to. Seeing her freshly fucked and covered in my cum, I feel the last of my anger dissipate.

"I'm going to clean myself up and we're going to go mingle before we go home. You'll stay as you are. Knowing your pussy is full of my cum soothes my beast."

She snickers and shakes her head. "You're a caveman. I'll end up with your cum running down my legs."

I lean over her and bite her ear. "Good."

I smirk as Six squirms beside me, my hold on her thigh tightening as I listen to Viddy.

"You think I'm nuts, don't you?"

"You are nuts, V, but not about this. You already took DJ in, why should this be any different?"

"I don't know, maybe because I'm pregnant. Plus, she is so much younger than DJ was. She needs..." her voice drifts off but it's Six that finishes for her.

"She needs a mom."

Viddy swallows at her words, looking up at Jude beside her.

He nods, pressing a kiss against her temple. "I've got you, V, always. And as for Kai, one look at those big sad eyes of hers and he'll be a goner."

"She's lucky to have you, Viddy. Nobody will keep her safer than you three," I agree, looking toward Cash sitting quietly beside me.

"You okay?"

He looks over and grabs his beer. "Yeah, you've actually helped with something..." He takes a swig of his beer as we wait for him to finish his sentence.

"Mack's ex-wife died, leaving his son an orphan," he admits.

"Fuck." Tough break for a kid who had already been through the wringer fighting off a rare form of leukemia while his mom faced her own battle with cancer. It was the beginning of Mack's downfall and the first step toward him turning traitor.

Cash never got the chance to take him out. Mack made a deal with the devil and the devil took his payment in blood, but that leaves the boy alone in the world.

"Layla wants him, but I wasn't sure. She's far more willing to forgive Mack for his sins than I am."

"The boy isn't his father," I reminded him softly.

"I know, but I didn't want to look him in the eyes and be reminded of the man who almost cost me everything. Listening to you all talk about taking in that little girl, I realize I'm being a dick." He drains the rest of his beer before placing the empty bottle on the table.

"Layla can't have kids of her own. The damage Dale did to her body was too much, but she has so much fucking love to give."

"Sounds like they deserve each other," Six whispers softly.

Cash turns to her and sighs. "Pretty sure even if Layla could have kids, I can't after you tried to unman me."

Six winces, making the rest of us laugh.

"But you're right. I'm going home to tell my woman to get the ball rolling. I'm grateful Tommy has a father and a huge extended family or I'm sure she'd want to keep him too."

"Tommy?" Six whispers to me.

"A little boy Layla saved. I'll tell you about it later."

She nods as Cash says his goodbyes and Orion and Diesel walk over to us. Six stands and hugs them briefly before I tug her back down beside me, making Orion smirk.

"We've gotta go too, but these guys have everything in hand. A couple of family members are flying in for their

381

missing loved ones. And the others who don't have anyone, well Carnage will help them get on their feet," Diesel informs us with a nod as King approaches.

In the end, there were only five survivors, but that's still five more people safe from harm now because of us.

"What about the little girl? Any news on possible family?" Viddy asks.

Orion glances down at his phone when it chimes, his eyes widening.

"Fuck yes," he grins before looking at us.

"Sorry, that was Luna. She has news about her brothers. I can't say anything just yet, but I have to go."

"If you need me, call," King tells him. It's not the order a father gives his son, it's the kind that comes from a man with a lot of power and resources.

"You got it, Dad."

King jolts at that and swallows.

They both leave, which I take as my cue.

Standing, I tug Six to her feet as Reign appears out of the crowd with a little girl beside her. She's clean and clothed so it takes me a second to realize it's the little girl Xavier was holding earlier.

"She hasn't spoken yet, but one of the other captives said they were taken from the same place. A commune near the Rockies. Dad was the pastor, mom a teacher. Both parents were killed. The man, John, says as far as he is aware, the little girl is alone now," King tells us quietly, shutting up when Reign steps up to us.

"Hey, guys." Reign greets us as Six drops to her knees in front of the girl.

We all stop to watch the scene play out in front of us, a

strange lump in my throat as if I'm seeing an odd flash into the past as Six looks at a little girl who was her ten years ago.

They stare at each other for a moment before the little girl steps forward and touches Six's cheek.

"Hey," Six whispers. "What's your name?"

Nobody speaks, waiting to see if she'll answer. She's quiet for a moment before she answers.

"Six," she says so softly I nearly miss it.

My Six sucks in a sharp breath. Even though Xavier told her the little girl was her replacement, this is a slap in the face. Viddy turns in to Jude, who looks like he wants to smash something. I focus on them, trying to find the right words to say.

"My name is Six too. But see this guy here?" She points at me, but her eyes stay on the girl.

"He calls me firefly. You don't look like a Six to me. I think you should get a new name too. What do you think?"

She nods slowly with a shy grin on her face.

"What did your mom and dad call you?"

The girl's face clouds over. "Sarah. But I don't want to be Sarah anymore either."

Christ, this kid is killing me. I bend down next to them and wrap my arm around Six. "Well, Sarah is too plain for a smart girl like you. I mean, none of us have simple names, apart from me. We have Viddy and Jude, my firefly of course, and then there is Reign and King." Her eyes light up as she takes us all in.

I look up when Bates steps up to Reign with a sleeping kid over his shoulder.

"How about Princess?" He winks at Reign, making me feel like I'm missing an inside joke somewhere.

"Princess?" the little kid asks, turning toward Bates, who scares off most grown men but apparently not little girls.

"Sure. You look like a princess to me and I saw for myself how brave you are."

She ducks her head and smiles, shying again. "Okay."

"You know what we need?" Jude asks, catching her attention.

"Viddy and I live with my brother Kai and a bunch of other boys and men who leave stinky socks lying around and forget to put the toilet seat down. Poor Viddy here is outnumbered and could really use a friend. Viddy is our queen so her new friend would need to be extra special," Jude tells her as she steps closer to him, enraptured by his words.

"Like a princess?"

"Exactly like that. Think you'd be up for the job? You'd get to see Six all the time too."

She looks back at Six, who swipes a tear and nods at her.

"Okay," she answers before shocking us all by climbing onto Jude's lap and leaning her head against Viddy's arm.

Viddy strokes her fingers down the girl's cheek, looking like she can barely keep it together herself.

"Friends?" Viddy asks her, offering her pinkie.

Princess wraps her little finger around it and smiles, showing a gap where her front teeth should be.

"Best friends."

EPILOGUE

SIX

J sip the glass of sparkling apple juice Will handed to me and look out over the lake, careful not to disturb Danni, who has fallen asleep on my lap. Her fiery red hair, so like her mama's, flashes in the warm sun despite us sitting under the shade.

"You know, it still blows my mind seeing these bunch of badass men turn into complete teddy bears whenever the girls are near." Jenna laughs rubbing her little bump.

She catches me watching her and grins. "What can I say? Wyatt has a thing about me being barefoot and pregnant. I know somewhere inside me I should be wailing about feminism, but getting pregnant is all kinds of fun," she teases.

Given how Jenna's first pregnancy went, we were all surprised how easy the second one progressed.

"Plus, he is more than hands-on. You spend just as much time at the club as you do at home," Viddy points out, tossing an M&M into her mouth.

"He's a keeper for sure," Jenna agrees as we all turn to watch Wyatt, who is in the pool with his son asleep on his shoulder and Esme attempting to drown Stuart.

"What about you, V? How are you coping now that DJ is off at college?"

Viddy throws an M&M at her and mutters a curse word, making me fight back a grin. Someone is having a hard time letting one of her babies fly the nest.

"I'm fine, he's fine. Everyone's fine," she answers before her shoulders drop.

"I miss him, okay? I know he's going to be okay, but I worry."

Layla chuckles from beside me. "I bet you sent a covert security detail to watch over him."

When she doesn't deny it, we all burst out laughing.

"Oh my god. That poor kid is never going to get laid," Jenna jokes.

"Good. He isn't allowed until he's thirty," Viddy snaps.

"Jesus, and I thought the men were bad."

"Look, Mom, I did it!" We all look up at the sound of Princess's excited yell and see her on top of Kai's shoulders after making her way successfully across the inflatable obstacle course Will had set up in the lake for them.

"That's my girl," Viddy hollers at her, making Princess laugh.

"She's come so far," I say softly to Viddy as I smooth my hand over Danni's hair when she stirs.

"They all have." She nods with soft eyes on Danni before looking out at the lake to Corey—Cash and Layla's adopted son, who is helping Lily over the obstacle course with Cash watching nearby ready to catch them if they fall.

"Not bad for a bunch of people as messed-up as us." Jenna laughs.

"Speak for yourself. I happen to be a fucking delight." Fisher stops to kiss my cheek as he runs past.

Viddy shakes her head and laughs as Baker chases after him with a giant super soaker.

Turning to me she frowns. "You're quiet. Even for you. Everything okay?"

I take a minute to think about my answer, trying to convey into words what I'm feeling.

"I'm happy, V. Honest to god happy. But with that happiness comes the fear of losing it all."

"Nothing lasts forever, Six. It's why you have to grab on to it when you find it and hold on tight. I deal in bullets and bloodshed but when I go home and hug Danni and see Princess's smile, it's worth it. Because being me brought me them. Being you brought you all this. We accept the bad so easily that it's hard to bask in the light without having your guard up. I get it, Six. I do. But if you shut your eyes and hope for the best, you'll miss all the best parts."

I take a breath and blow it out, letting my eyes rove around friends, knowing King and my brothers will be arriving soon too, and take stock of how blessed I am.

I have a house with windows, a heart full of love, and a man who looks at me as if I hung the moon.

Gazing up into the sky, I frown, then smile radiantly.

There's not a cloud in the sky, not a drop of rain to be seen, and yet stretching far beyond the lake and trees is a huge rainbow, framing my once dark world in a riot of color.

ALSO BY CANDICE WRIGHT

THE INHERITANCE SERIES

Rewriting Yesterday

In This Moment

The Promise Of Tomorrow

The Complete Inheritance Series Collection

THE UNDERESTIMATED SERIES

The Queen of Carnage: An Underestimated Novel Book One

The Princess of Chaos: An Underestimated Novel Book Two

The Reign of Kings: An Underestimated Novel Book Three

The Heir of Shadows: An Underestimated Novel Book Four

The Crown of Fools: An Underestimated Novel Book Five

The Mercy of Demons: An Underestimated Novel Book Six

Ricochet (Underestimated Series Spin-off)

THE PHOENIX PROJECT DUET

From the Ashes: Book one

From the Fire: Book Two

The Phoenix Project Collection

Virtues of Sin: A Phoenix Project Novel

THE FOUR HORSEWOMEN OF THE APOCALYPSE
SERIES

The Pures

SHARED WORLD PROJECTS

Cautious: An Everyday Heroes World Novel

Hoax Husband: A Hero Club Novel

STANDALONE PROJECT

Coerce

THE COLLATERAL DAMAGE SERIES

Tainted Oaths: A Collateral Damage Novel Book One

Twisted Vows: A Collateral Damage Novel Book Two

Toxic Whispers: A Collateral Damage Novel Book Three

ACKNOWLEDGMENTS

The Pretty Little Design Co – For my awesome cover.

Tanya Oemig – My incredible editor - AKA miracle worker. I'm so grateful to have you on my team. You're amazing and I adore you.

My Beta Angels – You ladies are everything. Thank you from the bottom of my heart for all you do. I heart you all.

Catherine Wilson– My mighty Alpha. I love your face.

Julia Murray — my amazing PA, friend and stealer of book boyfriends.

T.S Snow – my sprinting partner in crime. Thank the lord there is no actual running involved.

Aspen Marks— For the times you drop everything just to read my words. You're my ride and die and I couldn't love you more.

My Candi Shoppers– you are best readers group a girl could have. I love you more than muppet porn.

My readers – You guys are everything to me. I am in awe of the love and support I have received. Thanks for taking a chance on me and on each of the books that I write.

Remember, If you enjoyed it, please leave a review.

ABOUT THE AUTHOR

Candice is a romance writer who lives in the UK with her long-suffering partner and her three slightly unhinged children. As an avid reader herself, you will often find her curled up with a book from one of her favorite authors, drinking her body weight in coffee.

Printed in Great Britain
by Amazon

37653531R00229